I0618895

Imogene
of the
Pacific Kingdom

By Teresa Schapansky

REVIEWERS SAY...

"Imogene of the Pacific Kingdom is an adventure-filled chapter book aimed at older elementary school aged children. Nonetheless, this story is suitable for reading to younger audiences as well as for preteen to early teen readers. The storyline is fun and creative with lots of action, intrigue, and adventure. Imogene is loveable, adventurous, creative, imaginative, and a little stubborn. Every child will feel an immediate connection to this amazing girl. I look forward to more adventures from Imogene."

Tami Brady, Amazon Hall of Fame, Top 50 Reviewer

"Imogene discovers a magical kingdom, the Pacific Kingdom with her mom and of course the intrigue that goes along with it, the secret of the deep as well as the mystery of her own existence. Events are set in motion that take the reader on an electrifying ride. The book is riveting and moves on at an irresistible pace, and no matter what you have to keep reading. Forget about your worldly cares. This book is wonderful. This book is an absolute masterpiece of description, ocular worlds that wait for discovery."

Veronica Grant House, Veteran Reviewer

"Imogene kept me on the edge of my seat for the first few chapters, then allowed me to relax into an enjoyable reading experience in a fantasy world any

child would love."
Susan Valeri, President, Powerful Publicity Group

"Filled with suspense and interesting make-believe characters, the unique and suspenseful story line is the result of Teresa's highly refined imagination and her natural ability to entertain children of all ages. Her writing style and sense of enchantment captures the reader's interest immediately, making this self-published book a wonderful story for children as well as attracting the imagination of any age reader."
Rolli Gunderson, Columnist

"Teresa has done an amazing job telling a story that will grab your attention and not let go until long after you've read her book. "Imogene of the Pacific Kingdom" is a book to be loved by both adults and children for the characters are so full of life and become part of you after you read this book. Nothing could have prepared me (and most likely, Imogene) for the surprises that unfolded with each chapter - dealing with real and surreal subjects and stretching your imagination to the limit. A pleasant read and a definite must buy for lovers of an adorable and exciting adventure."
Marilyn Houle, Words Words Words

"Magic! Excitement! Beauty and splendor are some of the ingredients that make up this wonderful tale. The product of two different worlds, Imogene is a heroin that children will adore. One world is on the surface and is obsessed with material things. The other is beneath the Pacific Ocean, where peace and harmony exists for all those that live there. Teresa has created a story children will delight in. It is full of excitement and magic, as the forces of good and evil do battle. Once begun, the reader will not be able to put the book down. This is a book that all children will adore and want to read again and again."

Warren Thurston, Owner of Boggle Books

Teresa Schapansky

Imogene of the Pacific Kingdom

Copyright © 2025 Teresa Schapansky

All rights reserved.

The author may be reached at:

www.teresaschapansky.com

This book, in its entirety is a work of fiction. All characters appearing in this work are completely fictitious.

Any resemblance to real persons is purely coincidental.

Cover design and illustrations by Elly Mossman

Background photo credit: Vecteezy.com - Valentin Plugaru

Editor: Elly Mossman

All rights reserved.

ISBN 978-1-988024-36-3

DEDICATION

This book is dedicated to my children.

This book is also dedicated to every single person that believes in magic, the impossible, the what if's, and in particular, the what for's.

Thanks to Rebecca, Jorden and Aaron, for being my original Imogene, Marina and Rafe.

TABLE OF CONTENTS

1	Imogene Meets Auntie Agnes	1
2	Imogene's Adventure - The Beginning	15
3	Imogene - Five Years Later	23
4	Imogene and the Dolphin Pendant	37
5	Imogene and the Ocean	45
6	Imogene, King Roland & The Kingdom	59
7	Imogene and the Celebration	73
8	Imogene and Marina	89
9	Imogene and the Forbidden East Wing	103
10	Imogene and the Hidden School	117
11	Imogene and the Royal Dilemma	129
12	Imogene and the Return Above	143
13	Imogene and the Hypnotism of Kristine	163

14 Imogene and the Royal Ruse   179

15 Imogene and the Terrifying Tingle   193

16 Imogene and the Capture of the   211
    Kingdom

17 Imogene and the Grand Scheme   231

18 Imogene and the Royal Mission   257

19 Imogene Saves the Kingdom   281

20 Peace in the Kingdom   297

    Excerpt - Dager of the Tasman   309
    Empire

    About the Author   313

Imogene of the Pacific Kingdom

IMOGENE MEETS AUNTIE AGNES

Look ahead, Imogene!" Elsie exclaimed to her daughter. "There it is, see?" And then she pointed to the single, tree-lined driveway that lay ahead of them, and to the left. Imogene looked up quickly from her colouring book to see where her mother was pointing. The moment she saw the driveway, crayons flew from her chubby little fist and she squealed with five-year-old delight.

"Yes, Mommy! Is this really the place?" And then she giggled a wee bit. She had been considering how long they had been riding in the car and it had been since early morning. It was now well past the lunch hour and she had begun to think that if they drove for much further, they might easily just end up back home again. That would mean the entire day had been nothing but a big waste. But now she was relieved to learn that at last, they had indeed arrived at their final destination. Finally, she and her mother were at Auntie Agnes' estate! Imogene had heard so many wonderful things about her mysterious aunt, whom up until this point she hadn't even met.

"Yes, my love." Elsie answered, and she continued to stare straight ahead. A little reserved then, she added, "This is it!" She forced a smile, for her daughter's sake. She turned into the drive, and then parked her run-down station wagon in the empty stall a short distance from the main house. The two ladies exited the vehicle, and then hand in hand, walked toward the main doors. This was a majestic Tudor style mansion; one that Elsie's sister had inherited from her husband, who had died only the year before. The grounds were immense, and at the back of the property, and running the entire length of it, laid the seemingly endless expanse of the Pacific Ocean. Elsie knew with certainty, that her daughter would be safe here. And she could only hope with all her heart and soul, that in time, she might even find happiness.

Imogene, completely unaware of her mother's fears and misgivings, let go of Elsie's hand, and bounded happily up the stairs that lay ahead. The child was hardly even out of breath as she stood on her tippy-toes and reached up as high as she could possibly reach, to yank on the chain that belonged to the doorbell. It was not an ordinary bell either, but more like a great big smudged up brass monstrosity that looked completely out of place. After releasing her hold, Imogene only felt disappointed to hear the pathetic little *ting, ting* noise that she had produced with the chain. She just knew that a big bell such as this one was capable of a much greater racket.

As soon as Elsie reached the landing and joined her daughter there, they heard the echo of footsteps approaching from the other side of the door. Imogene's heart raced with anticipation. Then, suddenly the door squeaked open. Just a tad at first mind you, but open enough for each of them to catch the slightest glimpse of a man on the other side. The man looked at them too, and as soon as he recognized Elsie, he smiled the widest smile, threw the door open and motioned for them both to come in. Imogene and her mother were no sooner inside the building, with the door shut behind them, when Elsie and the man wholeheartedly embraced. Imogene stepped back, startled as she watched them greet each other in such an intimate manner. Elsie couldn't help but smile at her young daughter's horrified reaction.

"Imogene, dear," her mother started, "I would like you to meet Sampson. He is Auntie Agnes' butler, and when your aunt and I were little like you, he was our parents' butler." Imogene, her eyes still big and round, smiled politely and let out a sigh. She extended her hand to Sampson, fully expecting him to shake it. But she gasped in yet even more surprise when he knelt down on one knee, and kissed the top her of her hand! *Maybe he thinks I am a princess*, she thought happily. Now it was she who smiled broadly, as proud as could be. No one had ever kissed her hand before.

"I am delighted to meet you, Miss Imogene. And you are every bit as beautiful as your mother was when she was your age." Imogene felt the odd sensation of her cheeks flushing from pale to bright pink. Sampson rose then, and led Elsie and the embarrassed little girl down the hall and into the parlour. "Miss Agnes will be with us momentarily." Then he knelt again, and spoke directly to Imogene. "Miss, please wait in here while your mother and I fetch some milk and cookies." Imogene nodded, eager to please her newest acquaintance, and watched the two of them leave the room. She listened to the echo of their footsteps for what seemed to be the longest time, until she could hear them no more. And then Imogene wondered just how far they had to go to get the milk and cookies. She wished suddenly that she could have gone with them. This was the biggest house she had ever been in, and what if they couldn't ever find their way back to her? Imogene was becoming quite frightened at the very idea, and so being a smart little girl, she knew that she'd better do some exploring to keep her mind at ease. She began to roam around the parlour. All of the furniture, she noted, was dark in colour; the draperies a kind of red, but not quite red. Her favourite colour was blue, and there was so far, nothing blue here that she could see. She walked to the end of the room, where the fireplace sat. It was a large fireplace; so large that Imogene decided that she could probably stand up in it, and still not hit her head, it was that big. It was so clean; Imogene supposed her Auntie Agnes might not have ever used it. And then she smiled, wondering what the sense was in having such a fireplace, if it were never, ever used. She would have to ask later, if they could light a fire in it, if only for the pleasure of watching it burn.

Quiet as a mouse she was, as she turned and scanned about the parlour some more. She tightly clasped her hands together behind her back, in order to remind herself to not touch a thing; her mother had always warned her about not doing that in other people's homes. On the piano, to the left of the fireplace, sat some framed photos. She stepped closer to see them better, and with glee, she recognized her mother in one, and her father in another.

Imogene's mood turned slightly sour then and she swallowed hard. She was unexpectedly reminded of just how much she was missing her father. He'd had to leave in a big hurry, only a month before, after telling her that he would be back soon. Well, to Imogene this was far too long for soon. But she did understand that he'd left because of an emergency. Imogene wasn't certain exactly what an emergency was, but she knew that it just had to be important for him leave like that, in such a hurry and without taking even one single suitcase. She shook away her sad thoughts and continued to look at the photographs, only to become let down to see that she did not recognize anyone else. Imogene soon became bored, and decided to give up on her snooping about. There were no toys, no kids' books, and not one thing blue in this room. She began to ponder the idea that she might not ever like Auntie Agnes' home after all. She looked at the chairs and tried to decide which one might be the nicest for her to sit in. These chairs were not big and comfortable looking at all; very much unlike the ones she was used to in her mother's house. Instead, they were tall and straight-backed, with not even any sides for Imogene's arms to rest upon. They were made out of wood, Imogene guessed, and there were no cushions on the seats. She sighed; a disappointed little girl kind of sigh, and then sat down on one. There was after all, no use in worrying about which one to choose, as all of the chairs were identical. Sitting there like that lasted for only a few minutes, and then, without any warning whatsoever, Imogene found that she was very near tears.

Just then, Imogene spotted a small, round carpet on the floor in front of the fireplace. That, she decided, was more like it, and her mood brightened a little. She climbed down from the chair that she didn't like much anyway, then went and sat down cross-legged on the carpet. Before long, she was laying down on the carpet, and then the last thing she remembered was watching her imaginary fire burning bright; orange and yellow flames shooting high to low, then flickering gracefully about in the gigantic fireplace.

When Elsie and Sampson finally returned to the parlour with the milk and cookies, they found Imogene curled up, asleep on the small rug. The little girl had had such a long day already, Elsie knew, and must have gotten plum tired from just sitting and waiting for their return. She set the tray of cookies down on an antique serving cart, and knelt down beside her sleeping child.

"Baby, wake up! Hey, Imogene!" Elsie gently rubbed her daughter's back. The child stirred, mumbled incoherently and then began to rouse. "I'm sorry it took so long, sweet muffin. Look, Sampson made your favourite cookies, rainbow-chocolate-chip!" Imogene rubbed her eyes, and then focused on her mother. She *had* been *maybe* a little upset with her for leaving her alone for so long, but not anymore. Not now that she was back, in the flesh and right before her very eyes. To Imogene, her mother was the most special person in the world. And then, just as five-year old minds tend to switch subjects rapidly, she wondered suddenly how Sampson knew to make her favourite cookies?

Imogene, Elsie and Sampson had just sat down together and were beginning to enjoy their midday snack, when an odd tap-tap noise could be heard; faint at first but becoming louder with each tap. Imogene was anxious, as she *knew* that it just had to be her Auntie Agnes coming. She'd been waiting so long to meet her! Sampson immediately wiped the cookie crumbs from his hands, jumped up and quick as could be, straightened out his suit. Imogene wondered if it was because he wasn't *allowed* to have any cookies. But, he made them, she thought. She was about to argue that fact in her head, when she remembered the tapping noises, and looked back toward the door, just in time to see Auntie Agnes entering the room. Imogene's eyes bugged right out of her head as she stared at her in total surprise! Could this strange looking woman truly be her mother's sister?

Auntie Agnes stood stone still in the doorway, leaning on a shiny silver cane. She was a tall, thin woman and she was dressed in a black jacket, black pants, and white shirt. Imogene smirked when she realized that her aunt's clothes matched Sampson's. But then, Imogene immediately began to feel bad for her. Whoever had put in Auntie Agnes' ponytail had pulled it so tight; it had stretched her whole face sideways. Despite the rest of her face being pulled and stretched in that manner, her nose was long and beak-like. The *only* thing about her that even slightly resembled Elsie was her eyes. Auntie Agnes at least had her mother's eyes. Imogene breathed a sigh of relief, glad at last to have found some kind of likeness.

Auntie Agnes stood there in the doorway for so long, staring over them, that Imogene was beginning to feel uncomfortable. She shifted in her chair, nervously as it seemed no one was going to make any move at all. She wondered if she dared to breathe, for fear of attracting the wrong sort of attention. After what felt like an eternity, her mother stood up, and at the same time Sampson walked over to Auntie Agnes, and linked his arm through hers.

"May I introduce you," Sampson drawled, then paused. Imogene did as she had seen her mother do just the moment before, and stood. She looked at Sampson questioningly, and then he continued, "Your Auntie Agnes." And having said that, he walked with Auntie Agnes, arm in arm to where Imogene and Elsie stood waiting. Sampson released the woman's arm, then went and stood beside the door. Only then, did Auntie Agnes speak, but to Elsie, not to the child. She didn't even have the courtesy to acknowledge Imogene's existence. Strangely, and although it were to be short lived, Imogene felt relieved.

"Oh, Elsie! My dear little sister, it has been far too long. We have so very, very much to catch up on!" Auntie Agnes reached out then and patted Elsie awkwardly on her forearm. She then turned and faced Imogene.

"And you must be my lovely, dear niece, Imogene." She placed her bony hand upon Imogene's shoulder. Imogene thought it felt cold and hard, very much the opposite of what she would have expected from an auntie. Auntie Agnes scrutinized Imogene up and down, then up and down again. Her lips were drawn into nearly a straight line that began to curl up at each corner. "I am so very glad to have you as a guest in my home, dear."

Imogene's sincerest reaction would have been to run away, but her feet seemed to be at this moment, weighed down like cement. Instead of following her gut instinct, she did as she had seen her mother do in response to this woman. Imogene smiled and nodded, without uttering a single reply. Disappointed with the whole family reunion that she had been looking forward to, she decided that the best thing for her to do would be to sit back down and concentrate on her cookies. And so she did just that. She sat back down and with all her might, willed herself not to look up at her mother and aunt, lest sitting turned out to be the wrong thing to do. Instead, Imogene looked toward the door at Sampson. She marveled at his great height and extremely fair skin, and loved the way his short, red hair curled into the tiniest knots she'd ever seen. His freckled face was round and kind looking, and he stood so straight and tall that she had the notion that his back must be kinked. She knew that she immediately liked this man, and hoped that he would maybe someday be her friend. As she was thinking, she just about turned her attention toward the cookies, when out of the corner of her eye, she saw him wink! Not at her, mind you, but right at her mother. And then, he left the room. Imogene turned to her mother and opened her mouth to ask what *that* was about, when Elsie surprisingly gave her the *look*. It was the look that Imogene knew very well to mean, *never mind*. And so it was not long, as Imogene was very obedient, before she forgot all about the wink and the look, and concerned herself only with finding the cookie that held the most rainbows and chocolate-chips.

They were to stay the night, Imogene knew, as her little suitcase was packed and waiting in the car to be brought in. Her cookies gone, Imogene just continued to sit in her chair and listen to her mother and Auntie Agnes talk. She was bored out of her mind, but she knew better than to interrupt their conversation. Thankfully, a short while later, Sampson returned to the doorway and announced supper. Imogene was always hungry and eagerly followed him, her mother and Auntie Agnes to the dining room.

After eating a delicious meal that consisted of roasted turkey, stuffing, mashed potatoes, cranberries and yam, on an elaborate table that was surely large enough to seat twenty, Imogene followed her elders down another hallway that led an entirely different direction. This time she was taken into a sitting room, where Sampson served them tea. For the longest time, Imogene was forced to sit on yet another hard, straight-backed chair, and so she decided to twiddle her thumbs. First forward, then backward, then back the opposite direction, until she nearly cried out from boredom. She was just in the midst of making a desperate attempt to think happy thoughts, when the ordinarily quiet Sampson, who had been standing still at the doorway, cleared his throat. All three ladies looked up simultaneously.

"Miss Agnes, I do apologize for the interruption. I would like permission to take Imogene through the house. May I?" Imogene looked excitedly from one woman to the next. Her mother was smiling and nodding her head so much that Imogene thought she might like to tag along! Auntie Agnes' expression remained as sober as ever as she replied.

"Yes, Sampson, that would be fine. If Elsie and her daughter are to be our guests for the next few days, it is only right that the child should know her way around." She paused then, and her eyes narrowed even more, so much that they barely appeared to be open at all! Imogene felt goose bumps crawl up and down her arms. Auntie Agnes pointed a bony finger right at Sampson, and then added in her monotone voice, "Be sure to show her just where she is not allowed to go, as well." And

Imogene, as eager as she was to go with Sampson, knew well to remember her manners.

"Thank you, Auntie Agnes!" Imogene smiled gratefully at her, then at her mother, and then leapt from her chair and ran for the door. She was bubbling over with excitement. At last, there was something to do, and she just couldn't wait to begin her adventure with Sampson!

2

IMOGENE'S ADVENTURE - THE BEGINNING

Imogene held Sampson's hand, which practically enveloped hers, so much so that you wouldn't even know her hand was in his, as they toured the big house together. There were so many rooms, corridors and staircases that Imogene thought she'd better not ever, ever stray far for fear of not finding her way back again.

"Up the grand staircase," Sampson explained as he pointed to it with his free hand, "are the living quarters." And then they climbed the stairs together. It was a long way up, and Imogene was grateful for the handrail on one side of her, and of course Sampson on the other. Finally at the top, they stopped momentarily to rest. Sampson pointed to the left and said, "That, my dear Miss Imogene, is the East Wing. You are never to venture there."

Imogene questioned him with her big blue eyes, and waited for him to continue. "Not even Miss Agnes has been in the East Wing for so many years. There is nothing in the East Wing that would interest little girls anyway, but don't ever forget. It is *forbidden*." Imogene shuddered at that last long word that she had never heard before. It was scary and only helped to reinforce the "not to venture there" words that still rung in her ears. She nodded in compliance. She had no intention of ever going in the East Wing! Imogene looked over to her right, and then at Sampson. He smiled, and immediately put the child at ease.

"Yes, Miss Imogene. That is the West Wing, and we can certainly go there!" He pulled the little girl along, and nearly laughed with excitement. He was proud of the room that Miss Agnes had him set up for the child and couldn't wait to show it to her. The West Wing was all living quarters, and the only room there that was *forbidden* was Auntie Agnes'. They walked through the room that was to be Imogene's, through the room that was to be her mother's, and even through Sampson's own living area. All in all, it was a long hike; Imogene's feet were beginning to ache, but even that little bit of throbbing pain was preferable to sitting around in the company of that miserable Auntie Agnes.

Later that night, Elsie tucked Imogene into bed, in her usual loving way. It was a princess bed that she laid in; very big and very plush. The canopy above Imogene's head was made of bright white lace; it was a unique and an intricate design. The clear crystal beads that hung from the edges appeared like rain dripping eternally downward. The room that Imogene was to use was beautiful, indeed. Elsie was pleased to see that her sister, although she had never been blessed with children of her own, had at least the good sense to furnish it with a few toys, stuffed animals and books. It was the only childlike place on the whole estate. Elsie sat down on the bed beside her daughter, and lovingly caressed the child's face. She was deep in thought. Lost, almost.

Imogene, being as clever as she was, knew her mother well enough to see that she had become awfully sad. She wanted to ask, *aren't you happy to be here? No? Let's go home, then!* To a five-year old child, the solution was so simple. Imogene watched as Elsie's expression changed in hardly the blink of an eye, from sad to serious. With a heavy heart, Imogene recognized that all too familiar expression. It was the same expression her father had on his face, when he had announced to her that he had to go away. It was one particular expression, which she would never, ever forget.

"My dearest Imogene," Elsie began. Imogene sat straight up in bed now, on full alert. She could feel the hairs on the back of her neck shoot straight up, and her arms were growing goose bumps. *No*, she screamed inside her head. She knew exactly what was about to come. Elsie choked back her tears and tried again.

"Imogene, sometimes people have to *do* things. And these things they have to do, even if they don't *want* to do them. Sometimes people have to do things and in order to do them properly, they have to give up other things..." Elsie knew she was saying everything wrong. But, she wondered sadly, was there ever a right way to say goodbye to your child? And Imogene, well she just couldn't bear to be silent any longer. Manners or not, she let out a heart wrenching wail.

"But, Mommy! No! *You* can't go, too!" And then she burst into tears. Elsie took her shaking daughter into her arms and hugged. She hugged as though she would never, ever let go. This was harder than she ever imagined it would be. But alas, it had to be done. She stroked Imogene's long, blonde hair.

"Imogene, please. This doesn't change my love for you. You remember how your daddy had to go on that important emergency? Well, now he needs Mommy's help. I have to help him. You have to be brave enough and strong for both of us. We will come back for you." Now Elsie was crying, too. The mother and daughter pair sat on that big bed for a long time, locked in their loving embrace. After a time, their sobs subsided, and Imogene's breath came out in short and long gasps. Elsie held her tight until the child's breathing settled. And deep down, Imogene knew that her mother, like her father, would never, ever leave her unless it was really *that* important. For she knew just how loved she was by both of them.

"*When, Mommy? When* will you be back?" Imogene sniffed back the last of her tears and searched deep into her mother's eyes. Perhaps that was why her favourite colour was blue. Just like her dear mother's beautiful eyes.

"Well, honey. The thing is, that it'll be a long time. Can you be big and brave for me for a long time? Will you always remember in your heart, no matter what anyone else says, that I will be back for you? Mommy and Daddy both? You have to remember this above all else. It is important." Imogene pulled away and looked up at her mother in wonder. Now she knew that she was in charge of an important emergency, too. Her important emergency was to always remember. Yes, she could do that. She nodded, after careful consideration of all her mother had said. The poor child had so many questions, but she had the feeling that she would not have time to ask them all.

"But, where will I stay? Who will look after me?" For a brief moment, Imogene had forgotten where she even was. That Auntie Agnes and even Sampson were as far away from her mind as anything in the world could be. And once again, she asked her mother the most important question of all.

"When will you be back, Mommy?"

Elsie looked her daughter square in the eyes. Imogene's eyes were the exact same shade of ocean blue as her own eyes. In fact, they were the same blue as Agnes', the same as Sampson's, and the same blue as her very own husband's. She held Imogene's unwavering gaze fast as she answered.

"You will stay here, my love. Auntie Agnes will take care of you. But you must be patient with her, as she has never been as lucky as I am, to have children of her own. And Sampson, I'll bet he and you will become the very best of friends. You know, Sampson is my very best friend, too! You can trust him with everything, my love. I know that I do." Elsie paused; she waited for Imogene to absorb all that she had said. It was important that Imogene remember everything. When she was confident of that, she continued. "I will be back for you when you are ten. That is five years from now. I cannot come for you until then. But, you will always be with me in here." Elsie gently brought her daughter's hand to her chest, so that Imogene could feel the beating of her heart. She then took her own hand, and placed it on her daughter's chest. "And I will always be with you, in here." The two embraced again. Their tears all but spent, they sat there for a long time just that way. Elsie held onto her precious child for as long as she dared, even long after she knew that she had fallen fast asleep. With gentle hands, she reluctantly laid her back down upon the bed, and for a while simply stood over her, watching. She then reached back behind her head, and undid the clasp of her golden chain. On the chain hung a pair of glass dolphins, turquoise in colour, and between the dolphins, set in a ring of pure gold, rested a perfectly round pearl. Elsie knew how much Imogene adored this rare gem, and she laid it on the bedside table beside the lamp. She swallowed hard then as she took one last look at her very own sleeping beauty, then turned, and left the bedroom.

Elsie stole quietly down the grand staircase that led to the main floor. Sampson was waiting for her by the back service entrance. Quietly, they nodded to one another, held hands, and left the majestic Tudor style mansion, Imogene, and Auntie Agnes behind. Not once did either of them look back. Less than one hour later, Sampson returned to Auntie Agnes' estate alone. No one, other than he and Elsie would ever know that he'd gone anywhere that night. Nor would anyone ever guess that he'd had anything to do with her disappearance. Not until five very long years later.

3

IMOGENE - FIVE YEARS LATER

Imogene examined the waiting room. It was such a small room really, full of super big furniture that looked ridiculously out of place. The coffee table in the center, for example, was the size of a small dining room table, just not as tall. The couch was probably big enough to hold four large people. Imogene was sitting in the softest and most comfortable chair that she'd had the pleasure of sitting in for a very long time. It was overstuffed and oversized, and in her opinion belonged in a place much grander than this. It was sewn from the finest velvet, of that she was certain. And the colour was the most vibrant blue ever. Her very most favourite colour, at that. She tried to decide exactly which shade of blue her old grade two teacher, Mr. Eckert may have described it as; he seemed to be the colour expert. Sky blue? No, much too bright for that. Navy? No, it was too light and exciting to be navy blue. Navy was not such a happy colour, she decided. Azure? Yes! Imogene settled on that, satisfied at last with her descriptive choice. Although she never would have admitted this to anyone, but she wasn't really certain what azure was, or if it was a shade of blue at all. The important thing about it was, that azure seemed to fit. The walls of the room were painted two different colours. The top half was gray, and the bottom half was green. *Who'd ever think to put these colours together,* Imogene wondered. Certainly not that Auntie Agnes, who had to have every single wall in her great big house, white. Imogene put her ear to the wall then, where on the other side she knew that Auntie Agnes and the good doctor were conspiring together, about her. She couldn't make out one solitary word they were saying. She wished they would talk about her in front of her and not in secret, in another room. How rude was that? Imogene knew that if she'd ever tried to do such a thing, to talk about Auntie Agnes in another room with the doctor, she would have been punished but good.

Imogene was sure that nothing was wrong with her; this visit was nothing but a big waste of time. Oh well, it hadn't been too much of a bother to her, she supposed. And if the whole trip meant keeping that crazy aunt off her back even for a little while, it was definitely worth it! This whole examination was about the water. Imogene didn't see any harm in loving the water; however, she would never come anywhere close to confessing that she thought about the water more and more every day. In fact, water was first and foremost on her mind as soon as she woke up each morning. She guessed that was her last thought before her head hit the pillow each night as well, but after all. It *was* Auntie Agnes who had insisted that she'd better learn how to swim. *Learn to swim*, Imogene reflected with a smirk, *I sure did.* The fact of the matter was that as soon as she struck the water, she didn't have to be taught how to swim. She simply *began* to swim. From that first time, that first lesson only one year ago, Imogene knew that she was most in her element, when she was in the water. And now, she knew that being in the water was the closest feeling she'd had to really being home in five years. Who said water loving was a life threatening disease, anyway? Imogene just about laughed out loud at the very idea.

Bored now, after all she'd been sitting there alone waiting for some time, Imogene got up and looked around. She peeked through the open door, and down the corridor. Not another soul in sight! Not even any children to play with or watch. She decided to snoop through the magazine pile that sat on the large coffee table. She chose a magazine that perked her interest, and returned with it to the overstuffed chair. Snuggled deep into the folds of the velvet once more, she opened the front cover of the magazine and began to read.

In the meantime, Auntie Agnes and Dr. Doherty were going over Imogene's test results in the next room. The doctor was holding Imogene's medical report, and was trying to explain.

"But Agnes, she's a normal ten-year old girl. There is nothing in any of these test results that indicate anything being wrong with your niece! She's a little stubborn, perhaps, but even that won't show up in test results!" Exasperated, he put the papers back in their proper folder, and then returned the folder to the filing cabinet. Rather than sitting back behind the big desk opposite Agnes, he chose instead to sit in the chair directly beside her. Ordinarily the doctor felt most at ease when there was a comfortable amount of distance between him and Agnes. But on this day, his main objective was to stand up for the little girl whom this woman seemed so very fond of picking on, and so for that reason alone, he threw caution to the wind. He fought back a grimace as he reached over and laid his hand on her shoulder.

"You know, Imogene is so healthy that she borders on amazing. This is a child who has never had anything more serious than the sniffles, and for that alone you should be grateful. Truly my dear, I have known you for years, and you aren't one to jump to conclusions like this. Ten-year old girls have wild imaginations. So Imogene likes to swim and maybe she pretends that she is a mermaid!

She'll tire of that soon, and next she'll love to play soccer and pretend who knows what? After that... I think you get the picture. Really, Agnes. I will not run any more tests on Imogene. Not like this, not for this. Take your niece, go home and relax." Auntie Agnes narrowed her eyes and gave the doctor a dirty look. She was mortified that he would dare talk to her in such a tone of voice. Just as she opened her mouth to utter her usual cruelties, she realized that her powers of intimidation would not likely work here. Her mouth squeezed into a thin line, as she removed the doctor's hand from her shoulder. At that same moment, he thought her touch felt equivalent to receiving an electric shock. She stood then, and leaned on her cane. As she turned and began to walk away, without even the slightest backward glance, she said,

"All right, Dr. Doherty. You say that now, but you mark my words. Imogene is as far from normal as a child can get. I have been watching her for five years now, ever since my poor sister, Elsie disappeared. Granted, she is a good child. But she behaves in mysterious ways. You will see!" With a final huff, she slammed the door behind her and tap-tapped away.

"IMOGENE!"

No one could have mistaken that voice. Imogene leapt from her chair, and as she did so, cleverly allowed the magazine to fall behind it. The magazine was entitled, *The Mysterious Depths of the*

Seven Seas and if that Auntie Agnes had caught her anywhere near it, it would have meant a serious scolding. By the time Auntie Agnes rounded the corner to the entrance of Imogene's waiting room, Imogene was innocently standing at attention.

"Yes, Auntie?" she replied sweetly. "Are we done here, then? Ready to go home?" All the while she was talking, her hands were busy at work behind her back, folding up a full colour picture of an ocean floor which she then proceeded to tuck deep into her back jeans pocket. Imogene at first felt bad about taking the picture from the magazine, but then just as quickly, she realized that no one else in the world would possibly ever appreciate it as much as she did. And so she was able to convince herself that this one minor act of thievery was completely justified.

"Yes, Imogene! Stop dawdling and let's go home!" Auntie Agnes was yelling, and thus far she seemed incapable of changing the tone of her voice. She was able to change the volume however, from a little bit loud to very loud indeed. Right now, she was bordering on very loud indeed. Auntie Agnes turned on her heel and began to tap-tap down the corridor toward the exit. Imogene seriously wondered at times like this, what would happen if she never followed? She smiled at the very idea, shrugged her shoulders and then obediently followed her guardian. As soon as she left her waiting room, she saw that in complete contrast to earlier when she'd looked out the door and there was no one about, now absolutely everyone who was within an earshot of "IMOGENE!" was hanging out of doorways or milling about and watching their every move. Imogene was well used to being stared at whenever Auntie Agnes felt the urge to scream, and she had learned early how to deal with it. She held her head even higher, stared straight ahead and strutted down the hall. Within mere seconds, the valet had the car waiting for them by the front door, and within minutes, she and Auntie Agnes were in it and on their way home.

The ride to Auntie Agnes' was silent and long; it always was. Auntie Agnes did not believe in engaging in conversation while operating a motor vehicle, as she so often liked to put it. Imogene was used to that now anyway, but she would always remember taking car rides with her mother, half a lifetime before. She remembered easily, how fun those car rides were all the time. There was singing, the radio being played loud, and she could remember laughing, lots of laughing. Whenever Imogene thought of her mother, she smiled. And she knew that when the time was right, and soon, her mother *was* going to come for her. This was her secret now, one that Imogene kept only to herself. She had tried to tell Auntie Agnes before, and more than once, too, when she had first come to live with her; *not to worry, my mommy is coming back, Auntie Agnes. Just not yet.* Imogene could remember Auntie

Agnes ranting and raving like a mad lunatic, certain that Elsie had disappeared for good. That Auntie Agnes had the police and even hired private investigators, searching the four corners of the earth for Elsie, as Auntie Agnes so often liked to put it. And when there was not even a trace, after two long years of endless searching, Auntie Agnes sent the police and private investigators away. She sat Imogene down and explained to her that Elsie, Imogene's dear mother and her own dear sister, was *never* coming back. Imogene felt so very bad for Auntie Agnes, and she wished so very much that she could make her believe. But after some time, she gave up, and with a heavy heart, she quit talking to Auntie Agnes about Elsie altogether.

Imogene and her aunt arrived home, just an hour before suppertime. As usual, Sampson met them at the door. And as usual, he linked his arm through Auntie Agnes' and walked her to the parlour, or wherever else it pleased her to go. Imogene, as she trailed along behind, rolled her eyes into the back of her head and made a face at them both. She thought it was totally disgusting, that her aunt, who was a capable woman, needed to be walked everywhere! She wasn't crippled, after all. Sampson turned back, and saw the sarcastic look Imogene wore, then winked at her. Imogene smiled at him, before making a hasty retreat up the stairs to her room to admire her latest prize, the one she had stashed into her back pocket earlier.

She shut her bedroom door behind her, crossed the room, knelt down and reached into her closet, along the floor to the back, where she kept her special box of secret things. She slid it out, and as quietly as she could, emptied its contents onto the floor. She had clamshells and oyster shells, a piece of coral, smooth rocks and tiger rocks, and some stinky dried out seaweed that had washed up on the rocky shore. All of these, she had collected from just beyond Auntie Agnes' own backyard. Imogene took the folded up ocean picture and spread it out on the floor, too. The shells, coral, stones and seaweed she strategically placed on the picture to make it look more realistic. And then, she took out her mermaid collection and played for a short while. These toys were her most prized possessions, but sadly she knew, she was outgrowing them. For some time now, she found they weren't holding the same old magical appeal. Resigned to the idea that sometime soon she might have to discover new favourite toys, she began to place them back in the box, when something shiny and completely unexpected, from deep in one of the corners of the box, caught her attention. Instantly, Imogene tried with her fingers to pry it out, but it was definitely good and stuck. She couldn't even tell yet, what *it* was. *Oh, a chain!* She tugged at it gently some more, to no avail. Finally she used a little more strength, twisting this way and that, and it gave up and came free! She held her prize out high in front of her, and as soon as she realized just what it was, her mouth opened wide in surprise. It was the long lost and almost forgotten dolphin pendant; her mother's beautiful dolphin pendant!

"Oh, there you are!" She shook her finger at it, and then began to lecture, in an Auntie Agnes eerie sort of way. "Do you know how much I have worried about you? Have you been hiding in here all this time?" Imogene could not pretend to be angry with it forever, and so she undid the clasp and secured the chain around her neck. She stood and admired her reflection in her dresser mirror. *Was it glowing?* Imogene rubbed her eyes with her fists and gave her head a shake, then looked a little bit closer. It *was* glowing. At that moment, there was a knock at her door.

Knock. Silence.

Knock, knock, knock.

Sampson! It was their secret knock code, and it meant that she wouldn't have to hurry and hide anything. She ran to the door, and let him in.

"Sampson," she whispered hoarsely, "look what I found!" She proudly held up the dolphin pendant to show him. Sampson put his fingers straight to his lips and motioned for her to be quiet, and then shut the door behind him. Auntie Agnes did not know about Imogene and Sampson's secret visits. He knelt down in front of Imogene and held the pendant between his fingers.

"So beautiful, Miss Imogene. Your mother will

be so pleased that you found it. It is special, you know." He turned it around and held it up a little bit higher, so Imogene could look down and see it as well as he could. "And see how it glows!" *So, I was right*, Imogene thought. It *is* glowing.

"How was your doctor's appointment today, Miss?" Sampson let go of the pendant and went to sit on the edge of Imogene's bed as they talked. Imogene sat down cross-legged at the head of the bed, facing him. These were their usual secret talking positions.

"Well," she drawled. "You didn't *really* think there was anything wrong with me, did you? Of course you didn't!" She answered her own question. If it hadn't always been for Sampson's steady and normal presence, she may have been led to believe that there was something wrong with her.

"No, Miss. You are a normal little girl. More important than that, you are *Miss Elsie's* little girl. A *very* special girl, indeed. Maybe you should just be smarter about swimming. Maybe the trick is not to let Miss Agnes know about all the swimming that you really do. What do you think about that?" Sampson had a twinkle in his eye as he winked at her. She beamed with delight.

"Do you really mean it? Should I sneak?" Imogene giggled and rolled over onto her face. She tried in vain to stifle her laughter, to not let anyone hear. "Okay, I can do that!" She sat back up and looked at him. The very idea of having Sampson's permission to sneak around was without a doubt, hilarious.

"Now, Miss Imogene. How are your swimming lessons coming?" He looked at her more seriously now, and she immediately took the hint and stopped laughing.

"Oh, well they're done. I have just earned level twelve and that's as high as I can go until I'm fourteen. And that is a really long time from now!" Imogene yearned to be in some kind of swimming lessons, just so she would have the opportunity to be in the water. She had never even stepped foot in the ocean that lay behind the house. That Auntie Agnes was deathly afraid of it and all that was in it, as she so often liked to put it. And so, Imogene was forbidden to step even one little toe in the seawater. Imogene looked at Sampson hopefully. Maybe he would have a solution to her problem; he usually had the answers to everything, after all.

"Have you ever considered, Miss Imogene," he hesitated, and then chose his next words carefully. Imogene nodded her head up and down, waiting anxiously for him to finish. "Have you ever considered swimming in the ocean?" Imogene was startled. *Could he be serious?* "Yes, my dear, the ocean is what I said. Just because your Auntie fears it, does not mean that you have to. The ocean is a beautiful and mysterious place. It holds countless wonders that you couldn't even begin to imagine. And I know that if you really wanted to, you could have many great adventures there!" Sampson leaned in closer to Imogene, and Imogene, expecting a secret, leaned in closer to him. He said quietly, barely loud enough to be called a whisper, "Your mother, Miss Elsie swam in the ocean all the time!" And with that, Sampson got up from Imogene's bed. He reached over and patted the top of her head. She was still looking at him, searching for the wink that might mean he'd been joking all along. The wink was not there.

"Do you mean it, Sampson? Do you think I am good enough to swim in the ocean?" She wanted so much for his answer to be yes; in fact she knew it would be yes. She just needed to hear it for certain.

"Yes, Miss Imogene. Just please, don't let Miss Agnes catch you!" And then Sampson walked over to her bedroom door. He opened it quietly, turned toward Imogene and looked at her very seriously for a moment. And then he was gone.

4

IMOGENE AND THE DOLPHIN PENDANT

Imogene had just finished packing up her special box of secret things, and had no sooner shoved it to the back of the closet to its proper place, when she heard the distinct tap-tap sound coming toward her door. And then the *knock*; a different knock from Sampson's. This one was quick and harsh, and belonged to none other than that dreaded Auntie Agnes. Quickly, Imogene scanned the room for anything not approved of or out of place. Satisfied that nothing was left undone, she went to the door for the second time that afternoon, and answered the knock.

"Auntie Agnes!" Imogene tried to act surprised and pleased to see the woman. "Come in, please!" Auntie Agnes, without saying a word in reply, stepped into Imogene's room. Tap-tap, tap-tap

37

went the sound of her foot and cane. Funny, it had been five years since they first met, and Imogene had yet to notice even the slightest limp. She could not figure out what on earth the cane was for, but she lacked the courage to ask.

"Imogene, my dear." Auntie Agnes sighed as she spoke. Then she walked over to the edge of Imogene's bed, to the very spot where Sampson had been only moments before, and sat down. Here we go again, Imogene couldn't help but think; *now what have I done, or what have I not done, or what should I do?*

"Yes, Auntie?" Imogene replied, sweetly.

"About the doctor's," Auntie Agnes began. Then she thought for a moment, long and hard. She closed her eyes and dramatically placed her hand upon her forehead. Imogene was used to such acting, and patiently waited for this performance to end. Auntie Agnes continued.

"I regret to admit, my dear, that perhaps I overreacted. Dr. Doherty says you're normal, and so I will accept that, but only for the time being. We may find ourselves looking for a new family doctor. But! All that nonsense aside. I should be proud, I suppose if I must, of how well you swim. Not every girl your age can pass all twelve swimming levels within a single year, you know. Now tell me, how do you feel about soccer?" Imogene blinked hard as she looked at Auntie Agnes. She had no idea whatsoever that this soccer thing was linked to a point the doctor had tried to make with her aunt, or that it missed its mark entirely. All Imogene was certain of, was that Auntie Agnes was one step closer to the loony bin. For the woman to admit that she was wrong was one thing. To actually come so close to praising Imogene for her swimming ability was completely out of character. *But, soccer?*

"Well," Imogene knew she was walking on eggshells, and the less she said, the better off she would be. "Soccer is okay, I guess. We play it at school sometimes during gym." She continued to smile politely; never letting on for a moment that she thought Auntie Agnes had completely lost her mind.

"That is wonderful, child." Auntie Agnes got up from the bed and tap-tapped quickly to the door. For a fleeting moment, she nearly forgot to use her cane. At the door, she turned, looked at her wristwatch and said, "Imogene, supper is in ten minutes. Dress appropriately and don't be late." With that, she left, closing Imogene's door behind her.

After supper, and later when Imogene retired to her room for the evening, she lay flat on her back on her bed and daydreamed. She dreamt about the sea and soon found herself fantasizing about her and her mother swimming in it together. And then, as if a light were suddenly flicked on inside her head, she thought, *why not tonight? Why don't I just go and swim in the sea, tonight?* She got up from her bed and looked outside. *Perfect!* The moon was full and there didn't appear to be any wind. She wouldn't even be swimming in the dark. Imogene went to her dresser and took her bathing suit from the top drawer. And then, making as little noise as possible, she slipped into it. In case she was caught, she put a shirt and pair of pants over top, and then looked in the mirror to make sure the suit wasn't visible from underneath. Imogene slipped out of her bedroom, then quietly stole down the grand staircase that led to the main floor. To her surprise, Sampson was standing silently by the back service entrance. They nodded to each other, held hands, and left the majestic Tudor style mansion and Auntie Agnes behind. Not once did either of them look back.

Imogene and Sampson followed the pebble path that led to the back of the property. They walked under the shade of the huge palm trees that lined the yard, so as not to be seen, should anyone happen to be looking their way. Once Imogene was sure they were far enough away from the house to be heard, she asked.

"But, how did you know? How did you know that I would swim tonight?" She was happy to have her best friend with her, but she was confused at the same time. Imogene was sure that he didn't just stand there like that at the service entrance every single night. But tonight, he stood there waiting for her. She just knew it! They kept walking until they just about reached the shore of the Pacific Ocean. And then, Sampson answered.

"My dear, Miss Imogene. There is so much for you to learn. Come," he said, as he led her to a fallen log that had long ago washed ashore. "Sit with me awhile, and we'll talk before you swim." Obediently, she followed him to the log, which they both sat down on. The two friends faced each other. An odd pair, one who didn't know them might have thought. Sampson held Imogene's attention fast, as he never had before. She was curious to find out what on earth he was talking about. And as patient as she was, she sat quietly and watched him, waiting for him to continue.

"Now first of all, Miss. Are you wearing the dolphins?" He peered closer at her chest, and she promptly pulled the chain and pendant out from under her shirt to show him. She looked down at the dolphins and was amazed to see they were glowing even more brilliantly than before! She was speechless, and even more so when she saw that Sampson was pleased. Very pleased, indeed.

"Good, I thought you would be wearing them. Now listen to me, child. When did your mother say she and your father would come for you?" Imogene wondered what that had to do with glowing dolphins and swimming in the ocean, but she barely hesitated as she replied.

"Now! I mean sometime when I'm ten." Then she explained, "She left when I was five, and said she'd be back for me when I was ten. Why?" Sampson smiled at her and answered.

"I knew you'd remember. Elsie is waiting for you now, Miss Imogene!" Sampson couldn't have been happier as he watched the expression on his little friend's face. She was thrilled beyond words.

"What? Where? Where is my Mommy, Sampson?" And then Imogene began to cry tears of pure joy. She had been waiting for this moment for so long, she was at times afraid it would never really happen. Sampson moved closer to her and pulled her tight up against his chest. Gently, with a father's touch, he rubbed her back.

"Now, child. Now is not the time for tears, now is the time for happiness! Your mother and father have also been waiting for five long years. Wipe away your tears, Miss Imogene, for it is almost time." Imogene was more anxious than ever now, as she sniffed away the last of her sobs. If only she knew what it all meant. Imogene and Sampson both straightened out on the log and turned, facing the ocean. Her attention was drawn to the moon, and she saw that it shone directly downwards. She followed the beam of moonlight with her eyes, and observed that right on the ocean's surface, where the moon shone, there was not even the slightest ripple on the water. It was as smooth as a sheet of glass. *Impossible!* No movement at all. But all around it, the waves crashed and rolled about just as they normally would. She looked up at Sampson, and she was eager to ask him about the water, but as though in a deep trance, he just stared straight ahead. It was then that she realized that he was waiting. *But waiting for what?*

Just then, the dolphin pendant that Imogene wore began to move. Ever so slightly at first, so slightly that she just about didn't even notice it at all. Sampson however, saw it right away.

"Miss Imogene, now would be an opportune time to remove your outer clothing." Imogene nodded and stood, and then did just as she was told. She folded her shirt and pants, and placed them on the log beside Sampson, and then sat back down beside them. The dolphins began to move insistently, and pulled completely away from Imogene's chest! If it were not for the chain they were attached to, Imogene was sure they would have flown straight away. The dolphins pulled Imogene to her feet and toward the ocean, in a straight line to where the moonbeam shone. Imogene allowed them to lead her, as it seemed like the natural thing to do. Quickly, she turned and looked back at her trusted friend. Sampson nodded his head and winked back at her. And it was then that Imogene knew, that everything was happening exactly the way it was meant to.

5

IMOGENE AND THE OCEAN

The dolphin pendant pulled Imogene relentlessly toward the sea. As she stepped foot into the saltwater for the first time ever in her life, Imogene began to tingle. She tingled like she had never tingled before. It wasn't the little tingle she'd felt right before Christmas, or before her birthday or even before Halloween. This was a major, whole body kind of tingle. And the dolphins kept on pulling. Somehow, Imogene knew they were bringing her right to the very spot where the moon had shone down. She also knew, or hoped she knew, she had absolutely nothing to fear. Perhaps this was just one of the great adventures Sampson had talked about!

The water became so deep, that Imogene could no longer touch the bottom with her toes. She began to dog paddle. She would have preferred to do the front crawl, but she was afraid of accidentally bumping against the dolphins with her arms. Finally they reached the spot, and Imogene and the dolphins both glowed brightly in the moonlight. Imogene looked back and tried to see Sampson sitting on the fallen log on the beach, but he was nowhere to be seen. Suddenly there was a *hush*, and she could no longer hear the waves crashing around her. There was no sound at all! The dolphin pendant stopped moving altogether, and fell lifelessly back upon her chest, and for a moment time stood still. Imogene treaded water and waited. And then, before she knew it, an enormously strong current came up and sucked her right down, underneath the water's surface. How she wished desperately that she'd had time to take a deep breath first. Poor Imogene began to panic. Deeper and deeper she was being dragged, and she had been holding her breath for so long now, that she thought for sure she would burst. Sadly, Imogene realized that this was it, she was doomed. She looked upwards, to try and see the moonlight for one last time, but all she could see was darkness. Having given up all hope, she was dizzy from holding her breath for so long. A certain feeling of calm washed over her, and she opened her mouth, having accepted her fate. She expected it to hurt as the water came rushing in, but surprisingly, it did not. She inhaled as deep as she could, with what might she had left. No water filled her lungs and there was no pain. Imogene could breathe under water. She was stunned. It was no different at all, from breathing in air.

Excited now that she knew she wasn't about to drown in the ocean, Imogene looked around and took notice of her surroundings. It certainly wasn't dark, as it had been when she'd been holding her breath. With a funny underwater laugh, Imogene realized that it probably hadn't been dark at all. She had held her breath for so long, and was on the verge of passing out - that's why she had been unable to see. She looked straight up then, and sure enough she could easily make out the light of the moon.

Imogene discovered that she was strangely warm. Not too cold, and not too hot, her body temperature was just perfect. The current kept pulling Imogene down, down until her feet lightly touched upon the ocean floor. She bounced back up again, ever so slightly. She felt almost weightless.

On the way down, Imogene had gone through an incredible amount of seaweed, but now at the bottom the blades were scarce, and only grew thinly and in patches. She was glad for that, for if there were a lot of it, she would have wondered what might have been hiding behind each blade. Cautiously, Imogene took her first underwater steps. With each step, the water became murkier, and she could see less. The sand began to swirl around and around between her toes, and then it gradually rose to just above her knees, until she couldn't see where she was going at all. Imogene decided to try and tread water instead, and give the floor a chance to clear up. She gently jumped up a tad, and found that treading water was going to be easy. She floated there for a few moments and looked around. Ahead a little and to the side, she saw a large school of fish. The fish were absolutely dazzling in colour! Bright yellow with blue stripes, and hundreds, maybe thousands of them, at that. Imogene tried to keep as still as she possibly could so as not to disturb them. She was mesmerized by their pure and natural beauty and was unable to look away.

Suddenly, the fish at the front turned sharply and headed straight for Imogene, and it was leading the whole school toward her! She was too afraid to move. She tried convincing herself that they were harmless, yet she braced for the worst. Before she knew it, the whole entire school of fish was upon her. They swam under her arms, between her legs and straight above her head, and then kept going. Aside from learning that she could breathe underwater, it was the most exhilarating experience of Imogene's young life. She turned to watch them go, and it was at that same moment, when she saw the cave. The entrance of the cave was quite small, yet Imogene could tell that it would be large enough for her to squeeze through. But would she dare? What if she couldn't get out again, and who knew what dangers lurked there in wait? Wait a minute! That voice in her head did not belong to her; it sounded like something that Auntie Agnes might say. And then, rather defiantly, Imogene smirked and forced her body through the opening. The cave was narrow and pitch black, but once she swam ahead for a ways, she found that it became roomier. She could swing her arms right around and so she began to do the front crawl. Imogene found it dangerously exciting, the whole thing. The breathing under water, the school of fish, seeing the cave, and finally the swimming in the dark cave without a clue as to where she was going or what she may find. She couldn't wait to tell Sampson. She swam on.

THUD!

Imogene landed suddenly on her head. She felt along blindly with her hands, only to discover that the cave had, without warning, turned and led another direction! She continued to swim, but her arms and legs were beginning to tire. She hoped desperately that she might end up *somewhere* eventually, because she felt too tired to turn around and swim all the way back to the cave's entrance anytime soon. Just as she started to worry about getting back, she saw a light further on. It was not a bright light, but it was a light just the same. Imogene's adrenaline kicked in and she swam harder now; she couldn't wait to see what waited ahead.

The light became brighter with each stroke and kick, and now Imogene could make out the cave walls. They were shiny and smooth, and looked almost as though they'd recently been polished by hand. The cave was basically a deep gray, and she could see faint streaks of colour throughout it, as she swam on. She smiled as she saw each and every colour of the rainbow. The very idea of a rainbow, in a cave, at the bottom of the sea almost made her laugh. At long last, Imogene reached the cave's end. She stopped swimming, cautiously pulled herself to the edge, and peeked out.

Fish! Nothing but more fish! Sadly, Imogene found that she was getting a little bit tired of the whole ocean thing. The novelty was at last, wearing off. Granted, the fish were beautiful creatures, but she wanted to walk on solid ground and stretch her legs and feel the wind in her hair. She wondered just how long it had been now, since she had first entered the ocean. She turned her head, and looked above, and wait a minute! *Was that daylight? Daylight? Down at the bottom of the sea?* Excited, Imogene climbed the rest of the way out of the cave. Once she was out, she realized just how snug and safe she'd felt in there, but it was too late now. She treaded water for only a moment, and then stood once more on the ocean floor. To her complete surprise, when she did that, her head popped completely out of the water. She was breathing air again! She looked off into the distance, beyond the water's edge. *Dry land?* Imogene found that she was hidden by short, fat little green bushes. They completely surrounded her. The bushes were thick, floating kind of things and she wondered if they grew there, or if they had been deliberately placed to conceal the entrance of the cave. And then she had to wonder, *but hide it from what?* She shuddered at the very thought and looked around some more. On second thought, she was grateful for the placement of the bushes, regardless of how or why they came to be. At least this way, she would not be seen, unless she wanted to be seen.

She looked to the shore, which she estimated to be maybe one hundred feet from where she stood. She judged the distance by picturing in her mind, the length of the pool she'd spent so much time in. A hundred feet was not that great a distance. She saw buildings far off on the land. They weren't anything like the buildings where she'd come from. These all had rounded tops. *Were they made of cement?* She couldn't be sure. *Domes*, she recalled from her lessons in school. Real, dome roofed buildings that were so far off that she couldn't note any other particular details about them. Then, she saw movement. Fuzzy at first, and so far away. *People?* The movement was so slight; it was hard to be certain, until Imogene heard the faint murmur of voices. *People on dry land, at the bottom of the sea?* Imogene shrank deeper under the cover of the branches, and quiet as a mouse, she waited, watched and listened. The people were approaching the shore, and their voices were now audible. Imogene couldn't believe her ears.

"Oh, yes, Miss Elsie. She's on her way, now! Your little Imogene is such a fantastic swimmer; I'm surprised she hasn't found her way here, yet." *It was Sampson.* Imogene was stunned to hear his voice, and in disbelief at the mention of her mother's name! She peeked out further to see them clearly, and tears welled up in her eyes. She dared move closer, and her mother was in full view now. On Elsie's head, sat a delicate golden crown; adorned with the same kind of perfectly round pearls as was on the pendant that Imogene wore. Imogene saw that Elsie wore a long, white flowing robe, trimmed with gold. The robe was so long, it drug on the ground, as graceful as a feather, behind her. And Sampson? If Imogene hadn't known better, she wouldn't have recognized him at all, based on the way he was dressed. He also wore a robe, though not nearly as long as Elsie's. Imogene had never before seen him in anything other than his butler's uniform. His robe was cream coloured with no trim, and on his sockless feet, he wore open toed sandals. Imogene's breath caught in her throat, when she heard her mother's voice for the first time in five years.

"I don't know how to thank you, Sampson. For all you've done for us, and for the kingdom. I am forever in your debt, you know that." Elsie hugged her friend. Imogene stood, stone still, just watching and listening. She just knew she couldn't bear to be silent for much longer. *Mother! At long last! And Sampson? What kingdom?* Elsie and Sampson looked toward Imogene's hiding place, and she knew they were waiting for her to come out and show herself. After all, hadn't they all waited long enough for this moment? On shaking legs, Imogene waded out from under the cover of the bushes.

Elsie wasted not even a second's time. The moment she saw her precious daughter emerge, she jumped into the water and swam to her with lightning speed. Imogene was so exhausted, both physically and emotionally, it was all she could do to stand there and wait. Elsie scooped the child up into her loving arms.

"My darling baby, how I have longed for this! How I have waited for you. I love you, Imogene, and I'm so glad you made it safely!" Elsie let go then, and took a long look at her daughter. "My, how you have grown." Tears ran uncontrollably down Elsie's face. Tears for the five very long, lost years she'd spent without her daughter. Imogene hugged her mother tight. How she had missed her, too. The soothing sound of her voice; the warmth of her touch. Together then, hand in hand, they waded the distance back to the shore, back to where Sampson stood waiting. Sampson smiled as he rested his hand upon Imogene's shoulder.

"I knew you could do it, Imogene. You are so

brave and strong and smart. I have never, ever been more proud." Imogene smiled, and then for the very first time ever, she winked at him! They all had a good laugh, and then together the three of them walked away. Imogene knew that there would be answers to all of her questions later, maybe once she had the energy to ask them.

She was expecting to be led toward the dome-roofed houses she'd seen earlier, but instead they veered off a different direction and travelled up a long, winding pebble road. This road had so many twists and turns in it that Imogene had no way of knowing just where they were going to end up. The pebbles were almost spongy, but smooth; not at all unkind to her soft, bare feet. She began to stumble; her legs were aching so, when finally they turned the last corner of the road. Downward, and straight ahead of them, in the middle of an endless, green grassy valley, sat an enormous, stone castle. In an instant, Imogene snapped out of her exhausted state, and stopped and stared. Elsie pulled away from her daughter and laughed, a wholehearted belly laugh, which was music to Imogene's ears. Elsie sat down on the grass beside the pebble road and motioned with her arms for Imogene to join her there. Imogene did so, and snuggled up against her mother.

"Welcome home, sweet muffin! This is our true home!" Imogene still hadn't spoken a word; she was mystified. *How could it be? How could any of this be?*

"This..." Imogene stammered as she pointed to the castle, "is our home? We live in a castle? But... but Mommy, wouldn't that mean that... I mean, wouldn't we have to be..." Poor little Imogene was lost for words. This was all so dreamlike. For an instant, she thought perhaps she had hit her head a little too hard on that tunnel wall. Maybe none of this was real!

"Yes, Imogene, it means that we are royalty. It means that we rule this land and everything in it. Imogene, I am *Queen* Elsie, and you are *Princess* Imogene. Your father is the kindest and most just king that this land has seen for a long time. He is *King* Roland." Just then, Sampson sat down on the other side of Imogene. She looked at him, and he was ever so eager to shed the light on his own true identity.

"And I am and always have been your faithful and loyal servant, Princess Imogene!" He then gently picked up her hand and kissed it. Imogene remembered exactly what she had thought five long years before. *Maybe he thinks I am a princess!* The difference was, now Imogene realized that Sampson had known all along that she really was a princess. Imogene fell silent again, as the three of them looked over the kingdom. She couldn't see a single soul, and was about to ask, *what kind of kingdom has no people in it*, when her mother began to explain.

"Everyone is so busy, preparing for tonight's

celebration! It is a celebration in honour of you, Imogene, in honour of your return to the royal family!" And then Imogene was about to ask how Elsie knew what she was going to say before she said it, when her mother did it again.

"Some people in the underwater kingdoms, meaning for example, my mother and I; even her mother before her and so on, we are gifted. We are able to communicate using mental telepathy. And it just so happens that more women than men have this special talent." Imogene looked worried for a moment, and thought about all the things she may not want her mother to know. Again, Elsie replied, "Don't worry, Imogene! There are ways around it. For example, if you're not thinking about something directly associated with me, I won't know about it. If, however, you want to tell me something or ask me something, I will know it. And when you are ready, you will be able to read my mind the same way. It is an ancient method of communication, the way that our ancestors communicated with one another when they survived solely under the water. They had no air; it was the only way to talk to one another." Looking at her young daughter's puzzled expression, Elsie realized that it was probably way too much information for Imogene to take in all at once. "But, Imogene, you will learn it all in time. Right now, you have nothing to worry about!" Elsie stood up then, and Imogene and Sampson followed her lead. The three of them, hand in hand, walked the rest of the way down the pebble path, across the wooden bridge that was suspended high above the castle's moat, and through the castle's entrance.

6

IMOGENE, KING ROLAND & THE KINGDOM

Imogene kept as close to her mother as she could without bumping into her, as she followed her into the castle. They turned a sharp left the second they were inside. Elsie talked and talked as she led the way down a dim, candlelit narrow hallway. She knew better than to expect Imogene to remember even half of what she was telling her. She also knew that her daughter would feel better and be able to retain more information later, after a nice, long rest.

"This, darling Imogene, used to be the servants' corridor. In the days of old, the servants used to be seen when they were needed only, and they were never, ever heard. They had to move quietly and undetected throughout the house between these walls, so as not to disturb any member of the royal family or their guests." Imogene wrinkled up her nose at the very idea of people treating other people in such a demeaning fashion. She couldn't bear to think about never hearing Sampson or seeing him.

"Well, Mommy, I hope that's changed! The servants these days can be seen and heard, can't they?" Imogene certainly hoped so.

"Yes, of course. But you know, it wasn't that long ago, when that was how it was. In fact, before your father came into the throne, his parents' servants were treated just that way!" And then Elsie stopped, as they had arrived at an intersection. Imogene turned to make sure Sampson was still with them, and she was relieved to see that he was. His steps were so light, she hadn't been able to hear if he was behind her or not. She smiled at him, then looked to her mother again.

"Now," Elsie started, as she pointed to the left, "that's the way to the kitchen. From the kitchen, you can get to the main house and stroll freely from room to room." Then she pointed to the right and explained. "This is the way to our living quarters." Imogene wondered about the secrecy.

"Why do you use secret hallways and entrances? Why can't you just go through the castle to get where you want to go?" Elsie chuckled before she replied.

"Sometimes even *we* don't want to be seen or heard! Yes, we can use the main entrance to walk through the castle, if we so choose. I opted to show you this way first, because you will have so much attention over the next few days that you may wish to use it!" Then Elsie turned to the right, "Follow me, sweet muffin, for your father has been waiting to see you all day!" Imogene grinned from ear to ear at the idea of seeing her father at long last, and she and Sampson trailed behind Elsie a little ways more.

Just then, right out of the clear blue, a funny thought struck Imogene. She realized that it was daylight down in the kingdom, but when she'd left Auntie Agnes', it had been dark. She shook her head; it was all so new and strange. She decided to ask her mother about it later. They came to the bottom of a very tall, spiral staircase. Elsie pointed upward. "This leads to our house." Imogene hadn't really considered that there might be *houses* within the castle, although now she recalled her mother saying *house*, earlier. Elsie continued, "Sampson, would you like to follow us up? You are welcome to, unless you have other things that need tending."

"Thank you, Miss Elsie, but if you ladies don't mind, I would like to go home and see my family now. Is there anything else you would like me to do for you tonight?" He winked at Imogene, who was thunderstruck by the news that Sampson had a family of his own. She couldn't help but ask him.

"Oh, Sampson! Do you have children?" What an exciting prospect! He smiled as he replied.

"Yes, indeed I do, Miss Imogene. I have two children. My boy is twelve years old, and my daughter is ten, the same age as you!" Elsie knew that Sampson must be eager to see them, and so she stepped in.

"Imogene, dear, you will meet them all tonight. Let's let Sampson go to them for now, okay?" Imogene nodded enthusiastically, but then her smile fell as she realized that her questions were actually keeping him from his family! She'd never had the faintest idea that Sampson was a father, but then how could she? There were so many things she was just now, finding out.

"Oh, I'm sorry, Sampson. I didn't mean..." But Sampson put his fingers to his lips to shush her, knelt down on one knee, took her hand and kissed it.

"Miss Imogene, for the last five years it has been my absolute pleasure to be with you. There is no need now, nor will there ever be a need for you to apologize to me. Besides, I know it will be hard for you to believe, but I have been seeing my family just about every night for the last five years! My burden has not been nearly as great as yours or your family's." Sampson rose, winked at them both, turned and left. Imogene's heart felt as though it might burst, she was so happy for him. She and her mother began to ascend the staircase together. There was a humongous lump in Imogene's throat, which seemed to grow with each step she took. She swallowed hard a couple of times, but that did nothing to calm it down. They were near the top of the stairs, when Imogene had become so overwhelmed that she stopped dead in her tracks. Elsie turned to her daughter.

"Oh, Imogene. He is still your father; the only difference is that now you know he is a king. Don't be afraid, my dear." Elsie reached out her hand for Imogene to take, and she did. She felt better already. Imogene took a couple of deep breaths, and then climbed the last few steps behind her mother.

Finally they reached the top, and Imogene made a mental note for later, to go and look out one of those windows to see just how far up they really were. She was pretty sure it was more than three stories high, as the castle from the outside had looked very tall and they had climbed a great many stairs. She just had to ask, "Is this the top? The very top?" Elsie grinned at her daughter's question, so youthful and innocent.

"Yes, it is the top. The top is what we refer to as our house. The next floor down is separated into little apartments, and that's where most of the servants reside. Below them are the guests' quarters, but they aren't used often. And the two floors below that are considered the castle. It is where we hold functions; address the kingdom, you know, royal things." Just then, Elsie looked quickly over her daughter's head. Imogene whirled around to see what had caught her mother's attention so fast, and there he was. Right before her, stood her father.

"Daddy!" Imogene ran to him and jumped right

into his waiting arms. Any and all anxiety that she had felt only a few minutes earlier was completely gone and forgotten. Her mother was right; he was still the same person. She held onto him with all her might. How she had missed being held in those big, strong arms.

"Imogene!" Her father exclaimed. Tears ran without restraint as he held onto his daughter at long last. He had longed for her so much that his empty arms often ached. Now he knew that they would ache no more. He swung his daughter around and around, in big, full circles. Then, he gently put her down and stood her up in front of him. He looked his child up and down, almost in disbelief. "Elsie!" He looked at his wife. "Do you see how much she's grown? How tall she's become? Can you believe it?" He shook his head, and then hugged her again. "Our Imogene. You've come home at long last!" The happy, reunited family of three then walked together through the royal chambers. Imogene was pleased to see that every drapery in sight was her favourite shade of blue. The furniture was all plush and big and comfortable looking and there wasn't even one plain dreadful wooden chair in sight. This was definitely more like it. She followed her parents into the royal bedroom, and feeling very much like she was five years old again, ran straight for the bed. She flopped down on it so hard, that she bounced! She looked up just in time, to see her parents take a running leap for the bed! Imogene braced herself as her mother and father landed with a soft thump on either side of her. She had never been so entirely happy, as she and parents lay together on that great big bed, laughing and hugging. Things were exactly the way they should have been all along.

There was one question that had been gnawing away inside Imogene for five long years; since the night her mother left. Elsie, who had such a strong connection with Imogene, felt the question. She would wait to allow Imogene to ask it out loud. She and her husband watched as Imogene flipped over onto her stomach, and propped her chin up with her hands. Her eyes remained downcast.

"Mommy, Daddy. Why? Why did you have to leave me, and why did it have to be for so long?" She waited a moment, thought carefully, and then looked at each of them in turn. And then, "If Sampson could see his family just about every night since then, why couldn't you and I see each other?" They were hard questions for Imogene to ask, but despite the lump in her throat, she needed to have the answers.

"Well, my dear child." Roland began. He sat upright on the bed and turned to face his daughter. She sat up and moved to where she could look at both her mother and father. "You are certainly old enough to know the truth. It is a long and difficult story to tell, Imogene, so please be patient and bear with us." Roland got up from the bed, walked over to the window and looked out. How he had rehearsed this speech over and over in his mind; yet he was still not prepared. Imogene yearned to go and stand beside him, to hold his hand; to make it all better. But she was glued to the spot. *So much mystery.* She began to wonder if she really needed to hear it, after all. Roland cleared his throat.

"My parents had two sons. Myself, and my older brother, Serenito. Don't be fooled, Imogene," Roland was quick to add. He saw the look on her face when she appeared delighted to learn that she had an uncle. "Serenito is as nasty as the day is long! Anyway, he was groomed for the throne for his whole, entire life. I was raised to become his advisor, and the next in line for the throne should the need ever arise. When I turned eighteen land years old I went to the surface. It was not the first time for me; I had visited the surface many times before. This time was different. I went up to learn. I had to learn about the ways of the surface people. I had to fit in and become one of them. It wasn't hard to do. The surface people have many luxuries and conveniences that we don't have here, below. But that, my dear, is a matter of choice. For example, we could easily generate our own power down here." He paused then, and asked his daughter, "Have you learned anything about hydro electricity in school, yet?" She nodded enthusiastically, knowing that he was referring to power generated by water.

"Why don't you have power down here? Why would you choose to live without power?" And as she asked, she thought about all the things they couldn't do below, without the use of it. She was perplexed.

"Simple, dear. For generations, our ancestors have lived the way we do now. Our land and way of life has not changed a lot. Up above, the people depend entirely on technology and power. They have forgotten how to live off the land. It is important to know how to provide for yourself completely. We are, after all, one with nature. They..." he pointed upwards for emphasis, "...are ruining the environment, animal life and plant growth, and now all of that technology and power that they have worked so hard to obtain is destroying the ozone layer. So where does it get them in the end?" Imogene nodded. She was beginning to understand. "That, my child, is why we choose to live the way we do." Roland had strayed way off topic, he knew, but he was determined to answer each and every one of Imogene's long, overdue questions. Elsie interrupted.

"Roland, perhaps we should go back to Serenito. Imogene can learn about all the rest, later, my love." Elsie snuggled up to Imogene on the bed, and held her daughter's hand in her own. "It's quite a story, Imogene and very important that you learn it. Everything else will come in due time." Imogene agreed, but she wanted so much to know everything at once. There was, as Sampson had put it, so very much for her to learn. She looked up at her father again and nodded, urging him to continue his story.

"Serenito ruled for six years. During those six years, your mother and I met and wed. She and I decided that together, we could better benefit the kingdom if we both went back up and learned the surface way of life. And on the surface we had you! We were a typical surface dwelling family, and we did learn a great many things during our time up there. But in the meantime, my brother, who for as long as I could remember, was a mean and selfish person, became a mean and selfish king. He made all of the people in this, our beautiful kingdom, work for his benefit only. They weren't allowed to do anything for themselves at all. He always took away, and never gave back. Eventually, the kingdom fell apart. Our people were trickling out, sneaking away one by one. It wasn't noticeable at first, but before long, they were grouping together and fleeing our land."

"But, Daddy! Where would they go? Did they all go to the surface?" *They must have*, she assumed, *for where else could they go?*

"That's right, Imogene. But only a handful of people went to the surface. Those who did scattered like lost souls; in fact we still search for them. They need our guidance, as they were ill prepared for the ways of that world. As their true king and friend, it saddens me to think of what may have become of them." And then, predicting Imogene's reaction to what he was about to say next, he knelt down on the bed close to where she sat and looked her straight in the eye. "And some of the people went to *other* underwater kingdoms!" Imogene smiled a great big smile. This adventure was just getting better and better with each passing minute. She didn't dare speak; she wanted to know more. Her father understood. He took a chair from beside the window and brought it over to sit on while he continued his tale. He had to watch Imogene; he needed to drink in every single wondrous expression she made! He couldn't even envision, being in her position; a ten-year old child hearing it all for the first time. He straddled the chair and leaned in closer toward the bed.

"Another kingdom, Imogene, is where I met your mother! But, you have lots of time to learn about that. Anyway, back to our story. Only the loyal servants and people of the kingdom remained. It is important for you to know, by the way, that the servants we have now, *choose* to be our servants. They are here doing what they do, because they want to, not because they have been forced or born into it, as it used to happen. So, some people left, and the ones who stayed knew that Serenito was cruel and unjust and eventually they revolted against him. The numbers were too great for him to stand up against, and he had to leave. The kingdom was kingless for a short time. It was not long after that, when our dear Sampson came up to the surface and sought me out. I was the only person left who could rule. That is one regulation that will never change, Imogene. The proper bloodlines must rule this kingdom. And so, I had no choice but to leave the surface world and return to my own. There was six years' worth of turmoil to undo, and none of it was easy. To make matters worse, Serenito returned once he heard that I sat on his throne. He was very upset, as he honestly thought that one day, he would return to rule this kingdom again. But, he could not undo the unkind acts he had committed during his six years of rule. I had to banish him from this kingdom. Serenito became crazy with rage and vowed to seek his revenge on me. He was absolutely mad. He learned that I had a daughter, and threatened to spill your blood before you reached the age of ten. We took his words very seriously and could not take the risk that he might carry it out. And that, dear Imogene, is why we had to leave you up there." But, Imogene still did not understand it all.

"That tells me why you had to stay away, but why did my mommy have to go, too?" She looked from one parent to another as she asked. Elsie, who had been silent for a long while, felt that the time had come for her to answer.

"It was because Serenito had my scent. He could have found me anywhere, and if he found me, he surely would have found you. Serenito had not once met you, Imogene. And so there was no way for him to pick up your scent, as long as you were far away from us. And now you see, why it was that we couldn't have you back until you had safely reached the age of ten! It was for your protection. Sampson, on the other hand, was originally from *my* kingdom, which lies deep beneath the surface of the Atlantic Ocean. Until he went above to find your father, he had kept to himself here, stayed in the background. Serenito had never met him, and never found out about his connection to us. Sampson was the only person I could trust, who could really look after you without posing as a danger." Finally, Imogene understood. There was so much to learn and she supposed she could live to be one hundred years old, and still not learn it all. But at the very least, she was content for the time being, with all that she'd been told. Elsie got up from the bed and held out her hand for her daughter to take. Imogene rose immediately and stood beside her.

"Come now, Imogene. It is time for you to rest. Your father and I will bring you to your room." Roland took Imogene's other hand and together, as a real family, they left the royal bedroom.

Imogene was disappointed that the curtains in her room were closed, and the room was completely dark. She wanted so much to see what it looked like. Before she had the chance to say anything, her mother explained, "Imogene, the curtains are closed on purpose. You need to rest. You may not feel like it now, but you will appreciate the nap before your celebration, tonight! When you have slept long enough, I will come and let the light in so you can wake up." Imogene didn't really feel that tired anymore, but she wasn't about to argue. So she nodded, and allowed her parents to lead her to bed. It was just as big and soft as her parents' bed, and she eagerly climbed into it and under the covers. Her mother and father each kissed her cheeks, bade her goodnight, and quietly crept out of her room. Before she knew it, Imogene had fallen fast and hard, into a badly needed sleep.

7

IMOGENE AND THE CELEBRATION

Imogene was neither fully awake nor coherent when she swung her arms up suddenly to shield her eyes from the bright light. At the same moment, she remembered her mother's words, *"When you have slept long enough, I will come and let the light in so you can wake up."* And then Imogene sat bolt upright in bed, realizing that it certainly had worked! Her eyes quickly scanned the room until they fell upon her mother's form in the chair directly beside her bed. She rubbed the sleep from her eyes.

"How long have you been here, Mommy? Did I sleep too long?" Imogene felt so well rested, she was worried that perhaps it was already the next day. Maybe she had missed her own celebration!

"Don't worry, sweet muffin. You have slept for only three hours, and I've just now come in to wake you. I've only been sitting here for a few minutes. I thought you'd want to be woken up early enough to check out your bedroom, freshen up and dress!" Elsie laughed at the look of relief on Imogene's face, then hopped up from the chair and began to dance around the room! Imogene giggled, sprinted from her bed and joined her mother. They held hands, laughing and dancing around the room together. And as far as Imogene was concerned, everything in this new world was just perfect. They stopped finally and came to rest on the window seat. Imogene took a good look around her room; it was like a dream come true. The bed was covered in the softest blue satin. Satin covered quilt, satin sheets and satin pillowcases. *No wonder I was so comfy*, Imogene realized. The draperies were blue, but made out of heavy velvet, not satin. Imogene was thrilled to see a fireplace of her very own sitting against the far wall. Rather than being made from bricks, like most of the ones she'd seen on the surface, this one was lined with stones. And then Imogene peered closer at her walls. They too, were constructed with stones. The fireplace stones were a little bit different in size and colour than the wall stones, and Imogene thought it was a very clever way to set them apart. Her mother explained, "All of our buildings, Imogene, the walls, floors and even the ceilings are made of stones. They are stuck together with mud, which is very similar to the cement used on the surface." She paused a moment, and then pointed out the window. "You see that we have no window panes? No glass? We don't need it down here. It never rains; it doesn't need to rain. We have enough moisture in the air without rain. The wind, when it blows, it's so slight, that we actually welcome what little breeze there is. And snow? Down here, my dear, there is no such thing. Our seasons do not change. In fact, we have only one season and this is it! It is the way it has always been." Elsie stopped then, as Imogene nodded and looked around the room some more. She saw no lights or candle holders. She was about to ask her mother about it, when her mother began to answer. Imogene laughed, as she had already forgotten about the mental telepathy. Her mother smiled. "The reason our draperies are so thick and heavy, is so we can shut out all of the light when we want to go to sleep. We have daytime and nighttime, much the same as they do above. The major difference is, that it doesn't get dark here, ever." Elsie hesitated again to watch Imogene's reaction. She was truly fascinated. Who wouldn't be? There were *so* many things she still needed to ask.

"My love, you cannot really expect to learn about everything on your first day! You have already found out so much. Give yourself a break for the rest of the day and just enjoy it, okay?" She then led Imogene by the hand to the great big wardrobe that stood tall and noble looking on the other side of the room, across from her bed. Elsie let go of Imogene, as she needed both hands to pull open the two giant doors at the same time. The doors open wide now, Imogene could see just how big the wardrobe actually was. It was amazing! She watched speechless, as her mother climbed into it.

"Aren't you coming? Surely you would like to pick out tonight's outfit?" Imogene giggled as she stepped up and into the closet with her mother. On either side of them, hung rows upon rows of beautiful clothing. Elsie led the tour, as she pointed to the first rack, which held the fancier looking materials. These garments were longer and obviously fuller than the rest, and each piece was trimmed with a different colour of silk. They were all, without a doubt exquisite. "All of this," Elsie waved at them with her arms, "is your formal wear collection." They continued on, and Elsie pointed to the next row. "Here is your casual wear." Imogene felt the material with her hand, and looked questioningly at her mother. Some of these pieces were very small, and they looked like wetsuits. Elsie nodded her head in total agreement. "That's exactly what they are! Wetsuits, for when we go riding."

"Riding?" Imogene's eyes grew wider.

"Yes, Imogene, riding! We have our own line of seahorses. We have maintained the bloodline all the way back to our earliest ancestors. I can show you in the record book later, if you like. Ours is a beautiful, thoroughbred collection and it is the envy of all the other kingdoms." Elsie couldn't for the life of her sound nonchalant about it, and her excitement was definitely contagious. Imogene couldn't wait to get on the back of a real, live seahorse. Elsie shone with pride, as she continued. "I picked out a seahorse for you two years ago. I trained her myself and I just know the two of you will get along famously!" Imogene could not believe her ears. In the blink of an eye, she found herself living smack dab in the middle of a real, live fairy tale.

They finished going through the wardrobe, and finally Imogene chose a robe to wear that evening, with of course, her mother's approval. It was a silk robe; shiny as can be; a soft shade of blue, trimmed in emerald green. She picked out sandals that matched it perfectly. Imogene felt like she was playing dress up. On the surface she had never even seen clothes such as these, let alone try any on.

Later, before the celebration was about to begin, the royal family prepared for it together. Imogene watched in utter fascination as her mother lovingly placed her father's golden and jewel-encrusted crown upon his head. Once it was in place, Roland brought Elsie's crown to Imogene. He nodded toward her mother, and asked, "Imogene, would you like to have this honour?" He beamed down at his beautiful daughter.

"Oh, Daddy! Can I really?" She was eager and didn't wait for him to answer. She took the crown from her father's hands, went over and placed it upon her mother's head. It was fancier than the crown Elsie had worn earlier, and Imogene supposed this one was used for the important, royal occasions. It was adorned with rubies, emeralds and diamonds. The combs on the bottom slid into Elsie's hair with ease, and the crown came to rest midway across her forehead. Imogene thought her mother looked radiant, with or without it. With her fingertips, she gently pushed the stray wisps of her mother's hair away from her face. And then they were ready.

The royal family was truly stunning. The entire kingdom, servants and followers included had been waiting for this special moment for five years. The younger children, who had not yet been born during the time of Serenito's rule, grew up listening to the tales of the time when Princess Imogene would arrive. She was the most famous princess of all the ages; nearly a legend! She was surrounded by mystery and secrets; a captivating subject, indeed. As King Roland, Queen Elsie and Princess Imogene's impending arrival was announced, every waiting face in the crowd glowed with joy. And then, a hush of silence rippled through them all until at last there wasn't a sound to be heard. The royal entertainers sounded their horns, strummed upon their harps and hit softly upon their drums with well-rehearsed hands. Every eye was focused on the great velveteen curtain at the top of the stairs. Necks were craned upward until they ached; yet no one complained. There were six people on either side of the curtain, ready to pull the draw chords at only a moment's notice. There was one final drum roll, and then the curtain slowly began to rise. Finally, before one and all to see, stood at long last, the entire royal family.

The crowd clapped and cheered! King Roland stepped forward and lifted a large funnel shaped shell to his lips. The crowd was silent once more, and readily awaited his speech.

"My good people of the Pacific Kingdom! How long we have waited for this moment. For the royal family to be reunited!" He paused then, and looked around at all of his loyal subjects. How he loved them all. How fortunate he was to have them share this moment with him. "May I present to you all, at long last," and then he turned to Imogene and offered her his arm. She stepped forward and draped her arm through his, before her father continued, "Princess Imogene!" The crowd cheered some more. There was clapping and whistling, and then just as suddenly as it had begun, calm. Imogene stared wide-eyed at her people who, two by two, began dropping to their knees. *They're bowing before me*, she realized, and gasped in surprise. She was glowing; she was so thrilled. She reached back and felt for her mother's hand, who then stepped forth and took it. The royal family stood there together, proudly looking over their great many people. Even Imogene could feel their love and loyalty radiating toward her, and quietly, in her head, she swore that she would never, ever do them wrong. Whatever it took, she would do right by these people. And she had forgotten again for the moment, about the telepathy until her mother gave her a quick, knowing squeeze. Elsie was so proud.

The royal entertainers sounded their horns again, and the people of the kingdom rose to their feet. The royal family descended the stairs then, and started to mingle with the people. Imogene met so many, that she didn't think she'd ever get all the names right. She was disappointed, that so far she could not see Sampson. It was Sampson that she was so looking forward to seeing again. She approached her mother.

"Mommy, where is Sampson and his family? Please tell me they will be here, tonight?" Elsie smiled at her young daughter and she knew just how important Sampson had become to her.

"Yes, my love. Sampson wouldn't miss this event for the world. Don't worry, he'll be here before the feast begins, and I'm sure he'll seek you out right away. His daughter... do you remember Sampson telling you about his daughter who is your age?" Imogene smiled and nodded, after all, how could she forget? She couldn't wait to meet her! "Well," Elsie continued, "Marina is her name and she has been dying to meet you! She just couldn't wait to turn ten land years, for the simple fact that it meant you would also be turning ten and coming home." Imogene felt better knowing that Sampson and his family were coming, and especially knowing that Marina, who sounded like so much fun, was excited about meeting her!

Imogene felt strange in the pit of her stomach, to learn that *all* of these people, and virtual strangers at that, had been waiting for her to turn ten. And until this very day, she hadn't known anything about them! Imogene left her mother's side and wandered slowly through the crowd. She wanted to walk among them; to watch and to listen. It was, as she had found so many times over in the past, the best and fastest way to learn things. It occurred to her to ask her mother later, *what is the difference between land and underwater years?*

Elsie and Roland, having finished their walk-about, took their seats on their royal thrones. The royal thrones were set high on a stage at the front of the room. King Roland had tried to change that arrangement years ago. At first when he had become king, he felt that sitting higher than his people like that, made him appear superior. He felt that he was at the very most, equal to his people. When he brought those concerns to his wife's attention, Elsie wisely answered, "My dear, Roland. The people need a ruler to look *up* to. You have to lead by example, and pray tell me! How can they look up to you if they cannot see you through the crowd? You must leave the thrones high where they are." And that was that. From that day on, Roland made a point of asking his wife's opinion before considering even the slightest change to his monarchy.

And so they sat there like that, high upon their thrones, and scanned the room for their daughter. Elsie spotted her first and she watched Imogene as she silently slipped through and around the people below. Roland clapped his hands twice, signaling the entertainers to begin playing their harps, horns, and drums again. As soon as the music began, Imogene looked up at her parents. Elsie motioned to her with her hand to join them, and so she did. Up on the stage, a little higher than and in between the king and queen's thrones, sat Imogene's. Imogene took her position on her own royal throne, and everyone cheered! King Roland and Queen Elsie stood up, and the entire castle was quiet once again. Imogene just sat and watched, for she had no clue what was supposed to happen next. Just then, a servant rushed up onto the stage, and presented a wrapped package, which sat upon a blue velvet pillow, to the King. The king opened it and Imogene gasped when she saw what it was. King Roland held in his hands, high for all to see, the royal tiara! It was gold wrapped and laden with diamonds and sparkling blue sapphires. Imogene sat as still as she could as her father placed the tiara upon her head. The crowd cheered and clapped some more. Then the king and queen took their seats again, which signaled to the people to resume with their festivities. The royal family remained there, high upon the stage and watched. It was the perfect opportunity for Elsie and Roland to subtly point out to their daughter, just who each person was, and what role if any, they played in the kingdom. Soon Imogene was trying to memorize the face of every labourer, cook and seamstress. She learned who the teachers were, and who the homemakers were. And she knew most of all, that already she loved it in the kingdom.

Dinner was announced a short time later. Imogene discovered that the royal family would be the last to eat. King Roland explained, "The king must look after his loyal subjects first and foremost, my dear Imogene. This is how I show my gratitude to them for all that they do for us. Without these people, there would be no kingdom. Let us rejoice!"

Finally, after every single person, royal members included, had had their fill of fruits and breads and vegetables, it was time for the dance. Imogene watched as every able-bodied person, servant or not, helped to clear away all of the leftover food and dishes. It took no time at all for the floor to be cleared, and the entertainers took their positions at the bottom of the stage. They played soft and slow at first, and the music was so beautiful that Imogene and her parents tapped their toes and swayed in time to the beat. Then King Roland stood, turned toward his daughter and asked, "Princess Imogene, may I have this dance?" He held out his right hand, and bent his left arm behind his back, bowing slightly. Imogene giggled until she saw that he was completely serious. She straightened in her chair and tried to act as proper as she could.

"Of course, sir!" The giggles began again as she added, "But, please don't step on my toes!" The king tried not to snicker on such a formal occasion, but his daughter's giggling was contagious. Elsie laughed openly as she watched Imogene follow her father to the dance floor.

At first, no one else in the kingdom noticed King Roland and Princess Imogene dancing amongst them. But once they did, the word spread through the crowd like wildfire. Soon everyone around them moved off to the side, and stopped dancing. And then, as though on cue, they began clapping and stomping their feet! Imogene was caught up in a complete whirlwind of emotion. She had never had so much attention as this. Gradually, pair by pair, the people began to trickle back onto the dance floor, until there was no one left clapping and stomping. A good time was indeed, being had by all. The very second that the song ended, and directly before the next one was to begin, King Roland felt a tap on his shoulder. It was Sampson!

"Your Majesty, may I cut in?" King Roland stepped aside to allow Sampson to dance with his daughter. Imogene was thrilled to have her trusted friend back. He whisked her across the room and they gracefully circled the dance floor together. Imogene took this opportunity to thank him.

"Sampson, you know I never, ever had any idea about all of this. But you are the one who has guided me and protected me for all those years. How can I thank you for all that?" She was entirely sincere and straight-faced. It meant so much to her to know how much he had willingly given up for her. He smiled back.

"My dear, just as there is no need to apologize, there is no need to thank me. It has all been my pleasure." And that was all he said. She didn't realize that he was choked up with sentiment. He recovered quickly, and asked, "Would you like to meet my wife and children? I would have introduced them earlier, but you have been so busy!" Imogene smiled happily.

"Yes! As soon as possible, too! Where are they?" She abruptly stopped in the middle of their dance and looked around. Sampson laughed again, and then led her by the arm to the other side of the room where his family sat waiting. They rose from their chairs the moment they arrived. His wife started to bow; and as she did so, nudged her children with her elbows to do the same.

"Please!" Imogene cut in, "Really, please don't bow down to me." And then she held out her hand for Sampson's wife to shake. The woman smiled modestly and accepted it. Although she had heard nothing but good things about this little girl, she felt the need to address her the way one should always address a member of the royal family.

"Miss Imogene, this is my wife, Diploma." Sampson happily introduced the two.

"Hello, Princess. It is so good to meet you!" Imogene nodded eagerly, looking the woman up and down at the same time. She liked her immediately and was relieved to see that Sampson had such a nice wife. She was a small thing compared to Sampson, and was blonde haired and fair skinned. Just then a girl Imogene's exact size, pushed herself rudely in between Imogene and Diploma and hopped back and forth from one foot to another! Suddenly she came to a full stop and clasped her hands tightly behind her back. Sampson and Diploma both laughed, as Diploma laid both hands on the child's suddenly still shoulders.

"And this is our overly excited daughter, Marina. Marina, where are your manners?" The fact was that Marina had forgotten all about her manners; she was itching so badly to meet the princess. She held out her hand. Imogene took it immediately, and smiled back at the delightful girl and realized that making a new friend had never been so easy.

"Hi, Marina!" And then Imogene winked at her. Marina burst into hysterics and winked back. She leaned in closer to Imogene, who she just knew was about to become her closest friend. Imogene asked, "Want to come over tomorrow and play?" Marina began hopping around again and bobbed her head up and down in agreement. She liked Imogene instantly, even from a distance, when she'd spotted her for the very first time sitting high upon her royal throne. Sampson pointed to his son, who was standing a little ways behind his mother.

"Miss Imogene, please meet Quosmo." A tall boy came out from behind his mother. Without a moment's hesitation, the handsome young man knelt down on one knee, took Imogene's hand and kissed it! Her cheeks turned hot and a deep shade of red. Embarrassed, she snapped her hand from his and took a step back. With a sudden and strange new feeling creeping over her, she smiled apologetically to Quosmo, then rather abruptly turned her attention back to Marina.

"So how about tomorrow, right after lunch?" Marina readily agreed and Sampson reassured them both.

"My dears, I promise to bring Marina to the castle directly after the noon meal. For now, however, I'm sure the king and queen would like to have their princess returned to them." At that, he offered his arm to Imogene again and led her away. Her stomach was doing flip-flops, she was that excited. She could already tell that she and Marina would become the best of friends. But that Quosmo; Imogene shivered and felt her face turn red again, just thinking about the way he had kissed her hand.

8

IMOGENE AND MARINA

Faithfully, Imogene spent the rest of the evening at her parents' side. She could hardly wait for the night to be over, just so she could see all that the next day would bring. She danced with her father some more, and also watched her mother and father dance together. She could certainly see why all the good people appeared to be enchanted by their very presence. They were in every sense, royalty.

Finally, the celebration drew to a close. As much as Imogene appreciated the fuss made over her, she was glad when the time came to say goodnight. Once every last guest had gone home, the royal family climbed the staircase that led to their house. And at the entrance to her bedroom, Imogene hugged and kissed her parents and bade them goodnight. She retired to her room and changed out of her formal wear. From the wardrobe she picked out a plain pajama to wear to bed. It felt like flannel, much the same as her pajamas up above had been made of. Everything here was so different and new, she surmised, but it was all good. Good different and good new.

Imogene fell into a blissful sleep, almost as soon as her head hit the pillow. When she awoke the next morning and looked outside, she found that she couldn't even tell what time it might be. She would have to ask her mother later, about the underwater method of telling time.

She dressed into a simple robe that ended about mid-calf, and skipped from her room to find her mother. She found her in the royal bedroom, sitting at her dresser, brushing her beautiful dark brown hair. Imogene inhaled deeply, her mother's scent; the same scent she had remembered fondly over the last five years. She reached out and ran her fingers through Elsie's hair. That was probably her second strongest memory of her mother; the soft and beautiful long brown hair.

"Good morning, Mommy!" Imogene sat on her mother's lap. Elsie wrapped her arms around her daughter and squeezed.

"Good morning, sweet muffin!" Did you sleep well, my love?" Elsie watched her daughter's reflection in the dresser mirror as she spoke. Imogene nodded.

"Yes, I did. I think I sleep better down here than I ever did on the surface." And then Imogene's smile faded, and she turned serious. It was all Elsie could do, to not use her telepathy to find out why. She sat patiently, with her arms still wrapped around Imogene, and waited. Imogene moved and sat on the edge of her mother's bed, facing her.

"Mother," Imogene began, realizing that it was the first time she had ever called her, *Mother*. She continued, "What about Auntie Agnes? I have been gone since... how long have I been gone in land time? I don't understand what the difference is! And if Auntie Agnes is really your sister, she must have come from under the ocean too, right?" Imogene wrinkled up her nose; she was weighed down by her inability to know and understand everything at once. She was so frustrated, she was near tears. Elsie sat her brush on the dresser and calmly folded her hands, and set them on her lap.

"I knew these questions would come to you, Imogene, and don't worry. It *is* very confusing. Our calendar down here, the original one had three hundred and seventy-five days in it. Five years ago, your father decreed that it be changed to run the same as the calendar is used above; it is just easier that way. The little bit of difference that a few days make is not a lot to worry about, anyway. And that is why, you've probably heard us say, *land years* as opposed to simply saying, *years*." She saw Imogene let out a big breath of relief.

"Oh, thank goodness. I've been wondering how old I am down here. So I'm still ten, right?"

Imogene felt silly for asking, but she had to know for sure.

"Yes, Imogene, you are still ten!" Elsie laughed then, but not at Imogene. She laughed because she realized just how ridiculous it all must seem. "You have still been gone since last night. The reason Sampson was late making it to your celebration is because he had to return to Auntie Agnes' for a while." Imogene nodded. *So that was why he was late.*

"My dear sister, your Auntie Agnes, grew up in the same kingdom as I did. She was four years older than I, and was the first of us to go up to learn the ways of the world above. But when she learned how much it would mean to the surface dwellers to find out about us, to really find out about us at long last, she jumped at the chance to tell them!" Elsie looked down and shook her head. It was like reliving it all, the whole sordid affair. Her heart still ached for Agnes. Imogene almost felt bad for ever bringing the subject up, when she saw how much it disturbed her mother. Elsie took a deep breath and then continued, "Agnes was a self-centered child, and she grew up to be a self-centered woman. Her main objective in life always seemed to be centered on her own personal gain. While on the surface, she ran into some people who were interested in searching for the real Atlantis. The real Atlantis does exist, Imogene." Imogene's eyes grew as wide as saucers, but she didn't dare interrupt. "I know this for a fact, for that is where I come from. The

Atlantic Kingdom! But could you imagine what would happen to our way of life if they found out? The consequences would be eternal. Irreversible. Luckily for Atlantis and the Pacific Kingdom and all the other kingdoms, Agnes made a grave error in judgment. The silly woman; thankfully, she confided in Diploma. She told Diploma about her plans to share the story on social media, and even worse, *sell* the story to the highest bidder! Just imagine if word got out and spread like wildfire. If the wrong people ever got hold of the truth about us, there would be no end to it. We would be called freaks, and they would capture all of us and put us on display. They might even dissect us in laboratories. It just wouldn't do, Imogene. Ever." Elsie got up from her seat and began to pace around the room.

"Now Diploma cared more about our way of life and the disastrous results that were sure to ensue if Agnes had her way." Imogene squirmed in her seat, and raised her hand as if she were in a classroom.

"Why would Auntie Agnes want to destroy this world? Did she hate it so?" Although Imogene knew firsthand how cold her aunt could be, she just couldn't see her wanting to destroy an entire population.

"No, my love. She didn't hate anything. In order to hate, one must first be able to love. I don't think Auntie Agnes has ever been capable of either emotion. But, like I said before, she was self-centered. As I understand it, a few publishers were ready to give her any amount of money to get their hands on her story. Then she would have been able to have her heart's desire. Anything and everything she ever wanted. But, here's another twist; money means nothing down here. She wanted to use it up there. Her plan was to stay up there permanently; to become rich and surround herself with material things."

"Oh, no. How did Diploma get her to be quiet?" Elsie answered her with a sly look.

"She didn't! Diploma talked about it with Sampson, and then she and Sampson came to me with it. The three of us then talked to your father about it. At that time, your grandfather was still the king, and I know, you have yet to meet him. You will. Anyway, we all went to him with the information and a plan was put into place to lure Agnes back down here before any serious damage was done on the surface." Imogene's mouth gaped open. She hadn't thought her parents or Sampson would be capable of such trickery. She listened intently; it was truly an amazing story. Elsie moved her chair closer to the bed, and then sat down in it again. She leaned toward her daughter, as though she were about to reveal something secret and special indeed.

"Sampson is a doctor, Imogene, and I'll bet you didn't know that!"

"A doctor? No, I had no idea. I always thought

he was just a butler, and a friend."

"Sampson is special, Imogene, he is a doctor of hypnosis. He is the only one this kingdom has, that is until his own children, Quosmo and Marina come of age." Imogene thought she understood, a little.

"Do you mean that it runs through the bloodlines, just like royalty does? Only Sampson's children and their children and can become doctors of hypnosis?"

"Yes, my love, although there are always some exceptions to every rule. Anyway, Sampson's twin brother, Duluth, stayed in the Atlantic Kingdom to practice, while Sampson came here with me. Duluth also has a son to take over for him when he retires. Sampson has always been close with my family. And you probably have guessed by now that he was not ever my parents' butler! He is far too young for that. He and I grew up together. Although he appears much older, only two years separate us." Imogene wrinkled up her nose. How they had deceived her! Elsie caught on right away.

"I couldn't tell you when you were five, that Sampson was an underwater doctor of hypnosis and that the two of you would become the best of friends, Imogene!" Elsie laughed at the sound of that, as did Imogene. Apologetically, Imogene murmured.

"Well, Mother... when you put it that way..."

"That's right, my love. So back to the hypnosis thing. We had to be absolutely certain that Agnes wouldn't carry through with her plans, so we came up with this scheme. The king, your grandfather was involved, only because none of us would ever dream of doing such a thing behind his back or without his approval. And he did give us his consent, because the well-being of every single underwater kingdom was at stake. What happened was, Diploma invited Agnes for a dinner at her home, in Agnes' honour. Agnes, being none the wiser, was glad to attend." Imogene blurted out.

"Let me guess. Being as selfish as she was, she came just because she was the guest of honour?"

"How quickly you catch on. She had to think that she was the honoured guest, because it was the only way we could be certain she'd show up. So, she came all right, and without her even knowing it, Sampson hypnotized her. From that moment on, she has believed that she is and always has been a surface dweller. She remembers nothing of this." Elsie waved her arms around to emphasize. And then Imogene thought of something else, and added.

"And the cane? Why does she walk with a cane?"

"Awesome question, dear. When anyone of us goes to the surface, first we recognize others of our kind by their eyes. Have you noticed that we all have the same colour of eyes?" Imogene nodded. "Well, then there's the scent, but that only works if we've met them before." Imogene nodded again; she remembered being told that, the day earlier. "We also had to have a method of recognizing those of us who have been banished forever from our underwater world. And although there aren't many of us like that up there, it is very important to be able to tell those ones apart. The banished ones must walk with an old, shiny silver cane." It was slowly but surely beginning to come together for Imogene, but not quite.

"Okay, but she knows that she's your sister and that I'm her niece. Where does she think we came from? And Sampson?"

"When Sampson hypnotized Agnes, he imprinted a totally different past into Agnes' memory. To her, those memories are as real as the day is long. She thinks we grew up and lived like any other surface dweller. And she remembers Sampson as being our parents' butler, when we were young. Oh, and her husband who died the year before I brought you to Auntie Agnes? No such man. But she *thinks* she had a husband that died. The estate that she lives in, it actually belongs to your father and me. We pawned a few treasures here and there to pay for it. It has proven its worth to our kingdom, many times over and again." Imogene nodded and stood up. She was satisfied for the time being, with the knowledge she now possessed. Not only that, but all this learning was exhausting. Her stomach growled, and she realized that she hadn't had any breakfast yet.

"Um, Mother... where do we go to eat?"

Imogene didn't know if they were allowed to help themselves to the fridge.

"No fridge, dear. That would require electricity. The only way we have of keeping things cold here, is by immersing them in the deepest part of our lake." Imogene snickered a little, shaking her head the entire time. So much to get used to.

It was almost noon when the two ladies arrived in the dining area. They were served immediately. After enjoying a very late breakfast of fruit and nuts with her mother, Imogene asked, "What should Marina and I do, when she gets here?" Elsie smiled kindly, knowing full well that Imogene didn't know her way around the kingdom at all. And she had already figured that Imogene would most likely enjoy touring around with bubbly, fun Marina. But, she also had something else in mind for the girls.

"Why don't you start by taking her to your room, and showing her your special box of secret things?" Then Elsie gave her daughter that sly look again.

"My... but how did you know? How did *that* get here?" Imogene was surprised at the mention of it!

"Sampson insisted that he bring it back for you. It's in your room, under your bed. Oh, and I forgot to tell you. When he went back to Agnes' last night, he put her to sleep until we can figure out exactly what to do with her!" Imogene laughed as she visualized Sampson standing over her Auntie, putting her unknowingly into a zombie-like state. And then she meandered outside the castle, sat on the grass near the courtyard, and waited for her new friend to arrive.

True to his word, Sampson arrived a short time later with his hopping daughter in tow. Imogene squealed with delight. In her aunt's home, she had never been allowed to have friends over. She hugged them both.

"How is the Miss, this morning?" Sampson asked, with a twinkle in his eye. He knew that she must be in her absolute glory, in this fantastic new world.

"I love it here, Sampson!" And then Marina impatiently placed her hands upon her hips and jumped in between her father and her friend.

"Hey, Dad! *When* did you say you were coming back for me?" Her tone of voice had a funny, sarcastic ring to it. Sampson knew exactly what his daughter was getting at. He smiled as he answered.

"I do believe I said I would fetch you after supper. Now off you girls go, and don't find any trouble!" The girls bolted away from him and ran down the hill and into the valley.

"Marina!" Imogene called to her friend. "If you don't mind leading; I don't know where we're going!" Marina laughed at her and ran faster than before. Imogene struggled to keep up; she was laughing too hard to run. "Wait!" And then she was overcome with hysterics! Imogene gave up and flopped down on the ground. Marina stopped when she couldn't hear Imogene panting and puffing behind her. She ran back to help her friend up, when Imogene grabbed her by the hand and pulled her to the ground. Marina landed with a soft *thump* clumsily beside her. They both broke into giggles again.

The whole entire day was an unforgettable one for both Imogene and Marina. Marina learned about Imogene's life on the surface, and Imogene was able to find out more about the underwater world, which she was now very much a part of. They chatted back and forth the whole time, while they explored the kingdom. They strolled through bountiful orchards and rice fields. They wandered by the honeycombs where the bees lived and they walked through the markets. Imogene was surprised but delighted to find out that there were no stores here to speak of. And that meant of course, no swinging doors, no escalators and no elevators! There were only outdoor markets where people sold or traded their wares. No canned goods of any kind. In fact, she realized, things were just as her father had described, that if it didn't come from the land, then it didn't belong here. He was so right! There was no litter on the streets, and she couldn't see garbage at all, for that matter, lying about anywhere. Very different from the world where she'd grown up.

It was nearing suppertime when the two girls agreed to head back to the castle. Marina had never before stepped foot in the royal chambers, and she was thrilled beyond words. It was all she could do to not hop from foot to foot. They went straight to Imogene's room, where Imogene pulled her special box of secret things out from under the bed. Marina stared at Imogene's mermaid dolls with wonder.

"Is this *us*, Imogene?" At first, Imogene didn't understand what Marina meant. Then it dawned on her, and she looked upon the dolls with the same amazement as Marina. She answered as best she could.

"Well, the surface dwellers don't really believe that there are people living down here, in the first place. But the fairy tales, the stories us children grow up listening to, are about merpeople like these." And then she picked up one of the dolls and ran her hand down the length of its long, scaly looking tail. Marina thought for a moment before saying,

"You know, the historians say that before we walked on this land, we really did have tails like these. They say that before we evolved, we only breathed in the water and lived like fish. And that is where the telepathy comes in. Has your mother told you about any of that?"

"Yes!" Imogene yelped. "And I can't wait to learn more. Go on!" Marina was only too happy to comply.

"Well, once we started to evolve, we eventually lost our tails, began to walk on land and breathe in the air, and we could also live in the water. But then we started living more on the land and less in the water until finally this is where we ended up. Isn't that *cool*?" *Cool* was a new word that Imogene had added to Marina's vocabulary earlier, and Imogene was pleased to hear her using it in the right context, at last.

"Yes," Imogene agreed. "It is very *cool*. So then you learned to talk?"

"We," Marina corrected her. "We, not you. Remember you're one of us?" Marina had felt the need to point that out to her friend more than once throughout the course of the day.

"Yes, we. But where did the English language come in? How come it just so happens to be the same language as they speak above? That's a coincidence, or is it? Why not speak some silly sounding made up language that only the underwater people understand?" It was a valid question indeed, and Imogene could see Marina desperately racking her brains before she dared answer.

"I think, my dear Imogene, that is a question for the historians! Now let's play!" Both girls had enough of the serious chatter for the time being, and they started to play with the mermaid dolls. And, Imogene decided, that it was much more fun playing with them now that she had a friend, than it was when she used to have to play alone.

9

IMOGENE AND THE FORBIDDEN EAST WING

After that very first day that Imogene and Marina spent together, they had become inseparable. King Roland, Queen Elsie, Sampson and Diploma could not have been happier for their daughters. Marina enjoyed showing Imogene all of the everyday kind of things, that until now she hadn't realized how much she either overlooked or took for granted. And she hoped secretly, that someday she would be able to go above, so that Imogene could show her all there was to know about that world. The surface dwellers were so mysterious to her! She couldn't even begin to visualize what it might be like up there.

After Imogene's second week in the underwater kingdom, her parents decided that it was time she begin attending school. They were sitting in the dining room, having just finished eating their evening meal, when Roland brought the subject up.

"School!" Imogene cried out when he approached her about it. "I had forgotten all about school! Are you serious?" She had kind of hoped they didn't have real school under the ocean.

"Of course we're serious, Imogene." Her mother replied. "In fact, the children here in our kingdom have year round schooling. But the good side to that, my dear, is the four day weekends, all year long!" Imogene slouched in her chair. That would mean her playtime with Marina would be restricted to after school and weekends! She wasn't happy about the whole thing. Roland and Elsie, on the other hand, tried hard to hide their smiles. This was their first real indication that Imogene, although a princess, was still a normal ten-year old girl. They were almost relieved.

"Come on, Imogene. Surely you didn't think that it was play, play, play all of the time! And if you're at all curious as so why no children have been in school since your arrival, it is because they were all given two weeks off in your honour!" Imogene laughed at her mother, and then gave her a quizzical look. Now her interest was really perked. She sat straight up in her chair.

"What kind of subjects do they teach down here?"

"Well, we have science, math, history, language, social studies, study of the surface..." Roland began, but Imogene interrupted.

"Daddy, did you *really* say, "study of the surface?" Roland nodded as though it wasn't anything out of the ordinary, but Imogene laughed loud and hard. At that Roland and Elsie both realized how funny it sounded to their child. "Oh, my! Can I teach that?" Imogene asked, trying to sound serious. It didn't work and she broke into gales of laughter again. It was contagious and her parents giggled, too.

"Okay, so let me finish." Roland cleared his throat and tried to stop laughing as he spoke. "We also have weaving and sewing classes, gardening and food preservation. All of these skills you will need to learn as you grow up, Imogene! Oh, and we mustn't forget the fun stuff; riding and ocean exploration!" Now Imogene was super interested. She had already heard about the riding, but ocean exploration?

"Ocean exploration? What is that?" She pictured herself swimming about, looking at fish and shells, but she just knew there had to be more to it than that.

"Ocean exploration is just about what it sounds like, but not quite. We go on quite large expeditions, which can last anywhere from a day to a week long! We search for sunken ships and learn about the people who sailed them by the things left behind." Now that was something Imogene would really look forward to.

"I can't wait for that! What kinds of things have we found, so far?" Roland was glad that his daughter was so genuinely concerned with the expeditions, especially since it was his own area of expertise.

"Well, for one thing, we have found a lot of treasure; you know, gold, jewels and the like. But that doesn't teach us a whole lot about the surface dwellers, aside from the fact that they have always placed a lot of value on monetary things."

"Monetary, what does that mean?" Imogene could not remember ever having heard that word before.

"Monetary things, for example, kind of means things that would fetch a high price. Something that is worth a lot of money. Down here, we tend to place more value on sentimental things. We value them in our heart, instead of in our wallet." Imogene nodded, then replied.

"I think I know what you mean now. Is it like mother's dolphins? Like maybe they wouldn't cost a lot to buy them in a store, but I wouldn't sell them for any money in the world?" Roland and Elsie both agreed at the same time. Elsie answered.

"Exactly, Imogene! You see, you already know what sentimental value is. And my mother handed those dolphins down to me. They have played a great role in all of our lives."

"That reminds me, Mother. Why did they glow the night I arrived, and why have they stopped glowing now? And they moved! They really did and they pulled me into the ocean, and it was magical!" Elsie nodded again, eager to explain. Roland leaned in closer, as he was just as keen on hearing more about the dolphins.

"Okay, you know Sampson is a doctor of hypnosis? Well, he cast a hypnotic spell on the dolphins. He made the dolphins bring you to us; it was the only way we could figure out for you to come." This only confused Imogene further. Elsie could tell by the way her daughter's nose wrinkled up. She continued.

"We people of the kingdom, are unable to physically *bring* someone down here who has never been. Surface dwellers have found us, some of them, anyway, but on their own. Now Agnes is a good example. She was going to show the world the way, by drawing it on a map. She wouldn't have been able to *bring* them. It's just impossible. The same thing rings true with you. You had never been here before ever, even though you are of the Pacific Kingdom. Sampson could not bring you, and yet there was no way that you could have found the way on your own. And that is where the dolphin pendant came into play." Imogene was completely awestruck, and another question came to mind.

"Okay, I think I get all that, kind of. But do tell me, how in the world did Sampson get here before I did?" And then, just as she'd asked it, the answer came to her as clear as day. "Oh, my, there's another way, isn't there? There is!" She couldn't wait to find out where it was. Her father responded.

"Yes, Imogene. There are in fact, many ways to come down here! The tunnel or cave that you used is the main portal. There are four other underwater tunnels that branch into it, which is why the dolphins were so important; to make sure you didn't turn and go the wrong way."

"I didn't realize there were other tunnels in the cave! What if I had taken a wrong turn?" Imogene subconsciously brought her hand up to her chest to feel for the pendant.

"No," her father interjected. "The dolphins wouldn't have allowed it. Not with one of Sampson's spells! Anyway, speaking of Sampson, you wanted to know how he beat you here? You won't believe this, my dear." The suspense of it all hung thick in the air, and Imogene was sitting on the very edge of her seat. This time she didn't interrupt. Elsie saw how impatient her daughter had become, and smiled.

"In due time, Imogene! Yes, it's all very magical and mysterious, but it has to be. If it were so easy to find us from above, imagine the trouble we'd be in." Imogene agreed with her mother, but turned again to her father.

"Please, Daddy, do go on. I just have to know. Tell me, tell me!" And now the child was literally bouncing in her chair. She couldn't wait to find out more about the secrets and the magic.

"Okay, okay. Now do you remember the East Wing in Auntie Agnes' house?" Imogene's eyes almost popped right out of their sockets. Her mouth dropped open in astonishment, then with her sense of humour kicking into high gear, she brought her hand up and tapped her jaw shut, again. Her parents chuckled at her antics.

"Are you about to tell me, that the East Wing, in the same house that I spent the last five years in, has anything do to with this?" She was near shock.

"No, my darling child." Roland answered quickly. Then he leaned toward her with a mischievous look and said, "The East Wing has absolutely *everything* to do with this!"

Just then, one of the dining room servants, Elena, came in and asked the royal family if there was anything else they needed. It was getting late now, and Imogene was disappointed at the interruption, but only briefly; she realized how thirsty she had become. Elsie answered gratefully.

"Yes, my dear, and thank you for asking. I would like a pot of tea, please." Roland nodded in agreement and Imogene asked for a cup of juice. She stopped herself short of asking for a *glass* of juice, as she would have done up above. Down here, the only items made from glass were of the absolutely necessary sort; eyeglasses, medicine bottles and mirrors were the most common. Drinks were always served in earthenware cups.

"Thank you, Elena." Roland called out as she left

to fetch the refreshments. They could all use a drink after all the talking they'd already done, and Elsie and Roland were very much aware, that they were nowhere close to being through as long as Imogene kept asking questions.

"As you were saying, Father, about the East Wing? What do you mean it has *everything* to do with this? Please tell!" She was sure that this would be a bigger mystery than she had ever begun to imagine. Roland put his fingers to his lips and then turned to Elena, who had just returned with their drinks.

"Thanks again, Elena. And do tell me, do you begin your week long holiday tomorrow?" Roland loved keeping in touch with all of his servants, and he knew them all by name.

"Yes, Your Majesty! My husband and I are going to take our son to see the wreck on the south side. He's very excited about going!" Roland could tell that Elena was excited as well.

"And where will you stay, my dear? That's a long way to travel." He looked up at her questioningly. He had a way of asking questions that did not make him seem nosy. He appeared, and rightly so, to be genuinely concerned. He was always, in fact, genuinely concerned about everyone in the kingdom.

"We'll stay for a night on the Coral Reef. One night on the way there and one night on the way back. We're only planning to explore for a day, as we have too much to do at home to be gone the entire time. Thank you for asking!" And then Elena curtsied gracefully to the royal family, turned and left the room.

"Where does Elena live, Daddy?" Imogene asked once the servant was out of earshot.

"Elena lives at the bottom of the valley, adjacent to the first rice field that you see on the right hand side," her father explained. "You will get to meet her son, Rafe, who is ten just like you! But of course, you won't meet him until he and his family return from exploring the wreck. His father is in charge of most of the rice harvesting in the valley." Imogene nodded, and silently wished it were she who was going to explore the wreck with her family. Elsie heard, and as she poured tea into her and Roland's cups, she thought how best to dissuade Imogene from taking on such expeditions so soon. She set the teapot back in its place and looked at her daughter.

"Imogene, dear, in due time! You can't do everything at once, and you especially cannot go exploring yet. Not until you have been properly educated about the dangers." Imogene hadn't even considered that it might be dangerous, but now she understood that exploring for the time being was to be completely out of the question. She sipped her juice, and then turned again to her father.

"*Please* tell me about the East Wing!" And then she threatened, "I'll go crazy if you don't." Her parents smiled.

"Okay, okay, Imogene. Are you sure you want to know?" He was teasing her now, and Imogene folded her arms across her chest; she was slightly annoyed. He soon gave in, for she really had waited long enough. "The East Wing, of course is a secret. The only people in the kingdom who know anything about it are us and Sampson and Diploma. As you may have guessed, Sampson and Diploma are our most trusted friends." He was right, Imogene had already assumed as much. But silently, she urged him on. *East Wing, East Wing!* Elsie heard her again, and Roland wrinkled his brows and looked from his wife to his child, then just shook his head. He continued, "When we go on our expeditions, like I mentioned before, sometimes we find gold and jewels. You know that we have no need for them down here, and so we store them in the East Wing of Auntie Agnes' house."

"Oh, my! Daddy, what does Auntie Agnes think of that?" Now it was Roland's turn to laugh.

"Agnes? She hasn't got the faintest idea! Sampson brainwashed her into thinking only that the East Wing is forbidden!" Roland just about roared with laughter now, and he tried desperately to finish his sentence. Elsie covered her mouth with her hand. She knew that the last thing he needed, was to hear her giggling, for then he'd never be able to finish what he wanted to say. "The funniest part about it," he sputtered as he smacked his hand on his knee, "is that she thinks it was her idea!" Now the entire royal family burst into laughter. That was hilarious.

A few moments later, they settled down again. Quietly, Elsie and Roland sipped away at their tea, and Imogene drank the rest of her juice.

"Daddy, you can't be finished telling me about the East Wing and Sampson, are you?" She hoped not, and tried to be polite as she gently reminded him.

"No, as a matter of fact, I'm not. I'll tell you some of the rest, but your mother will have to tell you more about Sampson and the East Wing. The jewels and gold, the ones we take are the ones that have been on the ocean floor for hundreds of years. Therefore we prefer not to think of it as stealing, because whomever it belonged to has been gone for a good, long while. We store what we can up in the East Wing, and use it as we need it."

"But," Imogene was quick to point out. "You said there is no need for gold and jewels down here. What do you use it for?"

"Valid question, my dear. I am a good example of that. When I went up to the surface and acted like one of them, I decided to go to school to improve my experience up there. In order to go to school, and by school I mean college, right? I took a course in marine biology to learn what they teach the surface dwellers about sea life. School costs money, and we don't have money. So, little by little, we sell off the gold and jewels as we need, to fund our causes. In the long run, it's for the betterment of the kingdom. As you can guess, there are more gold pieces and jewels sitting there in the East Wing, than I think this kingdom will ever need. So much in fact, that recently we've stopped bringing it up." And then Roland was done explaining. He took another sip of his now cold tea, and motioned for his wife to begin.

"My turn!" Elsie shouted happily. It was her pleasure to tell Imogene how Sampson had made it to the kingdom so quickly. "So there's the East Wing, right? Well, it isn't just on the second floor, you know." She watched Imogene wrinkle up her nose, then continued. "There is a very narrow, three story staircase hidden within one of the walls in a bedroom on the East Wing." She paused dramatically, expecting Imogene to cut in at any moment with one of her many questions. But she didn't. She just sat and stared at her mother, silently coaxing her to go on. "It leads from the upstairs of the East Wing straight down to the basement!" Now that was too much for Imogene to take quietly, and she burst out.

"Basement, what basement? There's no basement!"

"Oh, yes, there is dear. The secret staircase is the only way into the basement. There are no windows to it. So now the basement has a dirt floor. But there are many rooms and hallways down there, just like there are on the first and second floors. In this one particular room, there is a pool of water in the floor. That pool is the entrance to a tunnel which leads to the main portal that you took. It is indeed, a faster way of travelling, and Sampson uses it daily." Imogene shook her head and looked from her mother to her father. She had no more questions to ask on this day. The royal family unanimously decided that there had been enough discussion for one night, and they brought their dishes into the kitchen. Imogene had so much to think about, she thought her head might explode! She and her parents climbed the stairs to the royal chambers. At her bedroom door, she kissed and hugged her parents, and bade them goodnight. And once again, just as soon as she had tucked herself into bed, she had fallen fast asleep.

10

IMOGENE AND THE HIDDEN SCHOOL

The next morning, Elsie arrived in Imogene's room quite early to wake her up. "Imogene, it's time to get up, dear!" Still drowsy, Imogene turned away from her mother, at the same time pulling her pillow down and over her head.

"But, Mother," she complained. "It's so early... why do I have to get up at this crazy hour?"

"Crazy hour, my dear Imogene. Perhaps we've spoiled you rotten by allowing you to sleep until noon for the past few weeks!" Elsie exaggerated as she teased her daughter. "It's only six-thirty in the morning and you *must* get up. School starts at eight."

"Eight? Oh, my. Up above, school doesn't start until nearly nine! Now I guess you're going to say it lasts until suppertime." Imogene was disgusted.

After all, who ever heard of school beginning at eight?

"No, actually. That's where the good news comes in. School is over at quarter to two." Imogene pushed the pillow away from her face, and then pulled her covers off. Sitting up straight now with her feet dangling off the edge of her bed, she looked at her mother in wonder.

"Really?"

"Yes, really. Now supposing that you don't want to be late on your first day, and especially since no matter what time you show up, all eyes will be upon you..." And having said that, Elsie walked over to her daughter's great big wardrobe and pulled the doors wide open. While Imogene freshened and washed up for the day, Elsie picked out a school uniform. Imogene's nose wrinkled up instantly at the sight of it.

"Yuck! I can't wear that thing!" She didn't want to believe that her mother was actually going to make her wear that. Elsie had lain out on Imogene's bed, a cream coloured peasant-style top, pulled tight at the neck with a drawstring cord. The sleeves were neither long, nor short, they were just plain odd. And the pants weren't even long enough to reach her ankles, but they were too long to be shorts. They too, had a drawstring cord at the waist. The cords looked like they were made from braided seaweed.

"My dear, this is the school uniform. The sleeves

are called three quarter length and the pants are called knickers. Every child; girl and boy alike must dress pretty much the same. The boys' clothes have more of a masculine look to them than these do," she explained. "When you are in school, you will dress the same as the other children, royalty or not. We can't have it appear that you are too good to dress like the rest. And besides, Imogene. You've made such a wonderful impression on the kingdom so far, it would be a shame to ruin it over some silly clothes!" Imogene felt ashamed of her behaviour, and she really was far from feeling superior to anyone. She nodded solemnly to her mother, who then left the room to let Imogene dress alone.

After the usual delicious breakfast of fruit and nuts that Imogene never tired of, a servant announced that a guest had arrived for her. Imogene was pleased to see Marina hop into the room! She had arrived just in time to walk with her to school, and Imogene was even happier to see that Marina was wearing an outfit identical to her own.

"Marina! Good morning!"

"Hello, Princess Imogene," Marina replied formally, and as she did so, curtsied to her and the queen.

"Don't be silly, my dear," Elsie addressed the child. "Please don't curtsy or anything like that when it's just us around! The only time that would be necessary is when we are in public; at royal functions and the like." She smiled at the girl, who was beginning to flush. Elsie was quick to add, "And Marina, please consider our house to be your second home! You are welcome here, anytime." Marina relaxed and smiled back appreciatively at the queen.

"Thank you, Your... I mean, Elsie?" Marina stammered, as she was now totally unsure as to what to call her. Elsie laughed and put the child at ease again. How she had a way with children.

"Yes, Elsie will do just fine, as long as *I* can call *you* Marina!" At once, the little bit of tension that had been there momentarily, dissipated. And Marina knew she would not have any problem at all, considering this fine castle, to be her second home. How lucky she was, to be Imogene's friend.

Imogene and Marina bounded out of the castle, across the bridge and headed toward the school that was nestled deep in the valley. Imogene was happy now, to be going. And Marina was just as happy to be bringing her there for the first time. She so adored her new friend.

"Imogene," Marina began, as they skipped along the path. Imogene looked at her friend, who had a troubled expression on her face.

"Yes, is something wrong?" Imogene's nose wrinkled at the very idea.

"No, nothing is wrong, at all! I've just kind of been wondering, do you think that you and I will ever be able to go to the surface? I mean, together?"

Marina had always dreamt of going there, at least once, but now that she had Imogene, she thought it could be an adventure they could share. Imogene laughed, as she hadn't before, actually considered that.

"Yes! Wouldn't that be fun? *Me* showing *you* around for a change? Oh, I hope so, Marina. I think that whatever we do, we'll always have fun together!" Marina smiled wide. She couldn't wait.

They reached the pebble path now; the one that Imogene had mistakenly assumed would lead them to the school building. But, she still couldn't see the school anywhere, and finally, she couldn't stand it any longer and had to ask.

"Where is it, Marina? How far do we have to walk to get there?" And just as she'd asked, groups of children joined them on the road. Although they were all walking in the same direction, it didn't appear that they were going to reach the school anytime soon. Marina laughed.

"Oh! I forgot to tell you, and I guess your mother did, too. The school is hidden..." And then she pointed down the road to a little hill that looked like nothing more than a raised field. "...right there!" Imogene peered closer at the field. They were closer to it now, but is still didn't look anything like a school.

"What do you mean, *hidden*? Why hide a school?" Marina raised her eyebrows and gaped at Imogene. She was stunned that Imogene had no idea why the school was hidden. After all, *everyone* knew that!

"Why, the school is hidden to protect *you*. I can't believe you didn't know any of this!" Imogene's mouth dropped open in surprise, but she remained silent. And there was no time for Marina to do any more explaining, as the road was full of children now. The two friends filed in with the rest, as they all made their way across the road, *opposite* of where the hill sat! Once across, they walked among the tall bushes and trees, which hid the entrance to another path that lay underneath the road they had just crossed. Imogene tried to act casual about the whole thing, as though it were a purely natural thing to do; to walk on a road that was beneath another road to get to a hidden school. Marina's words still rang loud and clear in her ears. *Why, the school is hidden to protect you.* As soon as school was over, Imogene would have to find out from her parents, exactly what kind of danger she might still be in.

Imogene was surprised to find that the school was quite large. There were different rooms for each of the different grades, and hallways and bathrooms, a library and even a gymnasium. If she didn't let herself think about the school being hidden in the ground under a hill, she might have even thought of it as a perfectly normal school. There were skylights to let in some light, but not much as Imogene figured that they too, were hidden by bushes, and therefore the light that filtered through was dim. The air was fresh, and

Imogene supposed that was due to the paneless skylights above. Candles that hung high on the walls were responsible for most of the light that lit the rooms and halls.

"School begins every Tuesday with an assembly in the gym." Marina explained. She held onto Imogene under the arm and led her along.

"Please don't let go, Marina. If I become distracted, I may get lost!" They both laughed, but Marina kept a firm grip. There were after all, hundreds of faces that she could easily imagine her friend becoming lost in. They arrived in the gym, and the two girls took their seats along with the rest of the students.

The principal began his speech on this day, no different than his speeches were on any other day. He briefly outlined the rules and discussed the upcoming schedules. Imogene was relieved, and yet surprised to find that he made no mention at all about her arrival in the kingdom. She looked questioningly to Marina, who was quick to enlighten her, in a hoarse whisper, "Your parents asked that the principal and teachers not make a big deal about you. My mom and dad told me, and that's how I know. Anyway, your mother and father thought the best way for you to fit in, was if you were treated just like the rest of us students." Imogene nodded and made a mental note to thank her parents for it when she got home. She'd pretty much had enough of being the center of attention, everywhere she went. The principal closed his speech and the students were dismissed. Marina hung onto Imogene's arm again and told her, "You're to stick with me; we have all of our classes together!" Imogene smiled gratefully at Marina, who continued, "Our parents thought it would be best, so if you need help catching up, I can help you. I am, after all, an honour student." Marina was very proud of her scholastic accomplishments and wasn't the least bit afraid to brag about it.

The school day came to an end, and Imogene was nearly dizzy from all that she had to learn. It had been so overwhelming. On the way back to the castle that afternoon, Imogene, a little embarrassed, confessed to her friend, "Oh, Marina. I am so glad we have our classes together. I can't remember anything I was taught today." Marina poked her friend in the side and snickered at her.

"Imogene, give yourself a break. It was your first day. So many new things to see and do, and so many faces to remember. You weren't expected to learn anything yet, really. Just get used to everything for now, is all." Imogene had to agree; it was like her mother kept repeating, *in due time*. Marina suddenly began hopping from foot to foot, as only she could do, and then she sprinted away. "Come on, Imogene. Let's go play!" The girls ran the rest of the distance back to the castle.

That night, after supper and once the servants had all gone home or to their quarters for the night, the royal family remained in the dining room. They had instantly fallen into this routine; sitting and talking after a day's meal and it had become an event they all looked forward to. On this particular occasion, the king and queen could tell that Imogene had something pressing on her mind.

"Mother and Father," she began directly, as there was no use in beating around the bush. She had to know now. "Please tell me why I attend a school that has a hidden road and why the school is hidden underground? I heard, and maybe it's only a rumour, that it is hidden that way because of me!" She was indignant; her voice rising up a notch with every word she spoke. She looked at her parents accusingly, because as far as ten-year old Imogene was concerned, there was no excuse good enough this time, for her to be kept in the dark. Roland and Elsie exchanged quick looks, and then began to laugh. Imogene sat taller in her chair and folded her arms across her chest; she was growing more defiant with each passing minute. The silence was unbearable. Elsie placed her hands flat upon the table in front of her, and having become as serious as her daughter, replied.

"My dear, Imogene. We could no longer tell you about the school you would be attending, than I could first tell you about why your father and I had to leave you way up above, back then. Some things must simply run their course and happen in due time. If your father and I had tried to tell you about the hidden road that leads to the hidden school, before you actually went and saw it for yourself, do you really think you would have been more prepared? Or perhaps would you have been more nervous about your first day than you already were?" Imogene was beginning to hate it when her mother was always right. Her cheeks turned hot and flushed with embarrassment. She managed to stammer.

"Well, when you put it like that..." And that was the closest that Imogene would ever get to admit to being wrong. Knowing she was wrong was bad enough, without coming out and saying it! Her father cleared his throat then, and began to speak.

"It is not a rumour, Imogene, that the road and school are like that to protect you. It is the truth. After I came into the throne, you had of course, already been born, and your mother was still on the surface with you. Then Serenito threatened your life! Although that threat seems to have passed ever since you reached the age of ten, and thus far no harm has come to you, we still refuse to take the chance that he may come after you. So, as soon as I came to rule this kingdom, we changed the way of the school. We enacted a law that said every child must dress the same when they attend school. That way, should Serenito return and try to find you there, he could not easily pick you out from the crowd. And that would be, only if he *found* the school in the first place! Anyone who doesn't live here, could ever suspect that there is a school hidden in that hill. Now, as a double safeguard, the children who live across the valley actually pass through the old school. To anyone looking in, it looks as though they are entering that school and not coming straight out the other side. But they in fact, do." Imogene was amazed at the foresight and trickery that had been put into place while she had been living on the surface with Auntie Agnes. She sat quietly and waited for her father to finish.

"Anyway, they come out the back of the school, and exit the building underneath another road, on yet another hidden road. That road winds through some bushes and the orchard, until finally it meets up with the road that you took this morning with Marina. We have lookouts. Should anyone other than those students happen to enter the old school, a kingdom wide alarm would sound and we would all be on full alert."

"Oh, my!" And that was all that Imogene had to say about that.

During the second week of school, Rafe had returned from his holiday with his parents. Imogene knew immediately that he had to be Elena's son, the boy whom she'd already heard a lot about. He looked a lot like his mother, from his crooked glasses to his paler than pale complexion. Where his mother's hair was red, his own was jet black and looked more like a perfectly round thick carpet that had been ever so carefully placed upon his head. He was shorter and scrawnier than most of the kids his age, but he seemed to fit in well, anyway. Imogene readily introduced herself to him at her first opportunity, and she found out that he was just as nice as Marina was. Better yet, she was pleased to learn that Rafe and Marina were also good friends. And so it happened, that Rafe joined Imogene and Marina on their daily walk to and from school. They had now evolved into a threesome.

For the next couple of weeks, Imogene tried earnestly to concentrate on her studies. Marina proved to be a fantastic example for her to follow; especially because she was a child who never fooled around in class. If Imogene were to judge her friend by the way she hopped around from foot to foot out of school, she never would have guessed it. Marina always studied hard and her assignments were always handed in ahead of schedule. Imogene followed her lead, and was turning into quite the model student, herself. Rafe also had all of his classes with the two girls; he was quite scholastically inclined, and his biggest interests leaned toward history and language. In comparison to all the rest of the students, Imogene was fairing very well. Her celebrity status had calmed down considerably and her fellow classmates had begun to treat her like just another regular student. Imogene was more content than she'd ever been. This new life, in her opinion, was far more than she had ever hoped for.

11

IMOGENE AND THE ROYAL DILEMMA

Imogene sat up in bed with a start. She looked outside, and then feeling suddenly frustrated, she flopped down onto her back. *When am I ever going to stop looking outside to see what time it is?* She was annoyed with herself. She just had to ask her mother for her own clock; she couldn't bear not knowing the time.

Imogene washed up and dressed then, and took her sweet time doing it. It was Friday, and that was *another* thing she wasn't used to; there was no school underwater, on Fridays or Mondays! Not a bad thing to become accustomed to, she supposed. Marina and Rafe would be arriving to play with her after lunch, and Imogene planned to just laze around until then. She was now ready for the day, and left her room to find her mother.

Imogene had fully expected to find her mother in front of her dresser, brushing her beautiful long hair. But when she arrived in the royal bedroom, Elsie was nowhere to be seen. Imogene looked to the bed. Neither of her parents were in it, but stranger than that, it was left unmade. Her mother *never* left the bed in such a mess! In almost a fretful state, Imogene sped from the royal bedroom and through the royal chambers. She was in such a dither that she nearly tripped and fell down the stairs that led to the dining room. She caught herself just in time on the top step, and took the rest of them down, two at a time.

Imogene had made such a racket running down the hallway and stairs, that by the time she rounded the corner that led to the dining room, all eyes were upon her. And right there, sitting at the table as though nothing were out of the ordinary, were her parents and Sampson.

"Hello, Sampson,!" she spat, totally out of breath. "Good morning, Mother and Father!" She was relieved to find them healthy and well, but she was still suspicious about the bed being left unmade. Elsie heard her concerns and smiled at her daughter.

"Good morning, sweet muffin! Did you sleep well?" To which Imogene, who was still trying to catch her breath, only nodded. It was her father who spoke next.

"Hello, dear. And what mischief have you got

planned for today? I understand that Rafe and Marina will be joining you after lunch?" Imogene nodded again, but she was quick to add.

"No mischief, Father, I haven't learned how to be bad down here, yet. That's why my friends are coming over... to show me!" She giggled then at her own quick wit. She loved to tease her parents. Then she turned to her longtime friend, "Sampson, I'm sorry if this is rude, but don't you usually do doctor type of things at this time of the day?" This was the first time Sampson had been by for a visit, at least while Imogene had been there. What *was* the occasion? Roland nearly choked on his tea.

"Oh, Imogene. You and your sharp tongue never cease to amaze me. Sampson, do tell. Was our child this sarcastic on the surface, or do we just bring out the worst in her?" They all laughed, and Sampson held up his hands humorously to protest.

"It's not my fault! I only watched out for the child!" Even Imogene giggled at that. As far as she was concerned, her parents couldn't have asked for a better person to be her guardian. She smiled warmly at Sampson, and then looked at her parents expectantly. As soon as her father cleared his throat, she could tell that whatever he was about to say, was sure to be of a serious nature.

"Well, Imogene. Sampson does have a good reason to be here this morning. We have found ourselves in the unfortunate midst of a dilemma!"

"A dilemma? Oh, no." That sounded bad.

"No, dear," Elsie piped in. "It isn't necessarily bad; it's more like a problem. Yes, that's it. We just have a problem that we need to solve." Imogene calmed down a little, then wondered if she should stay in the room or go. Was she to be included in the problem solving? Elsie heard.

"You can definitely stay for this, Imogene. In fact, you may be able to help us." Imogene wriggled in her seat, excited now. She really hoped this would involve magic and secrecy.

"So is it a big secret?" She turned to Sampson then. "It has something to do with hypnosis, doesn't it? It does, I know it does!" Imogene squealed with delight.

"First of all," Elsie warned with a threatening tone. "I said it's a problem. Not a happy problem, however. Second of all, Sampson is here of course, because it has *everything* to do with hypnotism. And thirdly, yes it is a secret, and no, you cannot discuss it with your friends." As soon as she was through admonishing her daughter, Elsie gave her the *look*. Imogene understood immediately that she'd better behave a little more seriously, or run the risk of being left out of the conversation. She smiled apologetically then, and slumped down a little further in her chair.

"One of the reasons," Sampson started suddenly, as if to change the mood, "that I would like you to be involved, Imogene, is because your parents and I would like you to begin learning the art of hypnosis." Imogene looked at Sampson, shocked. There was no wink. She stammered.

"But, but I thought... doesn't it run only in the bloodlines?"

"Yes, to a certain degree." He answered. "But there is an exception, and only one exception at that. Any member of the royal family can learn it as well." Imogene was still taken back, and she had to make sure she was hearing this right.

"Aren't I a little young? I mean, Quosmo is learning, but he is twelve." It wasn't as though she didn't want to learn.

"No, dear. Quosmo was your age when he began apprenticing. And Marina is the same age as you. The two of you could learn it together. How would you like that?"

"Oh, yes, please! Does Marina know?" And now Imogene could hardly contain her excitement.

"No, not yet, she doesn't. We wanted to talk to you about it first, to see how you felt about it. Now we know, and I will discuss it with my daughter. But you must remember, nobody can know. No one can find out that you; especially you, will be learning hypnosis. Not everyone knows the exception to the rule, Imogene. And it would be best that we keep it that way." Imogene nodded in agreement then, and she was still waiting to hear about the royal dilemma.

"I promise not to tell a soul, Sampson!" And then she looked first to her mother, and then over to her father. "Father, what is the dilemma?" He cleared his throat again.

"Well, straight to the point; the dilemma is Auntie Agnes. We still don't know what to do with her." Imogene laughed then, remembering the conversation she'd had about her earlier, with her mother.

"I guess you think she has slept long enough?"

"That's exactly it, Imogene!" Her mother replied. "Is it right of us to just have her lay there, day in and day out the way she's been? We've been so busy down here, wrapped up with you, that quite honestly, until Sampson showed up this morning, I haven't given Auntie Agnes much thought at all." Roland added.

"But you know that we can't trust her any further than we could throw her. To release her from the hypnotic state would be to endanger too many lives! I can't see how we could risk it." He shook his head. Sampson picked up where the king had left off, and spoke directly to Imogene.

"And to wake her up only for her to find out that you and I have disappeared. It just wouldn't be fair, my dear. She has looked after you for so long, I hate to think what it would do to her to find you missing." The three adults then, all having said their piece in explaining the predicament, looked solemnly down at the table. They weren't naturally deceitful; in fact it was their honesty that they were respected for the most. Imogene thought too, long and hard. The four of them were still sitting there like that, staring at the table, when Elena came in.

"Excuse me," she said, and then curtsied. She tried not to give them all sideways glances, but the truth was, that she thought it was odd the way the four of them sat there so still and quiet like that. Elena had begun to wonder if someone had died. The royal family and Sampson looked up when they heard the sound of her voice.

"I'm sorry, Elena. What was that?" Elsie asked.

"Oh, Your Majesty! I was only wondering if the four of you would like some tea and cookies. Lunch is a ways off yet, and I know it was hours ago when you ate breakfast."

Elsie looked suddenly at Imogene then. She had just realized that the poor girl had not yet had a bite to eat. "Yes, please Elena. And double the cookies, if you don't mind!" And then she added, "And how is it, Elena, that you always know exactly when to serve us?" Elena smiled then, and turned and left for the kitchen. Imogene smiled gratefully at her mother.

"Thank you, Mother, I didn't even know how hungry I was until Elena came in." She had become so involved with the talk of hypnosis and Auntie Agnes and the whole dilemma thing, that the thought of food hadn't once crossed her mind. They continued to sit quietly, and deep in thought, even until a good while later when Elena returned with the snacks and drinks.

"My apologies," she started. "The cookies were not quite done baking, and so I waited for them to finish. At least they are fresh." She finished, with a hopeful smile; she hated being late for anything. And then she laid everything out on the table for them. She brought two teapots instead of the usual one, and a large cup of juice for the princess. Once the whole spread was ready and in place, Elena curtsied and was about to leave. Imogene helped herself right away; she was so hungry.

"Excuse me, Elena?" Imogene called over her shoulder to the servant. Elena stopped dead in her tracks. "Please, what kind of cookies are these?" They were so good! Elena smiled as she returned and stood next to Imogene.

"Oh, Princess, these are mineral weed, and actually, Rafe favours them as well!" Imogene nodded and kept on chewing. After she'd swallowed her mouthful, she thanked Elena, who promptly left the dining room. Imogene had to laugh out loud, for if anyone had ever before offered her a mineral weed cookie, she surely would have declined the offer. And then she realized that this was the first baked treat she'd had since her arrival in the kingdom.

"Mother, I can't believe I didn't notice until now. How were these cookies baked without power?" Cookie crumbs flew from her mouth; she was in such a hurry to find out. To Imogene, this was yet another mystery. Now that she really thought about it, she had eaten delicious bread... but hadn't given its origin a single thought. Her mother laughed.

"You're so funny, Imogene! And you know, it didn't occur to me that you might wonder about that. Such a curious child. There are, under this ocean like all the rest, underwater volcanoes." She saw the innocent look of skepticism cross her child's face. "No, really, dear." Anyway, we're fortunate enough to have some live ones right on our surface, right here in the kingdom. They stretch deep within the earth, and they lie beyond the valley. That is why you haven't seen one yet. So, we haul live, lava rocks to the palace every week. We keep them deep in the ground where they retain their heat. We take them out as we need them, and use them in our rock ovens." Imogene really looked doubtful. And she crossed her arms across her chest and gave her mother the look that said, *I don't think so*. At first, Elsie, Roland and Sampson all laughed at Imogene. Elsie forced herself to be serious for a moment and continue the lesson. This wasn't really fair to her daughter.

"Imogene, really. We have three rock ovens in our kitchen in the castle. Usually the small one is only used, but if we have a function and we are feeding the entire kingdom, we use the two bigger ovens as well. The rock ovens are pits dug into the ground, lined with regular stones. We then take the lava rocks and use them to fill the pit with. The lava rocks heat up the regular rocks and together they become hot enough to cook with, all day long! The neatest part about it, is when the lava rocks burn out, as they do by the end of each week, we simply return them. By the time our second week's supply is used up, we take them back and get the old lava rocks again." Imogene nodded then and made a mental note to check it out for herself, later. Elsie heard and chuckled quietly.

Sampson, while Elsie had been talking to Imogene about the rocks and ovens, had made very good use of his time. He'd been thinking long and hard until finally he had come up with the ultimate plan. And now it was his turn to speak.

"Elsie, Roland and Imogene! I think I may have come up with a solution to the royal dilemma." The royal family looked at him anxiously as they could not wait to hear him out. "What we can do, to be the most fair, is this. Now, wait; listen to me before you say anything. This *can* work if we truly want it to, and if we believe." He took another sip of his tea, and then continued on with a more serious note. "I go back to Agnes and wake her up. I then tell her that she had a fever that lasted for an entire day, and much to my relief, she's come to! She will not find out how long she's really been sleeping for, and what has that been now, a month? Oh my. We sure let that slip by us, didn't we? Anyway, I'll bring Imogene back with me, and you, Imogene will act as though nothing has changed!" Elsie just about jumped out of her seat. She couldn't, just couldn't give up her daughter again, for anything or anyone. She would rather let her sister lie there in that bed forever. Roland glanced at his wife, and subtly caught her attention before she had the chance to protest. Kindly, he motioned for her to wait quietly. And it was then that Elsie decided that he was right. She owed it to Sampson to at least listen to the rest of what he had to say. Sampson finished.

"The next day, Elsie, you arrive. You apologize for having been gone for so long, but now that you're back, you can take Imogene with you. And that will be the end of it."

"But," Imogene offered. "But, what if she doesn't want to let me go?"

"I've already thought of that, Miss. I will hypnotize her, ever so slightly into thinking that it's her idea to let you go." Elsie and Roland both agreed at the same time.

"Yes!" Roland exclaimed. "I think you've got it, Sampson. And then that way, we can return later and anytime for visits, and she won't think anything of it. If we happen to come and go, she'll think we're just passing through, right?"

"That's right. But we have to be very careful not to let on that anything is out of the ordinary. If Agnes ever suspects that I am Sampson, the doctor of hypnosis, or if she has any recollections of the underwater kingdoms, everything would be in jeopardy. Nothing about us can remind her of home." Roland and Elsie nodded again, but suddenly Imogene bolted out of her chair.

"Oh, no!" she yelped, and her face turned ghostly pale.

"What is it, Imogene?" Her mother asked as she rushed to her daughter's side. She put her hands upon the girl's shoulders and looked into her eyes. Imogene looked back at her mother and stammered.

"The smell. My scent. I can't go back there to Auntie Agnes smelling like this." Elsie looked to Roland who in turn looked to Sampson. Sampson only grinned back.

"You, my dear, are brilliant." Sampson announced as though he could never be more proud of anyone. Roland and Elsie didn't understand, and simply watched as Sampson and their daughter stared at one another; it was as though the two had just shared a special revelation. In the next instant, Elena returned to the dining room to clear the table. She took one look at the royal family and Sampson, just staring at each other and she gulped. Ever so careful not to disturb them, Elena silently set the dishes on her tray. She left as soon as she could; things in the dining room were getting stranger by the hour.

Imogene took her seat again, and Elsie returned to her own chair. Then the men sat down and all was still. It was Imogene who broke the silence at last. "Mother, when you were gone for so long, or I was gone... well, you know. We were apart! There was one certain thing that I remembered about you the very most. It was your smell. Of course at the time, I didn't know it was a special scent."

"Yes, dear! That is the scent that we talked a little about before. Just like how because you are of the Pacific Kingdom, and have always been drawn to the water. You also will always recognize the distinct smell." Roland nodded now, as he watched the exchange.

"Yes, Mother, that's exactly what I mean. But she is not used to me smelling this way. Sampson may return to her, and she'll think everything with him is normal. But I think, once she takes a good whiff of me; our plan would fail." And then Imogene looked despondently down at the table. Now what would they do?

"Imogene has much foresight for a child of her age," Sampson said to his friends. "I don't mind admitting, that it was one detail which even I had overlooked. And although it is easily remedied," he looked to Imogene and then back to her parents, "It would have proven to be disastrous if we had continued to overlook it. A scent such as this could trigger even the deepest, most forgotten memory!" Imogene sat up taller in her chair, happy that she'd been able to offer some assistance, too. And then she smiled mischievously at her mother.

"Mother, by the smell I don't mean that I always thought you stunk!" The three adults shook their heads at her and laughed openly. Imogene managed to find the funny side in everything, and her parents wondered how they ever managed without her. She had been a great help in solving the royal dilemma.

12

IMOGENE AND THE RETURN ABOVE

That night, Imogene had a hard time falling asleep. She lay awake for what felt like forever, worrying about the royal dilemma. It had been solved just that morning for sure, but the plan still needed to be carried out, and that was the part that troubled Imogene the most. It was kind of exciting to be included in the master plan to deceive Auntie Agnes, but then there was the nagging worry about getting caught. If the plan failed completely, then what? Imogene also felt really bad about having to keep such a big secret away from Marina and Rafe. As such, Imogene felt as though she'd spent the entire day lying to them, although she simply was not allowed to share the information. At last, Imogene fell asleep, but it was a fitful rest and for the whole night she had to cope with a gigantic knot in the pit of her stomach.

The next morning, Elsie quietly went into Imogene's room to wake her. She sat near the head of the bed, next to her daughter's pillow, reached over and was about to rub her back, when suddenly she changed her mind and pulled her hand away. At the last minute, she decided to just watch her child sleep. How she despised the idea of sending Imogene back to the surface, even though it would only be for a couple of days. Elsie didn't know how she had even survived while Imogene had been separated from her for so long before. She'd certainly spent more time involved with the royal duties, she supposed. And the volunteer work at the school had helped a little; although being with the other children only served to remind her of what she herself, could not have. Then, as Elsie sat and watched her daughter sleep, she marveled at her feelings for her. *Oh, how I love you. Imogene dear, will you ever really know how much?* And then as Elsie wiped away the small tear that had spilt down her cheek, Imogene began to stir.

"Of course I know how much you love me, Mother! Why would you ask that?" And then she muttered, as an afterthought, "Good morning." Imogene's eyes were still shut as she spoke out loud. Elsie just sat there, totally astonished. Imogene had *heard* her! She couldn't believe it. Most girls didn't begin to hear until they had reached their teens. She swallowed hard and tried to figure out the best way to approach this subject.

"Good morning, my love. Have you been lying there awake for long, with your eyes closed that way?" And then she proceeded to rub Imogene's back.

"No, I think I just woke up when you started talking. And it sounded like there was an echo in here. Was there?"

"No, sweet muffin. No echo. It must've just sounded funny because you were still half asleep." And then Imogene turned over and fully opened her eyes. Her eyelids were awfully heavy!

"Oh, Imogene! You didn't sleep well, did you?" Elsie already knew the answer, as she had not slept well, herself. They were both nervous about this day.

"No, Mommy." It had been some time now, since Imogene had called her mother, *Mommy*. "I didn't sleep very well. I wish that this didn't have to happen today! What if I bungle it up?" Elsie was fully aware that she, her husband and Sampson were placing a terrible amount of responsibility on Imogene.

"No, Imogene. You won't bungle it up. Sampson has promised your father and I that he will hardly leave your side at all. He's going to be stuck to you like glue, dear." And then they both smiled weakly at Elsie's feeble attempt to brighten up their moods.

"Imogene, I know it will be hard, but just be

yourself." Imogene sat straight up in bed now, folded her arms across her chest and looked at her mother crossly.

"How can I be myself? My *old* self? There is no way that I can go back to Auntie Agnes' home and pretend that nothing has changed. *I* have changed! I'm not the same person as I was a month ago. I've learned so much more; I feel so much more. I don't think she's going to fall for it. You don't know her the same way that I do, Mother. She's so suspicious all the time. Even where there's nothing to suspect!" Elsie half smiled. Imogene's concerns were valid, and she recognized that her daughter was feeling a tremendous amount of guilt over the upcoming ruse. She knew that she was going to have to employ a different kind of tactic in this particular situation.

"Imogene, you are so right. I guess we'll just have to call the whole thing off!" And having said that, Elsie got up from the bed and walked toward the door.

"Mother!" Imogene cried out. "No, I didn't mean..." Elsie turned back and faced her daughter dead on.

"You didn't mean what, exactly?" As soon as she gave Imogene the *look*, Imogene resigned herself to the facts.

"What I mean is that I will do my best back on the surface." Elsie smiled and returned to the bed. She had to be tough for Imogene's sake, if she expected her daughter to do this thing. She sat back down and put a reassuring arm around her daughter's shoulders.

"My dear, Imogene. Honestly, if your father, Sampson and I didn't think you were capable of this, we would have found another way." Imogene would protest no more. If Sampson and her parents had that much faith in her, maybe it was time that she believed in herself as well. Most of all, she didn't want to let them down.

"So then it's settled. Today, you return to the surface with Sampson. Once he has rid you of the smell of the Pacific Kingdom, he will waken Auntie Agnes from her sleep. For one entire day only, you will act as though nothing is out of the ordinary. And you know that it's the weekend, even up there; so you won't even need to go to school. How would you usually spend your Saturdays up there? At home?"

"Yes," Imogene thought for a moment. "The only time we'd go somewhere is if she or I had an appointment of some sort. The maid, Kristine, does all of the grocery shopping." And then Imogene gasped, "Mother, the maid! What about the maid?" She hadn't thought about the rest of Auntie Agnes' household at all.

"Don't worry, Imogene. Kristine is from the kingdom, also. She is actually Elena's little sister, although you'd never know it by looking, and the dark glasses she wears masks the true colour of her eyes! It was easy for her to play the maid, as she has no family of her own, down here. Although she is Auntie Agnes' maid, her knowledge of most things is very limited. She doesn't know anything about the East Wing or the basement. Until you came down to the kingdom, she didn't even know your true identity."

"Oh, my. And what has Kristine been doing for the last month or so?"

"Sampson tells me that she has been keeping house just as she normally would. Once a week she goes for groceries. She tends to the grounds as well, and of course uses the car on a regular basis. To the outside world, the estate looks very much the same as it always has. And right now, Kristine is the proudest maid in the world!"

"Why is that?" Imogene asked as she wrinkled up her nose.

"Once she learned about the grand scheme that she was inadvertently involved in, she realized that she had come to the aid of the royal family. Due to her good deeds of the past, present and future, she has earned a special place with us."

"Oh, wonderful for her! Doesn't she mind though, that she was tricked and for five years did not know that I was a princess?"

"Not at all, my dear. Kristine is as loyal as a servant could be. She doesn't mind because it was a means to an end. And a great end, at that!"

"So, will she return to the kingdom, now?" Her

mother shook her head in response.

"She was given that option, and for now, she has declined it. Kristine has decided to stay long enough for us to find a replacement for her. So far, we haven't anyone in mind who could take her place. As you can imagine, my dear, a servant of her devotion will not be that easy to find." Imogene thought for a moment.

"Well then, is she going to help us fool Auntie Agnes again?" Elsie nodded.

"Yes, but only to a certain degree. Sampson has advised her of everything that she needs to know."

Elsie and Imogene sat there together for a while, quiet and still; each lost in her own thoughts. Elsie tried with all her might to shake off the feeling of dread that had begun to eat away at her. *Why...* she asked herself. *Nothing can go wrong!* If only such hoping could make it so.

After nearly devouring a hearty breakfast, the royal family waited for Sampson in the dining room. Roland was also concerned about his daughter's return to the surface, and the truth was that he didn't want her to go anymore than his wife did. He was also worried about the little secret that Elsie had confided in him. They both agreed that Imogene was far too young to have telepathic powers; she couldn't possibly be mature enough to carry that burden. And so, the king kept bringing up happy, unrelated subjects in order to keep his wife's mind off of Imogene's impending departure.

In doing so, if Imogene happened to hear Elsie's thoughts again, she wouldn't know how worried she really was. Roland could not wait for Sampson to arrive; the whole morning had become very stressful. There was a quiet in the air, and Elsie's brows furrowed together. He knew she was worrying again, and so Roland had to think fast, for the umpteenth time.

"So, Imogene. Have you seen your seahorse, yet?" he asked her hopefully.

"No, not yet." Imogene answered politely. She was not at this moment, interested in seahorses.

"Um, then how are your studies coming along?"

"Great! I love school." And at that moment, she had not been thinking about school.

"That Marina and Rafe! You three are getting along famously, hey?" By now, poor King Roland was at a complete loss over what to say to distract the women in his family. Imogene's patience had reached the end.

"Okay, Dad. I have not seen my seahorse. School is good, and yes, I like Marina and Rafe." Then Imogene stood up from her usual spot, and walked to her parents' side of the table. She placed her hands on the table in front of them and stated, "I know you mean well, Daddy. And Mommy, too." She looked directly at her mother then. "You're trying to think the happiest thoughts," she hesitated, then turned and poked a finger straight at her father's chest. "And you are trying to keep me from hearing them! Guess what? It isn't working!" With that, Imogene folded her arms across her chest and returned to her chair. Elsie and Roland exchanged looks. But their daughter wasn't quite finished. "Mother, how did you know I could hear you?"

"Oh, Imogene. It was only this morning when I was in your room! When you heard me say how much I love you? Well, I hadn't said it out loud. But you heard me, anyway, and answered. That's how and when I knew."

"Oh! I thought you were talking for real. I guess because I was still half sleeping, and I didn't know." Her secret was out. Her father cleared his throat, loud and clear.

"Imogene, as thrilled as I might be for you and your new ability, please do tell. How long have you been able to hear?"

"Only for the past week. I started first, by hearing bits and pieces of sentences. Then the harder I listened, the more I heard. Now, it's really easy. But Mother, why have you been trying to think happy thoughts all morning? Is there something that you don't want me to know?" And that was exactly what had been troubling Imogene the whole time that morning, not knowing what they were trying to keep her from knowing. Now that she'd asked, she felt as though a great weight had been lifted from her chest.

"No, sweet muffin. Only the dangers that you

are already aware of. There is only the chance of getting caught. The one thing that I didn't want you to know was how uneasy I've been feeling about this whole thing. I don't need to be passing my fears to you. I know that you are afraid enough, for one little person." Imogene let out a huge sigh of relief.

"But, Imogene," her father began ever so seriously. "You have to be responsible with your telepathic powers. You are not to use them carelessly. And I suppose that once this little ruse with Auntie Agnes is complete, you and your mother are going to have to sit down and have a really good talk about it."

"Yes, Father. There is much that I need to learn, I know." She and her mother made eye contact then, and nodded to one another. "But, there is a question about it that I'd like to ask now." She waited for her parents' reply.

"What is it Imogene?" her father asked. "Although, be quick, as Sampson should be arriving any minute now."

"It's just that I understand that all of the underwater people used to use mental telepathy to communicate. Then once we began to live more on land, we began speaking out loud. Why is it though, that mostly the women can use mental telepathy? Why can't just as many men do it, too?" Roland chuckled at his ever-inquisitive daughter, and then thought how best to answer. They were not all simple questions that Imogene asked.

"To tell you the truth, we're not entirely sure why some men lost the ability. Your mother tends to think that it was due only to the natural process of evolution. She likes to believe that in the end, some men just weren't meant to retain that power." Imogene looked back and forth from one parent to the other.

"But, what do *you* believe, Father? It sounds like you may have a different idea about it."

"Yes," he answered. "You're right. I have just resigned myself to the fact that some of us can't do it. It changed so long ago that even my father wasn't able to do it. And I haven't heard of any other men in our family who could do it either. Maybe it's only because it wasn't kept active and taught from father to son down the line. Maybe the women, since way back then, just kept on practicing the telepathy and in doing so, were able to pass it down from generation to generation. And so, some men who are of the far less talkative persuasion..." and then he stopped short, after having become the target of a small glare from Elsie. Imogene was still waiting for him to go on, and so he continued on a slightly different note. "It would be unfair if I didn't mention this, and that is that there has always been the odd rumour, that there are more men now who can do it, than ever before." Roland quit talking again, as Elena had entered the room. She curtsied as always, and announced that Sampson had arrived. Imogene wanted to listen to her father some more, but she knew that they all had much more important matters to attend to now.

"Please show him in, Elena, and thank you." Elsie said quickly. The sooner Sampson was in and Elena was out, the sooner they could finalize their plans. Elena nodded and hurried from the room, and a few moments later, Sampson joined the royal family. Imogene hadn't expected to see him wearing his underwater clothes, and she was even more surprised to see that in his hands he carried a heavy, mysterious looking black bag. Sampson was very excited; he smiled at them all as he approached the table.

"Good morning, my friends! What a grand day for an adventure." He smiled at each of them again and then took his usual seat. Sampson noticed that Imogene was still staring at his robe.

"Don't worry, my dear Miss Imogene. And I suppose I'd better get used to calling you that, again. My suit and tie await me in the basement, as does a freshly laundered set of clothing for you. Oh, and Kristine is looking forward to your return." Imogene looked bewildered.

"But, I thought... does Kristine know about the basement, now?" She was sure she remembered her mother saying that Kristine wasn't aware of the basement. Sampson nodded.

"Yes, but only temporarily. We need her help a little bit more, this time around." Just then, Roland coughed and cleared his throat again. Imogene laughed at her father's habit. All eyes turned to the king.

"Excuse me, Sampson." Roland looked seriously at his friend. "I'm sorry, my dear," he directed toward his daughter. "But time is of the essence and you and Sampson will have lots of time for talk on the surface." Imogene nodded quietly. It was almost time to go. Roland asked Sampson, "Did you bring *it*?"

"Oh, yes. I sure did. The newest and latest, in fact." He looked over at the queen then, who had been unusually quiet since his arrival. He tilted his head and gave her a reassuring look. "My dear friend. Don't be troubled so. You know that I will take even better care of Imogene than I did before. As will Kristine!"

"Oh, Sampson. I don't doubt you." She replied sincerely. "I hope to be myself again once this is all done and over with." But Sampson shook his head at her.

"Don't fool yourself, my good queen. This will never be done with; only this particular ruse! And do not feel so bad or responsible for Agnes. We look after her well, you know that."

"No, I can't deny that. She lives better than most surface dwellers do!"

"Absolutely, she does," he agreed. "By all rights, she could have been turned out and made to live on the streets. And then what do you suppose would have become of her?" Just then, Roland stood up and joined Sampson in trying to comfort and at the same time, convince his wife.

"That's right, my dear Elsie. Your sister would have been the ruin of us all, without giving us even one backward glance! Now instead, she helps us, although she doesn't know it. It's best this way for all of us." He turned to Sampson, "Now, may I see *it*?"

Imogene, who'd been looking back and forth from one adult to another, was becoming just as impatient as her father. And she wanted so much to ask, *did Sampson bring what? Can her father see what?* Just as she was about to fold her arms across her chest, Sampson winked at both her and her mother. It was not the joking kind of wink. Instantly the royal women relaxed; but just a tad. They watched Sampson as he lifted his big black medical bag from the floor, and set it with a thump upon the dining room table. Imogene had no idea what he was going to pull out of it! She was so curious, she didn't even dare to blink for fear of missing anything. Sampson began to explain.

"Miss Imogene, in here we have the tonic that will remove any and all of the Pacific Kingdom scent from you." He displayed in front of them all, a dark brown bottle.

"Do I drink it or wear it?"

"No, you must drink it just as we are leaving, in fact. It will remove your scent from the inside out. But the effects will only last for two days. That's why everything has to go according to plan."

"In case it doesn't, why don't we just bring the bottle with us?"

"A good and fair question. Miss Imogene, I'm afraid that this tonic, in its bottled state would be completely useless up above. It will only work if you drink it down here." To which Imogene nodded again, as he had just answered her next question. She had wondered why her mother couldn't have stayed with her, drinking the tonic every two days for the whole five years. Her mother heard her thoughts and cried out.

"Oh, Imogene! Believe me, if there had been a way for me to be with you, I certainly would have done it!" Tears welled up in the woman's eyes. Imogene was ashamed, for she knew that if she possibly could have, her mother surely would have gone to the ends of the earth to protect her and be with her at the same time.

"Yes, I know. I know that it was for my protection. I just can't always help but remember how much I used to miss you." Imogene was feeling awfully sad and she bit her lip and tried to think happy thoughts to keep from crying. Sampson knew that this would be a good time to continue with his demonstration.

"In this can," he said as he held up a small container the size of a soup tin, "are the power beads. Imogene, if you should need me desperately; and don't worry because I won't ever be far away.

But it may happen that you and your Auntie Agnes are alone together. If that happens, and I repeat, if you should desperately need me, you squeeze one of these beads. I will come running to you like I have never run before." And then he held out a power bead to show them all. Imogene automatically reached for it.

"No, Miss, not yet. I'll give them to you once we have safely reached the basement. Your only concern between now and then will be to follow me. Anyway, the beads are directly linked to my mind, and that's how I will know... actually feel it when you need me."

"Wow, Sampson! Will I get to learn about that too, with the hypnosis?"

"Yes, Miss. Eventually. But you must remember to only use your powers in the most responsible fashion."

"Oh, you can count on me." And then Sampson, Roland and Elsie, all took a good, long look at the princess. Somehow they knew that truer words had never been spoken. They would always, no matter what, be able to count on Imogene for anything.

Sampson kept the little tin and bottle out, and buttoned his bag back up. He turned to Elsie and asked, "I'm sure you'll keep my bag in a safe place?" Elsie nodded as she strained to lift the bag from the table. She left the room with it and returned only moments later without it. Everyone stood. Sampson offered his arm to Imogene.

"My dear friends, please follow me. Imogene, will you walk by my side?" She draped her arm through his, and the four of them left the dining room. They walked straight out through the great castle doors, and up the pebble path that led to the lake. It was the very same pebble path that Imogene first took when she came to the castle, and she realized, she had not been on it since. Not until now, anyway. As sad as she had been about her upcoming departure, now that the time had come, she felt the familiar little tingles of excitement. She looked up at Sampson as they walked on, and he winked at her. She smiled.

Finally they had walked enough and rounded many bends, and the royal family and their friend made it to the lake. Imogene looked out and over the water, and saw the little bushes that had ever so briefly provided her with cover when she'd first emerged from the cave. She remembered hearing her mother's sweet voice for the first time in five years, and seeing her in that beautiful long flowing robe. She remembered her surprise when she saw Sampson! Surprise and relief, she knew. He was still, and probably would forever be, her best friend. And the four of them stood quietly for a moment, looking out over the water. Elsie broke the silence.

"Imogene, did you wear your bathing suit like I asked?" Imogene slid her shirt away from her shoulder to show her, then untied the drawstrings of her shirt and pants and removed them both. She folded them neatly and handed them to her mother.

"It's time for you to drink the tonic, Miss Imogene." Sampson handed her the bottle. She opened the lid, and smelled it. Yuck! Sampson and her parents laughed as Imogene wrinkled up her nose and made the worst face ever. Imogene tried her best not to gag; it tasted *that* bad.

"Now, we must go." Sampson retrieved the empty bottle from Imogene and handed it to Elsie. "Please return this to my bag, and I will see you tomorrow evening." Elsie gave her friend a hug. Sampson turned to Roland, teasing, "I trust that leaving the kingdom in your hands is a good decision?" They both smiled as they shook hands. And then it was Imogene's turn to say goodbye. Roland knelt down on one knee, and opened his arms wide. Imogene embraced him.

"Oh, Father. I will be okay! I'll be back at bedtime, tomorrow night." Roland hugged her back and wished that he had as much confidence as his daughter did. But he replied, with a smile.

"Yes, my love. Everything will be just fine. The kingdom will be desperately awaiting your return." He choked on the last two words and had to clear his throat. Imogene let go, turned and ran into her mother's waiting arms.

"Imogene, you be careful up there. We love you!" And now Elsie was crying. She just couldn't bear saying goodbye to her daughter again, no matter how short the length of time. Imogene fell to her knees and stretched her arms upward, mocking fear.

"Mother, I'll be waiting for you, come save me!" She pleaded with a small grin. The adults all laughed. Imogene gave one last glance at her parents, turned and stood beside Sampson. Sampson reached down and took his young charge by the hand. And then, without saying another word, they slipped into the water. Elsie and Roland watched them until their heads disappeared under the water's surface, and they could see them no more. Sadly then, arm in arm, the king and queen of the Pacific Kingdom walked with slow steps and bowed heads, back to their castle.

13

IMOGENE AND THE HYPNOTISM OF KRISTINE

Before Imogene and Sampson's heads went under, he had instructed her carefully. "Now remember, Miss. There are four tunnels that lead into the main portal. Don't lag behind, stay right with me. Now is not a time for exploring. Another time perhaps, we can explore the other caves, okay?" Little did he know, Imogene had no intention of losing sight of him.

"Don't worry, Sampson. I'll be with you all the way." And then they were under. It was funny again, for Imogene to be breathing in the water and moving amongst the fish. Funny but wonderful! Sampson led her past the bushes and into the cave's entrance. It was darker swimming in the opposite direction of how she'd first come, and harder to paddle and kick. It was as though even the tunnel itself was protesting and did not want Imogene to leave. They swam on and on until they reached the turn where Imogene supposed she had hit her head earlier. Sampson reached back, grabbed Imogene's hand, and pulled her a different direction. She could tell immediately that this was no longer the same route as before.

They were swimming just about straight up now and Imogene had to swallow hard to keep her ears from popping. The tunnel turned again and the upward angle tapered off until they weren't swimming upward anymore at all. Imogene's ears adjusted to the new elevation just when she was sure they would explode. At last, she thought she saw light up ahead, but were her eyes playing tricks on her? No, it *was* light; she was sure of it! No wonder Sampson had arrived at the kingdom so much sooner than she had. This route had taken hardly any time at all. And as she followed him toward the light, she thought about the secret basement. She could not wait to see it and the hidden staircase, which would lead to the East Wing. The *forbidden* East Wing, at last.

The light grew bright and she could now see Sampson clearly ahead of her. He suddenly let go of her hand, and she treaded water, and watched him. It looked as though his head was above the water's surface, but she knew that if he had wanted her beside him, he would have pulled her up, too. And then, very unexpectedly, she heard, "*Wait a*

minute, Miss Imogene. Let me see if the way is clear."
Imogene let out an underwater gasp; it couldn't
have been! But it was. She answered, "*Sampson, I had
no idea you could talk this way!*" And just then, he
tugged on her arm. He pulled her up so rapidly that
before she knew it, she was alongside him; their
heads raised above the surface.

"Miss Imogene," he exclaimed out loud.
"Welcome to the basement." Sampson winked at
her. And as she looked around curiously, she
blurted out.

"But, Sampson, I never would have guessed that
you had telepathy! Do my parents know?"

"Yes, Miss. It is a secret. But did they tell you,
that some men retained the ability? So at least you
knew it was possible?"

"Yes, but my father said that it was just a
rumour..." She didn't finish what she was about to
say, because just then, Kristine, the maid appeared.
Imogene looked her up and down and silently
compared her to her sister, Elena. Where Elena was
small, red haired and freckled, this woman was of
average height with blonde hair. There wasn't even
a hint of red in it and she bore no freckles that
Imogene could see.

"Sampson! Miss Imogene! I'm so glad you've
arrived safely!" And then she ran to them, with her
arms full of big fluffy towels. She set them on the
ground beside the pool and reached in to help
Imogene up. "My dear Princess, it is so good to see

you, again."

"Yes, Kristine, I'm glad to see you, too!" Imogene began to dry herself off, just as Sampson pulled himself from the pool. He reached for his towel.

"Kristine, I'm pleased you were able to follow the directions that I gave to you, to find the way here. Did you lose your way at all?" She shook her head excitedly. She was so worked up in fact, that beads of sweat were visible on her forehead. She reached up with her sleeve to wipe them away.

"No, Sampson, I didn't. I memorized the way you told me to take and by the way," she bubbled, "did you know that this is my first time down here? My very first time? It was even my first time in the East Wing. I have to admit, my knees were shaking, I was so afraid. But I'm not afraid now, can you tell?" She spoke so fast that her words bumped into each other and she'd begun to flush. All the mystery and sneaking about were right up her alley.

"Yes, I know, you are so loyal to the royal family and that is why it'll be tricky to replace you up here. Do you know how hard the royal family is looking, to find another like you? I'm afraid it will be a long and arduous task." The woman flushed deeper at the direct compliment. She then diverted her attention to Imogene.

"Oh, no! My deepest apologies, Princess. I haven't even addressed you properly." And then Kristine fell to her knees and bowed.

"No, please Kristine, don't bow down to me." She then repeated nearly the very thing that her mother had once said to Imogene's friend, Marina. "There is no need to bow down to me, Kristine. Only at public functions." And then she added humorously, "You have protected me for five years, and so it is I who should bow down to you!" In that same instant, Imogene bowed. Kristine giggled as she stood.

"All right, *Miss* Imogene. I suppose it wouldn't do anyway, to treat you like royalty for the next two days, now would it?" Imogene shook her head, no. "Come with me now, and I'll show you where you can dress. Sampson can wait for us here." Imogene did as she was told and followed the maid out of the room. Kristine led her away in the dark; only a few candles lit the short little hallway that led to another small room. "You can change in here, and I will wait just outside the door for you." Imogene nodded and entered the room. This room was better lit than the hallway had been, and she looked around. She spotted her regular old surface clothes right away; they were folded and waiting for her on the dresser. She began to change, still looking around as she did so. She noticed that this room was furnished just like a regular bedroom would be, and she thought, *why not? Why not have a real bedroom in a hidden basement that nobody knows about?* The bed was made and there wasn't a speck of dust in the room. She finished dressing, went to the door, opened it and called out.

"Kristine, would you come in here for a minute, please?" And Kristine rushed to the door.

"Yes, Miss Imogene? The clothes still fit, don't they?" Kristine proceeded to look her up and down with skepticism.

"Oh, yes. See?" Imogene twirled around and around to show her. "It's not the clothes. I was just wondering what this room is used for?"

"Ah, Miss. Actually, I regret to say that I have no idea what this room is for! It was part of the instructions that Sampson gave to me. He had me clean and prepare it and then all he said was, *"just in case"*. I don't know, Miss. It's all so mysterious, isn't it?" Kristine's eyes were all lit up with delight. "Ready, now?" Imogene nodded and followed Kristine back to the room with the pool.

"There you are!" Sampson said as soon as he saw her fully dressed. "You look just like you used to, Imogene. We have nothing to fear." Then he spoke to the maid.

"Kristine, the next day and a half is critical. I know that you've learned a lot in the last few weeks. I have but one more favour to ask you." He looked serious indeed, and his voice lowered to a most conniving tone. Kristine held up her hands in dissent.

"Sampson, whatever it is, my answer is yes. Whatever you have in mind, I know that it is for the good of the Pacific Kingdom!" She eagerly awaited his next set of instructions. Sampson nodded and patted her affectionately on the shoulder.

"I just knew that's what you would say, Kristine. That's only one of the many reasons you are so valuable to the kingdom." He turned to Imogene, then. "Miss, you are about to see hypnosis in action."

"HYPNOSIS!" Both Imogene and Kristine cried out at once. Within seconds the initial shock wore off. Imogene smiled in anticipation while Kristine nodded in agreement.

"Now, Imogene, this is not a lesson for you; by simply seeing it done once, you cannot learn the art. This is only meant for you to observe; to be used as only a small sample of what we can accomplish with our powers!" Imogene agreed and remained serious and quiet. Sampson turned to Kristine.

"Kristine, the reason I need to hypnotize you is for the safety of you, the princess and the kingdom. As I said earlier, this is critical. For the next while, and actually until you have been replaced up above, you must be made to forget about the world you come from. You will know nothing at all about the basement, the East Wing, and this pool, here." As he spoke, he pointed to the small pool of water set in the middle of the dirt floor. Kristine nodded again and Sampson further explained. "If anyone ever tried to sabotage our mission; you'll know nothing. Any objections so far?" He looked at her questioningly; he was asking a lot from her. To agree to be hypnotized to such an amazing degree! Such loyalty.

"Yes, Sampson, of course. I trust you with all my heart!" And Kristine was as sincere as sincere could be. Imogene just stood quietly, watching. She reminded herself, *watch and listen, watch and listen!* Sampson smiled at both of them.

"The one thing you will remember is how important Imogene's safety is. You won't remember why. You will only know that she is Agnes' niece and is worthy of your protection. Soon, we will begin." Kristine and Imogene remained quiet as they listened, each from their very own unique viewpoints. Sampson left the room then, without saying another word about it or where he was going. Imogene, quite frankly, was too scared to move and so she just stood there and waited. Kristine just stood there, too; she had never to her knowledge been hypnotized before, and she was just a little apprehensive about the whole thing. She quite hoped, in the back of her mind, that it wouldn't hurt a bit. It wasn't long before Sampson returned to the doorway with a big, black bag in his hand. It looked much the same as the one he had in the kingdom, only a little smaller. He called to them.

"Ladies, follow me; I will lead you back to the main house." And so it was, that the three of them made their way through the basement. Each time they came across candles, Kristine swiftly blew them out. Imogene secretly hoped she wouldn't be expected to find her way on her own anytime soon, as she knew it would be impossible. She saw that each room they went by, and even the hallways that connected them, were ever so narrow. That, she would have to ask Sampson about, later on.

Sampson came to an abrupt stop. He handed his bag to Imogene, and then reached his hand in along the bricks of a wall. To the untrained eye, that wall wouldn't appear to be anything but just that, a brick wall. Imogene watched in fascination as he removed one of the bricks, then reached into the gap where it had been. A soft, but definite *click* could be heard from somewhere to the left of them. Sampson closed the opening with the brick, and retrieved his bag from Imogene. He stepped closer to where the *click* had come from. Imogene blinked hard. A part of the wall, that had only a moment before looked like only a part of the wall, had moved aside! *A secret entrance! Another secret entrance!* Imogene shook her head comically and thought, *why not?*

The trio stepped through the secret entrance and then Sampson secured it behind them in much the same manner he'd used to open it. As soon as Imogene was through and had the chance to look around, she realized that she was now in another hidden basement. *A hidden pool in a hidden basement in a hidden basement in a hidden staircase in the forbidden East Wing. Oh my!*

This area was far brighter than the last one, as

the walls were lined thick with candles. Again, Imogene turned and saw that Kristine blew them out, as she went by each one. These halls were wider, the rooms were bigger, and Imogene wished that she could spend an entire day in these two basements, just exploring. What fun that would be! What a splendid time she would have, if she could include Marina and Rafe!

Once they arrived at the end of the basement all that stood before them was a huge fireplace. It was identical to the one upstairs in the parlour, and it too, looked as though it hadn't ever been used. Imogene wrinkled her nose, for she saw that there was no way out. Sampson must have gotten turned around somehow, and Imogene herself imagined just how easy that would be to do. She was about to say something about it to him, when he climbed quickly into the fireplace and completely disappeared! She clapped her hands with glee, and without any hesitation followed him in. The wooden logs that were placed on the grating, supposedly to burn, made excellent stairs. Imogene looked up just in time to catch sight of her friend's foot, as the rest of him slipped through a hatch in the wall of the chimney. She and Kristine kept close behind.

Once they all were safely through to the other side of the hatch, Sampson secured it shut with a latch. They now found themselves in the narrow little staircase that Imogene knew had to lead to the forbidden East Wing. Her heart was beating fast in anticipation. The East Wing! They climbed up and up and up until they reached the top. Imogene and Kristine stopped dead in their tracks as they watched Sampson; he put his ear to the wall and listened. No one dared move. At last, satisfied that there was no one lurking about on the other side, he opened yet another hatch and climbed through. Again, once the ladies followed him out, Sampson locked the hatch shut. He swung a portrait that hung to the side, over the hatch to cover it up. He then moved a small desk in front of it, and a small rug in front of the desk. Then he was done, and led the ladies through the room. Imogene looked up and saw a light bulb that hung from the ceiling in the middle of the room, but it was not turned on. It didn't need to be, as this room had a window large enough to let in some light. This was a storage room, Imogene realized. There were tons of interesting looking things in here, and Imogene decided that she'd like to explore it later with her friends, if she could. They quietly made their way to the door, where Sampson stopped and listened as he had done before. And then he spoke, for the first time since leaving the hidden basement, in hushed tones.

"Now Kristine, from here, follow us straight to Imogene's room." Seeing the strange look on both girls' faces, he clarified, "I can't hypnotize you here, for you wouldn't know how or why you came to be in the East Wing. We'll leave this room and nonchalantly make our way down the corridor, beyond the grand staircase and proceed to Imogene's room. But Imogene, Kristine and I will be pretending to give you trouble for having caught you nosing around the East Wing. We're bringing you back to your room. Do you understand?" Imogene was perplexed.

"Uh, no. Not really. If Auntie Agnes is asleep, why do we have to put on a show?"

"Because, Miss, we must always be prepared for the opposite of what we expect to happen. More simply put, there is always a chance that she's not asleep. Or someone else could be in the house, see us and wonder why the three of us are coming from the direction of the forbidden East Wing! Now, do you see?" To which Imogene nodded. She just couldn't wait to get this over with. They left the room then, and walked down the long, hollow sounding corridor. As they neared the grand staircase, Kristine began.

"Yes, Sampson, that's where I found her! Miss Imogene, you know better than to go anywhere near the East Wing." Kristine was doing such a good job, that Imogene's skin began to crawl.

"Imogene, it's a good thing we found you before you got all dirty. There is nothing, as you have been told before, for little girls in the East Wing." Sampson scolded.

"I'm sorry, you guys. And you're right. From

what I could see, there's nothing there but dirt and junk. I won't do it again."

"That's right, you won't!" Kristine started in again, and it was quite obvious that she was enjoying her role. "Now off to your room and get cleaned up!" And they marched straight by the grand staircase, a little farther down the corridor and directly into Imogene's bedroom. Imogene looked around, feeling very strange to be back. Not at all *glad* to be back, just strange. Sampson gently closed the door behind them and immediately motioned with his fingers to his lips, for all to be quiet. Quickly then, he searched the room for anything out of place. Convinced that nothing was amiss and it was just the three of them in the room, he turned to Imogene and spoke barely above a whisper.

"Imogene, quick! Here are the power beads. Please, put them in your pocket so they'll always be close at hand." And he handed her the tin. As fast as she could, she emptied the contents into her pants pocket. Sampson then, led her by the hand to her own fireplace.

"What is it?" Imogene asked, surprised by his extra urgency.

"Why, this is your fireplace, Imogene!" To which both she and Kristine, who was still standing near the door, giggled nervously.

"Yes," she agreed cautiously. "I know what *this* is." But right then it occurred to her, what he was really trying to show her. She let go of his hand, stepped *into* her fireplace and looked up. There it was; a hatch much the same as the one in the fireplace that stood in the hidden basement! She looked at Sampson and nodded hopefully. "Just in case, right?"

"Yes, Miss Imogene. Just in case. It leads to the same place." And then he turned to Kristine. "The time has come." She stepped forward.

"I'm ready!" Still, deep down, she wondered what she was getting herself into.

Sampson led Kristine to Imogene's bed. She sat down on the edge of it and smiled at both him and Imogene who stood at Sampson's side. Out from under his buttoned down shirt, he pulled out a gold chain. On that chain, hung a huge pendant, and it was unlike any other that Imogene had ever seen. She suddenly remembered hers then, and felt for it. It, like always, was still there. She continued to observe Sampson as he began to swing his pendant, back in forth in front of Kristine's eyes. Already, the maid was in a trance-like state. Imogene was amazed at how fast it happened. *Perhaps*, she thought, *it is a magic pendant*. Sampson chanted, in a low and mechanical sounding voice.

"Watch the pendant, Kristine. Watch the pendant, Kristine. Watch the pendant, Kristine. Blink once if you are watching the pendant, Kristine." Kristine blinked once.

"Watch the pendant, Kristine. Blink twice if it's

going back and forth." Kristine blinked twice. "You are so tired, Kristine. You've had a long day. Blink once if you are tired." Kristine blinked once. "Now, tell me who you are." Kristine's eyes remained transfixed on the pendant, never wavering. She answered.

"I am Kristine."

"Good, Kristine. Where do you come from and where are you now?"

"I come from the Pacific Kingdom. Right now I am in Princess Imogene's bedroom in Agnes' house."

"No, Kristine. I am afraid you are wrong." Sampson's voice remained steady and low, completely void of feeling. His hand was steady as he swung the pendant.

"Oh? Wrong?"

"That's right. Your name is Kristine."

"Yes."

"You are in Imogene's room."

"Yes."

"The same Miss Imogene who is Agnes' niece. Miss Imogene has lived here for five years."

"Yes."

"There is no Pacific Kingdom."

"No."

"You are from a family that lives in town, here."

"Yes."

"Fine. Now who am I?"

"You are Sampson, doctor of hypnosis."

"No, Kristine. I am afraid you are wrong."

"Oh? Wrong?"

"That's right. I am Sampson. I am Agnes' butler."

"Oh. Agnes' butler."

"Now, Kristine. What do you know of the East Wing?"

"It is forbidden."

"Have you ever been in there?"

"Yes. I mean, I think so."

"No, you are wrong."

"Oh? Wrong?"

"Yes, that's right. You have never been in the East Wing because it is forbidden."

"Oh."

"That's right, Kristine. Little by little now, I will slow down the swinging of the pendant. When it comes to a full stop, you will wake up completely and finish your chores. You came into Miss Imogene's room only a moment ago, to fetch her dirty laundry."

"Yes."

Imogene watched with eyes open wide as the pendant began to slow down. Soon it stopped. And then, Kristine stood up.

14

IMOGENE AND THE ROYAL RUSE

"Miss Imogene! Have you been stashing your dirty socks under the bed again?"

"Yes, Kristine. I'm sorry." As Imogene knelt down to search under her bed for the missing socks, she knew that if the circumstances were different she might have found this situation hilarious.

"And Sampson, what are you doing in here? Shouldn't you be tending to Miss Agnes?"

"Yes, Kristine," he agreed. "I only came to tell Miss Imogene that tea will be ready in the parlour, shortly." As he spoke, he hid the pendant and chain tight within his fist. And for Kristine, it was as though the events of the last month and even the events of that very morning had not happened. Sampson left the room to tend to Miss Agnes, although not in the manner in which Kristine had imagined. He was about to wake her from a very deep sleep.

"Here's one, Kristine!" At that instant, Imogene proudly produced from underneath her bed, one dirty, gray sock. It was more than enough to distract the maid from worrying about Sampson.

"Thank you, Miss." Kristine haughtily replied, as she snatched it from Imogene's hand. "Please take care to put them in the hamper from now on, as that would make my job a lot easier!" With a huff, she left the room. All the way down the corridor, and all the way down the grand staircase, and all the way to the laundry room, all Kristine could think about was how spoiled rotten that little girl really was. Why, if Kristine had left her dirty clothes lying around when she was a ten-year old girl, her mother would have grounded her from the television set in a heartbeat.

Imogene waited alone in her room for a few minutes after Kristine left with the sock. She sat on the edge of her bed, and carefully considered the entire situation. This, she knew, would take all of her courage, not to mention, her theatrical skills. As she sat there, she lifted her arms and sniffed. She brought her hair around to her face with her hands, and sniffed again. Of course, she couldn't tell, but she certainly hoped she didn't smell like the kingdom. Imogene took a couple of deep breaths and got up from her bed. Rather robotic-like, she walked to her door. Remembering how everyone she knew and loved in the kingdom was counting on her, she straightened a little, held her head high and left the room. She walked steadfast to the grand staircase, then took the stairs one at a time to the main floor that would lead her to the parlour.

"IMOGENE!" Auntie Agnes screeched, just as Imogene rounded the corner. Imogene thought, *some things never change...*

"Yes, Auntie?" she replied, ever so sweetly.

"Sampson said he fetched you ages ago for your tea and now you'll have to drink it cold." Auntie Agnes motioned to the hard wooden chair across from her own. Imogene, without a moment's hesitation went straight for it and sat down. She stole a quick look at Sampson, but he only stared directly ahead, obediently awaiting his next set of orders from Auntie Agnes. Imogene made herself as comfortable as she could in her chair, which was not an easy thing to do. These old hard chairs felt worse than they ever had. She cradled her teacup in her hand and sipped away at her tepid tea, and then as she set the cup back down on its saucer, she feebly tried to explain away her tardiness.

"I am sorry for being late, Auntie Agnes." Imogene tried her very best to look sincere as she continued, "I was looking for stray socks for Kristine to bring to the laundry room." Auntie Agnes shook her head repulsively. It was as if no one in the world other than Imogene had ever lost socks.

"There is no excuse for that either, Imogene.

When will you ever learn to put your dirty clothes directly into the hamper? And I do suppose," she added, placing one hand upon her forehead and feigning total disgust, "that you found at least one sock under your bed?" Imogene only nodded and hoped with all her might, that she looked dreadfully sorry for it. She sipped her tea again.

"SAMPSON!" Auntie Agnes suddenly barked. "I am ravenously hungry! Would you fix Imogene and I a quick, but nutritional snack? I shan't have any sweets until I am feeling better." It wasn't really a request, but an order. Sampson replied immediately from his spot near the door.

"Yes, of course, Ma'am. And would you and Miss Imogene care for more tea?"

"Of course we want more tea! Why would we want a snack and no more tea? And besides that, my niece and I have much to talk about. We will be in the parlour for a good long while, I'm afraid." Auntie Agnes didn't see Imogene shudder, but Sampson did.

"Yes, Ma'am. How silly of me. Right away, then." As he turned to leave, he winked at Imogene. She was relieved to see the wink, at last, as it was at this point, her only form of reassurance. She took another long sip of the now cold tea, and wondered how to distract her aunt from whatever it was that she so desperately felt the need to discuss. Too late.

"Now, Imogene! About our conversation last night." Auntie Agnes looked directly at Imogene with her hard blue, accusing stare. Imogene's brain absolutely raced. She had to think fast. *Last night? Oh my. Last night? What did we talk about when... oh! The last time I saw her? Soccer?*

"Yes, Auntie Agnes. Do you mean the doctor's appointment?" Imogene asked naively. Auntie Agnes only clucked her tongue. How could any relation of hers be this dense? Her snappy reply rang with an impatient edge.

"No, I do not mean the doctor's appointment. We have finished that discussion, and had you been paying attention, you would know that. What I am referring to, is soccer."

Just then, Sampson returned to the parlour with a tray that held a freshly made pot of tea and hot cups, straight from the dishwasher. Carefully, he took the cups that Imogene and Agnes had used, and replaced them with the new ones. Slowly, he filled them. He too, was trying desperately to buy some time.

"SAMPSON! I do declare that you are getting slower all the time! Don't think that I can't or won't replace you. Where are my snacks?" Sampson bowed his head and slouched humbly as he stood in front of her.

"I apologize, Miss Agnes. I will fetch the snacks now; it was only that I didn't dare carry it all at once." He took the tray with the dirty cups and left again. Imogene interrupted her aunt's hot burning stare into the butler's back as he departed.

"Yes, Auntie Agnes. Last night, I said that I like soccer well enough. Would you like me to join a team?" She smiled sweetly at her aunt, relieved that she had remembered what their conversation had been about, all that time ago. For Auntie Agnes, it had only been a single night that had passed.

"I think it would be best, Imogene. And the swimming? I am glad I had you take all those lessons. Never forget all the time and money I spent on them!" Imogene shook her head, no, as though she would forever be in her aunt's debt. Sampson came back in, this time with a tray full of fresh fruit and sandwiches. Of course, Auntie Agnes' favourite fruit, and Auntie Agnes' favourite sandwiches.

"Thanks, Sampson!" Imogene said honestly, as she reached for a strawberry. Auntie Agnes guffawed rudely.

"Imogene, really! Don't be so kind to the help. Next you'll be telling me that they have feelings, too. Sampson, do you need to hover so? Don't worry. If I need you again, you will be the first to know." And with that, she dismissed him with a callous wave of her hand. Imogene nearly choked on her strawberry; she had almost forgotten how nasty Auntie Agnes could be.

"I'm sorry, Auntie Agnes. I forgot again." She swallowed hard on the piece of fruit and forced it down. Then, out of the corner of her eye, she caught the slightest movement out in the corridor beyond the parlour door. It was Sampson! If Auntie Agnes had any idea he was hovering about, he'd be in it for sure. Imogene smirked, ever so grateful to know he was near.

Imogene and Auntie Agnes sat there in the parlour; they drank their tea and ate their fill until the tray was just about empty. To Imogene's great relief, her aunt didn't have the faintest clue that anything had changed, and she'd certainly eaten enough to make up for the month's worth of eating that she'd missed. Imogene watched as the woman dabbed at her pale lips with her napkin, and stared back at her again.

"Well, it's settled. I'll have one of the maids call the president of the soccer group first thing in the morning, and you will begin playing the sport as soon as possible." Auntie Agnes wiped the crumbs from her lap and took a final drink of her tea. She reached for her cane and leaned on it heavily as she stood. And then she glared at Imogene again. "Aren't you more quiet than usual?" She asked in an accusatory way.

"No, Auntie Agnes. I don't think so."

"What are you hiding? What have you done?" She demanded angrily as she stared at the young girl. Imogene shrank back in her chair, with mock innocence and fear.

"Nothing! What could I have done between last night and now?" Imogene pleaded to her aunt with tears in her eyes. Auntie Agnes shook her head, but she was not quite convinced.

"Lucky for you, that's true enough. Just try not to look like *that* from now on." With that, she turned and tap-tapped out of the parlour. Too fast though, for Sampson to make himself scarce. Imogene peeked around the corner just in time to see the woman nearly bump into him. She lifted up her cane and pointed it at his chest. "What have I said about loitering?"

"I am sorry, Miss Agnes. I was just coming now to take away the dishes." Shamefully, he looked down at his feet.

"Just watch where you're going next time. Since you're here though, you may help me to my office." She reached for his arm. Imogene stopped spying on them and went back to sit on the chair. She sat quietly and listened to the sound of Sampson's footsteps and her aunt's cane until she could hear them no more. And then she heard only the footsteps nearing the parlour. Sampson entered the room.

"Miss Imogene, is there anything more I can get for you this evening?" He asked loudly. Then he knelt down beside her chair and added, "How is the princess holding up?" She answered him honestly and in a panic-stricken tone.

"Not well! I can't wait until my mommy gets here tomorrow. I'll die before then, I'm sure of it." Sampson laughed and shook his head.

"No, you certainly will not. I'm here to take care

of you. You've survived the daily lecture from your aunt and now you'll only have to make it through the evening meal. Then it'll be bed time and you won't have to see her again until tomorrow morning."

"I know, Sampson. I'm just worried, that's all. I can do it and I will do it. Hey," Imogene added, as she'd suddenly come up with a great idea. "Can you speed up time?" Sampson laughed at her never faltering quick wit.

"No, that's something that not even I can do. If I had the power to do that, I would be high in demand, indeed. Keep your chin up." And then before Imogene could say anything more, he stood up, turned and left. Imogene felt so alone. It was the same kind of alone that she used to feel, for five whole years. She knew that she would never trade her life in the kingdom, her full and happy life in the kingdom, for anything in the world.

Imogene soon left the parlour and headed upstairs for the solitude of her room. At least there she could lounge on her bed and be kind of comfortable. She laughed out loud when she recalled just how soft she used to think that bed was. But then, that was only in comparison to the hard furniture that the rest of the house was stocked full of. That bed now, didn't even come close to measuring up to hers in the castle. She climbed the grand staircase, and was only halfway up when she stopped to listen. She could hear no birds singing and no water running, aside from that of the laundry machine. She looked over to the windows and peered through the solid glass panes that had never been opened. The whole entire world was locked out of this big, fancy house. *Funny*, Imogene realized as she climbed the rest of the way up; she had missed out on so much that was real and alive while she'd been stuck in this place. And she concluded that she would be very happy to leave it again.

She shut her door tight behind her and walked to the bookshelf. She chose an old and worn out comic book and then flopped down on her back, on the bed. As she read and turned the pages, she found that now, even the comics lacked appeal. It was obviously going to be a long day and night. She returned the comic book to its place and decided to browse around her old room to see if there was anything she might want to bring back with her, to the kingdom. She spotted her scrapbook, barely sticking out from a stack of books. She pulled it out and brought it back to the bed with her. Flipping through the pages, she saw each of her old class pictures from kindergarten straight through to grade four. Kristine had put the book together for her; Auntie Agnes would never bother with such things. The last few pages were empty; reserved for the rest of the grades. And at the end of her book, stapled to the very last page, were each and every one of her swimming badges. She closed the book and slid it under her bed. That, she decided, was where she would put the things she wanted to take. On second thought, she took the comic book back off the shelf, for after all, Marina and Rafe might find it amusing. It joined the scrapbook underneath the bed. Sadly, Imogene couldn't find one more thing to take. She had the books now, along with her special box of secret things that was already at the kingdom, and she guessed that would be enough.

She flopped back down onto her bed and stared above at the canopy. *What to do?* She watched the beads that hung toward her and began to count them. That at least, she hadn't done before. She was just at bead number three hundred and two, when a soft *knock* at the door broke her concentration. She sat still and listened. Silence. Then another *knock, knock, knock*. It was Sampson's secret knock code! Imogene bolted to the door and opened it. He stood there with his fingers to his lips. Imogene backed up and allowed him room to slip in. He did so, ever so quietly and closed the door behind him.

"How are you doing now, Miss?" He asked perceptively.

"Oh, I am so bored to death. I told you, Sampson, I warned you that I might die here." And then in a manner mimicking her Auntie Agnes, she threw her hand up across her forehead. Sampson smiled.

"I don't think there's a chance of you dying, Miss

Imogene. At least not with the sense of humour you've been afflicted with." Imogene wrinkled up her nose at him.

"Anyway, I came to fetch you for supper. Miss Agnes has asked me to inform you to wash up and dress appropriately for it." And then came the wink. "Please don't be late and don't give your aunt any reason to reprimand you!" Imogene nodded and her nose was still wrinkled up when he left. As soon as the door closed behind him, she ran to her shelf and grabbed the dictionary. She had to know what *afflicted* meant. She found the word and the meaning, then washed up and dressed into fresh, clean clothes. She made her way slowly to the dining room, in an attempt to hide her eagerness to get the evening over and done with.

Sampson and Kristine had just laid out the last of the dishes on the dining room table when Imogene arrived. Auntie Agnes sat prim and proper in her usual spot at the end of the table. Imogene took her spot, twelve seats down from her aunt, and then they waited with their hands folded neatly upon their laps, to be served. As always, Kristine filled Auntie Agnes' plate and Sampson filled Imogene's. The instant the servants left, the eating would begin. The quiet eating; nothing at all like the talkative and fun eating in the kingdom. And as Imogene ate in total silence, she thought about what life might have been possibly like for her mother and aunt, growing up together in the

Atlantic Kingdom. Probably miserable, she assumed and she knew that she disliked her aunt more and more with each passing minute.

Having finished every last crumb on her plate, and seeing that her niece had done the same, Auntie Agnes smacked the table with her hand. The servants came running, for that was the signal to clear away the dishes.

"May I be excused, Auntie Agnes?" Imogene asked sweetly, and it was at that exact moment that she noticed how phony her voice sounded, every time she spoke to her aunt. She didn't like not being her normal old self and dryly she thought, *tomorrow will not come soon enough.*

"Yes, Imogene. Is your homework done? Don't go leaving it until the last minute." Auntie Agnes ordered with a warning glare.

"Uh-huh! I finished it last night before I went to sleep. May I go to my room now?" Imogene smiled at the older woman pleasantly. But Auntie Agnes was becoming more and more suspicious with every breath she took.

"Why are you in such an all fired up hurry to go to your room, Imogene?"

"No reason, " Imogene stammered. The truth was that she wanted badly to run away from the woman's accusing watch. "I just thought I'd read for a while, is all."

"And what are you reading that's got you so interested?" And then the woman thought for a moment before reaching for her cane. "SAMPSON!" Auntie Agnes screeched. Sampson was not far away, and came instantly to her side. "Take me to the parlour. Miss Imogene is going to her room to get the book that she's so involved in." As he helped her stand, she turned, faced her niece, then added, "Then she will bring it to the parlour to read it to me." With one hand on her cane and Sampson steadying her under the arm, she threw her free hand upon her forehead. "My eyes just aren't what they used to be, Imogene. You can entertain me tonight." And then she turned away, and with Sampson's help, tap-tapped off to the parlour. Imogene sat and listened as the stepping and tapping grew fainter, and miserably she knew, that there was no getting out of this one.

15

IMOGENE AND THE TERRIFYING TINGLE

Imogene, upon returning to her bedroom, went back to her bookshelf to choose another book. She had no idea which one it was going to be, but she searched for the most boring book she had. If she was going to be made to read to her Auntie Agnes, she wasn't going to be the only one suffering. She found it. It was entitled, *"The Journey of the Mouse"* and it was about a mouse that that had become lost and had to find its way home. Perfect.

Imogene ran out of her room, down the corridor and bounded down the stairs. Proudly, she walked into the parlour and straight to her Auntie Agnes. She held the book out in front of her.

"Here it is, Auntie Agnes. My favourite!" But she was standing a little too close to the woman, who promptly reached over and snatched it right out of

Imogene's hands. She looked it over with a scowl.

"Well now, I must say, I don't see what is so interesting about a mouse. But if this is the book that has preoccupied you so, let's hear it." She passed the book back to her niece. Imogene took her place in a hard wooden chair across from her aunt.

"Auntie Agnes, would you like me to read it right from the beginning, or from where I last left off?" Again, Imogene was using that sickeningly sweet voice, and it was almost enough to make her gag.

"From the beginning, of course! Why would I want you to start from anywhere, but the beginning?" Auntie Agnes spoke to Imogene as though she had no brains at all in her head. And in the very next breath, she screeched, "SAMPSON!" Sampson appeared at the door so quickly that Imogene knew he couldn't have been far away. He was, as she had hoped, holding true to his promise to always be near. Imogene smiled.

"Yes, Miss Agnes?"

"Sampson, do bring us our evening tea now." She ordered, with a stern look. As if he would ever dare to disobey her.

"Right away, Miss Agnes. Miss Imogene, would you like anything?" He looked sympathetically at the young girl who was being made to read out loud. Sampson smirked as he read the cover of the book she was holding up. He knew exactly why she'd chosen it.

"Yes, I..." Imogene started gratefully to her friend. Her words were cut off by Auntie Agnes.

"Sampson, I do declare. I said, bring *us* our evening tea. Now wouldn't that mean to you that Imogene has already been taken care of? Or were you thinking that you and I would share the tea?" She glared at the butler.

"No, Miss. I just thought the young lady might prefer some juice. My apologies." And then quickly and to avoid further arguments, he left to fetch the tea.

"Imogene, I do hope you're paying attention. If we don't keep these servants right under our thumbs where they belong, why! They'd begin to think it is they who run things around here! Never let them get away with anything. Now. I'm waiting to hear you read this book that you love so much." And then Imogene wished that she could have asked for some juice; she was awfully thirsty. She cleared her throat, and then smiled as soon as she realized that was exactly what her father did whenever he was about to speak. Obediently, she began to read.

"Little Mike Mouse was a lonely mouse who lived in a nest he had built for himself in the trunk of an old fallen tree. The tree lay in the middle of a great big forest on a great big mountain. Poor Mike Mouse had never before had the pleasure of seeing another mouse! How he longed for the company of those of his own kind. True, he had Sammy Squirrel to chatter with, and often times he'd share wild vegetables with Benny the Bunny..."

"IMOGENE!"

"Yes, Auntie Agnes? But, I'm not done reading to you." Imogene exclaimed hopefully.

"Oh, yes you are. Are you trying to tell me, that you are in the fifth grade, and still reading stories about cute little forest animals?" Imogene nodded eagerly, before replying.

"Well, yes! This is my favourite book!" Imogene held it up again, but Auntie Agnes shook her head.

"Favourite book, my foot. At your age you should be reading about mystery and suspense. Not about happy little nonexistent characters that bounce around all day in search of food or friends!" Predictably then, the woman threw her hand up across her forehead. Imogene sat quietly, watching and waiting.

"Now, Imogene. I want you to go into my office. Don't touch a thing on my desk," she added with a shake of her cane. "Go to the little bookcase beside the desk, you know the short one with the glass doors?" She didn't bother to wait for Imogene to answer. "You know the one. In that bookcase there is a wide variety of books for children just your age. Go and pick one now. I don't care which one you choose! Pick one and take it up to your room and read it. And that, my dear, is the kind of book you should be interested in." Auntie Agnes, having said her piece, looked absently toward the fireplace, and

Imogene knew she'd just been dismissed.

"Yes, Auntie Agnes." She answered as she rose from the chair. Slipping the mouse book under the crook of her arm, she left the parlour and walked down the corridor to the office. Auntie Agnes' office was just about as *forbidden* as the East Wing. Even though she had just received permission to do so, Imogene was scared to death to step foot in it. She had always been certain that this room was full of secrets, and knowing what she knew now, as far as the Pacific Kingdom was concerned, *why not?* Anything was possible.

Imogene cautiously entered the little room, and went straight to the bookcase. She knelt down in front of it and with both hands, tried to pull the doors open, but they refused to budge. She took a deep breath and wondered what to do. She was afraid she might break them if she pulled too hard, yet she couldn't ask Auntie Agnes for help. That would definitely be asking for trouble. Imogene tried again, this time giving each door a gentle jiggle as she pulled. At last, just as beads of sweat began to form on her forehead, the doors came open. Imogene let go and sat down on her bottom with a soft thud. And then, she started to browse through the titles. Sure enough, as her aunt had claimed, the bookcase was full of mystery novels, although Imogene didn't find any the least bit interesting. She chose one anyway, and then jiggled the doors closed again. Imogene left her aunt's office with her nose in the book, when she bumped into Sampson.

"Whoa there, Miss," he exclaimed, startling her even more. She jumped back and the book flew out of her hands.

"Oh, I'm sorry, Sampson. I wasn't looking..." she began as she watched him expertly steady his tea tray. She retrieved her book from the floor.

"Aren't you joining your aunt for tea?" He asked, with a touch of sarcasm. He smiled at the young girl whom he knew was doing her very best to make it through the day. She shook her head, no.

"I'm afraid that my favourite book didn't pass inspection. I am to read this one now, to myself, in my room. And I really *wanted* to read to Auntie Agnes!" Imogene rolled her eyes into the back of her head as she spoke. Sampson winked at her, then continued on his way.

"Have a good evening, Miss Imogene!"

"Yes, Sampson. Goodnight!" She watched him leave; his head held high, shoulders back. One would think that he was the proudest butler alive. Not a person in the world could ever guess that Sampson wasn't a butler at all. Imogene smiled to herself as she turned and made for the stairs.

Imogene was glad once more to be in the privacy of her old bedroom. She changed into her pajamas, washed up in her bathroom, and then headed back toward her bed. She climbed in between the old familiar flannel sheets, and lay her head down on the pillow. Imogene wasn't tired enough yet to sleep; and she was dreadfully bored. She reached over to the bedside table and picked up the mystery novel that she didn't want to read, and began flicking through the pages. She soon found that the more pages she turned, the more interested she became. And so, she began to read.

It hadn't felt to Imogene as though much time had passed, when she happened to glance over to her window. The moon was high in the sky. She furrowed her brows together, very much in an Elsie-like fashion and looked at the clock. It was late! Imogene looked back to the book she held fast in her hands, and was surprised to see that she was already halfway through. *Maybe, just maybe*, she thought grudgingly, Auntie Agnes knew a thing or two about books. Imogene would gladly die however, before admitting it to her. She closed the book and put it back on the table. Just as she reached up to turn off the lamp, a strange feeling washed over her entire body. It was almost identical to the tingle she'd felt when she'd very first stepped into the seawater. Imogene didn't bother with the lamp now; she pulled her hand back and tried to lie still for a moment. Surely this would pass. And then it did. The sensation disappeared, and left Imogene feeling very empty and very alone. Then suddenly, she was overcome with a strange, suffocating sense of fear.

On shaking legs, Imogene raced from her bed to where she'd set her clothes. She reached into her pants pocket and pulled out one of Sampson's power beads. She studied it long and hard. *What if I'm only being silly? What if I'm only scared about tomorrow?* She asked herself these questions, over and over again. Was there something that she should be afraid of? Imogene realized that the feeling of terror had not quite disappeared and she knew there just had to be a reason for it! She was just about to squeeze the bead when she heard a faint *knock*. Silence. *Knock, knock, knock.* Sampson! As quick as she could, she returned the power bead, still shiny, round and intact, to the pocket.

She hurried to the door and opened it to let him in. As usual, Sampson entered her room without saying a single word, and closed the door behind him.

"Sampson! How did you know I needed you?" Sampson looked just as perplexed as she did.

"Princess, to be honest, I didn't know. I only came to tell you that I have to go back to the kingdom for a while! What do you mean, you needed me?" And now he was deeply concerned, for he knew that Imogene was not a little girl prone to crying wolf.

"I... I really d...don't know," she stuttered, very afraid now. "All of a sudden, I became terrified of... of... I don't know what. It won't go away! What is it? Something is terribly wrong, right? It is, I know it is!" Imogene was bug-eyed now, and her voice was becoming louder and shriller with every word she spoke. At this rate, she was going to wake up the whole mansion. And then, just before Sampson was about to soothe her with his calming way and wink, he stopped. He watched as Imogene's colour drained completely from her face, and then she began to shake uncontrollably. Sampson took her firmly by the shoulders and stared straight into her eyes. And then, in a voice so terrifying that it didn't even sound like Imogene's she cried out.

"It's my mother and father! Sampson, you must go to them now!"

"PRINCESS! Princess Imogene! What is it?" Her fear passed to him the moment he laid his hands upon her, and a battle of wills began. The two of them were locked in a stare, but Sampson's experienced telepathic powers soon defeated Imogene's. Right then and there; right in Sampson's arms, she trembled violently once more, and then fainted. Ever so carefully, he carried her to her bed and laid her down on top of the covers. He ran to the bathroom, dampened a face cloth and brought it back to her. He dabbed at her forehead with the cloth and whispered her name. Slowly, Imogene began to come around.

"Imogene, are you alright?" Sampson held up her wrist and felt her pulse. He was very glad to see that it was slowly, but surely stabilizing. Imogene looked up at him meekly, and even his years and years of medical practice could not have prepared him to see her lay in such a weakened state.

"Sampson, what happened to me?" Her voice was small, and it hurt her head to talk.

"Honestly, Imogene. That was the strongest case of telepathy that I have ever witnessed, or been a part of. The connection between you and your mother is so powerful, it is beyond compare!" He continued to dab the sweat away. She jerked up abruptly to a sitting position, obviously annoyed with him.

"In plain English, please!" He smiled at his young charge; she was regaining her strength *and* attitude with amazing speed!

"You'll be just fine, Miss. What happened is... don't be afraid, but you are correct; there must be something terribly wrong in the kingdom." Sampson shuddered at his own words. The kingdom had been so stable for so long, that he couldn't even begin to fathom the cause.

"Is that why you were going down there, Sampson?" She assumed it was, for what other reason would be so pressing as to drag him away? Anything else could surely wait for his return in one day's time. But he shook his head, no.

"Not directly, no. Quosmo has summoned me, and so I was going to meet him."

"Summoned you?" Imogene asked incredulously. "Does that mean that he can speak and hear the way you and I can?"

"Yes, he can. Don't be so shocked, my dear. Of course I would want to pass a talent such as this one, down to my own children. But, until I came to your room and saw the shape you were in, I wasn't at all aware that there is danger lurking below. Now it is imperative that I return, immediately!" Imogene became frightened again.

"But, what about me? What do I do?"

"Nothing, child. You must wait, is all. You cannot return to the kingdom until I am sure it's safe for you to do so." It looked to Imogene, as though Sampson had more on his mind than all he'd said. She folded her arms across her chest impatiently.

"And?" She reached out and took his face in her hands and turned it toward her own. "What is it that you're not telling me?"

"If it is not safe for you in the kingdom, Imogene, I'm afraid that your mother will not be able to come for you as planned." It pained him to say such words, but Imogene needed to know what they might be inevitably facing. He reached up, took hold of her hands and gave them a loving squeeze. Still holding on, he got up to leave. "I must hurry, Imogene. I have to find out what's gone wrong. Do you still have the power beads?"

"Yes." Imogene tried desperately to keep her voice from cracking. She was so close to bitter tears that she could taste them. *One night*, she thought. *It was only supposed to be for one night!* She had a million things going through her mind at once. Knowing she had to let him go, she let her hands drop. And then, just as quickly and as silently as he'd first arrived in her room, Sampson was gone again. Imogene crawled back under her covers and tried to go to sleep. She was so tired; but she had so much to worry about. She forced her eyes shut as she lay there, knowing she had to get some rest. After all, who knew what the next day would bring?

Imogene woke up the next morning, not feeling rested at all. She had just gotten dressed when there was a *knock* at the door. But it was not the *knock,* silence, *knock, knock, knock* that she'd been hoping for. This knock was the quick, sharp rapping that belonged to Kristine.

"Come in, please!" Imogene hollered politely. She watched the door swing open.

"Good morning, Miss Imogene. Dirty laundry?" Kristine smiled at the young girl, as she went to empty the laundry hamper. Imogene gave it to her, apologizing.

"There you are, and I'm sorry about the sock under the bed. I don't mean to make your job difficult." Humbly then, just as she'd seen Sampson do with Auntie Agnes, Imogene looked down at her feet. Kristine felt bad immediately for the girl; she realized that she'd probably been a little too hard on her the day before.

"No, Miss Imogene, that's all right now. It's just a sock, after all. You'll have to excuse my moods now and then, for I don't mean to make you feel bad." This time Kristine's smile was genuine, and she meant what she'd said about the moods. In the last twenty-four hours especially, for some strange reason, the maid felt like she'd been through an emotional whirlwind.

"Thanks, Kristine. Oh, and by the way, is Sampson out and about yet?"

"No, Miss. And that's unusual, isn't it? By this time of the morning, I often find myself tripping over that man somewhere in this big, old house!" Kristine saw an opening to comment further, and she took it, adding, "And if you don't mind a maid putting her nose in where it doesn't belong?" Then she waited. Imogene only smiled and nodded for her to continue. "You see, it's only that a young girl like yourself should have friends her own age! Most girls don't hang around with an old butler the way you do." And then she looked at Imogene in much the same way that Auntie Agnes usually would. Suspiciously. As though the two of them were up to something evil. Imogene had to do some fast thinking to talk her way out of this predicament.

"Well," she started, ever so sadly. "It's only that I hardly remember my own father at all." She sniffled then, for emphasis. "Sampson is like a father, don't you think?" Tears began to well up in the corners of Imogene's eyes.

"Oh, my." Kristine replied with a start. The accusing look she'd worn only a moment before disappeared and was replaced with a look of shame. She'd never once thought that Imogene might look upon Sampson as a father figure. Imogene, upon seeing the intended effect she was having on the maid, really laid it on thick as she continued.

"And I think Sampson and my father would have been friends, had they known each other, don't you think, Kristine?" She sniffled some more, and her tears spilled over and ran freely down her face. Kristine felt so sorry for the orphaned child; she quickly put the hamper down and took a freshly laundered hanky from her pocket. She dabbed at Imogene's face and then took her into her arms.

"Now, now, Imogene. I guess it has been a lonely life for you. If Sampson is like a father to you, far be it from me to interfere! That's okay, child." She held onto Imogene for dear life, feeling so guilty for bringing Imogene to tears. And Imogene, with her head hung over Kristine's shoulder like that, made a face and rolled her eyes into the back of her head. Imogene stopped sobbing then, and pulled away from the maid, but her performance was far from being over.

"And, Kristine?" She looked at her hopefully. Kristine was in the midst of picking up the hamper. She picked it up and looked to the child. "Would you mind if I pretend that you are my big sister?" Kristine dropped the laundry hamper like a stone and grabbed Imogene again.

"Yes, child, of course. And you will be like *my* little sister. You poor, poor sweet thing." And then she proceeded to rub Imogene's back. Imogene snuggled in closer to the woman, who at this point would surely go to the ends of the earth for her.

"Thank you, Kristine," and then rather abruptly, she added, "but now I have to go to the bathroom." Kristine let her go and without saying another word, picked up the laundry hamper and fled from the room. Imogene could see that she had begun to cry. As fast as she could, Imogene closed her door behind the maid. She walked around her room, wondering what to do next! In just a few seconds, the episode with Kristine was close to forgotten and Imogene thought she might lose her mind with worry. She simply could not spend a whole day without having the faintest idea about what was going on in the kingdom.

She sat down on the edge of her bed and thought about her tingling and feeling of terror, the night before. She hadn't asked for it to happen but it did. She hadn't been thinking directly about the kingdom and yet she sensed fear. She began to think. *If I concentrate hard enough, can it happen again?* Her mind was made up and she would give it all she had.

Not wanting to risk the slightest interruption, Imogene locked her bedroom door. She returned to her bed and sat down on it cross-legged. She waited. Nothing. Imogene thought about Sampson. She concentrated on his image with all her might. And then it began. A slight tingle at first. She concentrated some more. Another tingle. And then, inside her head, in a voice that sounded foreign but she knew was her own, she spoke.

"*Sampson! Sampson? Can you hear me?*" And then she felt another tingle. Her whole body felt it now; it was getting stronger. *What did it mean?* Imogene was excited now, as she waited.

"*Imogene!*" Sampson answered. She could hardly remain calm, but she couldn't risk losing the connection. She settled down and focused only on his voice.

"*Sampson, I can't bear it. Tell me what's going on down there!*"

"*Now is not a good time, Imogene. Be patient; I am swimming back right now. Hard to talk so much and swim at the same time.*"

"*Sorry, Sampson.*" Imogene straightened out her legs, swung them over the side of her bed and waited. And then she got up and began to pace around the room. Her tingling had stopped the moment the connection was broken, but she was feeling a little lightheaded. At least now she knew what the tingling meant. Suddenly it occurred to her, *had her mother been trying to reach her last night?*

She quickly returned to her cross-legged position on the bed. Taking a couple of deep breaths, trying to relax, she thought about her mother. Nothing. She concentrated harder on her mother. The tingling began, just like that. Slowly at first, but soon it took over her entire body. Imogene felt fear again, just before she heard her mother's voice.

"*Imogene! I can feel you. Talk to me, sweet muffin.*"

"*Yes, Mother, I'm here. What's wrong? I know something is wrong, I feel it. I felt it last night even, it was so strong!*"

"*Yes, my love. There is something very wrong.*" Elsie paused. "*Serenito has returned.*" Imogene groaned.

"*Oh, no. Now what do we do? I want to be with you, Mommy!*"

"*No.*" Her mother's voice was firm. "*You're much safer where you are. Serenito has no idea where to find you. It worked out well that you happened to go back up right when you did. Last night, when I was so very afraid, you also became afraid. I am so sorry that you didn't understand why.*"

"*Were you trying to talk to me, Mother?*"

"*Yes. I wanted to reach you to let you know that somehow everything will work out. It will only take a little bit longer. Your father sends his love.*"

"*Oh, Mommy, where are you and Daddy right now?*"

"*Promise to be strong and brave, Imogene. Your father and I are locked in the dungeon.*"

16

IMOGENE AND THE CAPTURE OF THE KINGDOM

Imogene couldn't have heard correctly. "*Mother, you didn't say, dungeon, did you? Are you hurt?*"

"*Yes, I said dungeon, and no, we're not hurt at all. Oh, no! Imogene, he's coming… I have to go. Please be careful and remember that we love you.*" And then, just like that, the tingle and the connection were both gone. Imogene jumped from her bed and paced the floor again. Then, right out of the blue, came a quick rapping at her door. Impatiently, Imogene went to it, undid the lock and opened it. It was Kristine again, and what did she want now?

"Yes?" Imogene asked curtly, as she poked her head out.

"Miss Imogene, what's wrong? You look like you've seen a ghost!" The maid looked truly concerned. But Imogene shook her head.

"No, Kristine. It's only that I'm not feeling well. Did you need something?" Kristine, in turn, shook her head.

"No, dear. Miss Agnes has asked me to fetch you for breakfast, since that Sampson is still not around."

"I'm sorry, Kristine. Please tell Auntie Agnes that I'm too sick to eat. I really am. I'm afraid it might be contagious and it wouldn't do for me to make the rest of you ill, would it?" Imogene rubbed her aching belly, in full view of the maid. Kristine had to nod in total agreement.

"Absolutely, Miss Imogene. What a thoughtful child you are. Would you like some ginger ale and dry toast, then?"

"Please, if it's no bother. Maybe my stomach will feel well enough later, so I can nibble a bit." Imogene grabbed the doorframe suddenly then, as if for support. Her knees shook slightly and she doubled over in pain. The maid backed right up, almost to the other side of the hall.

"No bother at all, Miss! Now please go and lie down. I will explain it all to Miss Agnes, and you shan't be bothered again. Shall I leave your tray just outside your door?" As Kristine asked, her head bobbed up and down hopefully. She surely did not want to catch whatever it was that Imogene had come down with.

"Yes, please and goodbye!" With that, Imogene slowly closed the door. It looked to the maid as though it had taken all of her strength. Imogene locked the door again with a soft click. She half-smiled, knowing that she likely wouldn't have to deal with her auntie or the maid, for quite some time. Now Imogene had some serious thinking to do. Suddenly, she remembered the hatch in her fireplace. Should she or shouldn't she? She should.

Imogene quietly unlocked her door. She wrote a quick note, took a thumbtack and stuck them together on the outside of her door, and then locked it again. Almost as an afterthought, she grabbed a roll of glow-in-the dark stickers from her desk drawer, and stuffed them into her pocket. Then, as though approaching one's fireplace was a very bad thing to do, Imogene tip-toed over to hers. She stepped in, climbed up and disappeared. Once inside the narrow chute, Imogene secured the hatch behind her. There was only one direction that she could go and it made perfect sense to her that she was in fact, travelling toward the East Wing. She was all bent over as she made her way to the end, as the chute was not the least bit high. At the end, she found herself facing another hatch. She wondered, as she tried to pull it open, if she might find the narrow little staircase right on the other side. The hatch was stuck. Imogene pulled again with all her strength, until it finally came free with a resounding *BANG*!

In the meantime, downstairs, Auntie Agnes had been looking through one of her magazines when she heard a loud, thunderous clap. She set her reading material on the table, stood up from her chair, leaned on her cane and stared up at the ceiling with curiosity. She waited. When there was no other sound to be heard, she sat down again. She decided that her foolish niece must have fallen out of her bed. She frowned, and then picked up her magazine to resume her reading, meaning full well to demand an explanation about the noise, from the child, later.

Back in the chute, Imogene didn't even breathe for fear of attracting attention from other parts of the house. Surely that sound could have been heard from a block away. Cautiously then, she poked her head through the opening and looked down. Sure enough, it *was* the staircase! But then she heard noises. She shrank back into her own chute, daring not to make a sound. And it was then that she tingled.

"Imogene, that'd better be you up there!" Sampson called silently, although he knew that it was. Imogene breathed a huge sigh of relief as the sound of his familiar voice filled her head.

"Yes, and I'm sorry but I couldn't wait. I spoke with my mother."

"I know. Follow me up to the storage room. Make sure to shut the hatch behind you." Soon after, he passed right by Imogene. She immediately followed, securing the hatch as she'd been told. Up and up they climbed, until finally Sampson stopped and

listened, before opening the last little hatch, and climbing through and into the storage room. Imogene was right behind him; but this time, Sampson didn't close the opening. Imogene guessed it was because she would have to go back, the same way, just as Sampson whispered, "Will you find your way back, okay?" She nodded and proudly held up the roll of stickers she'd taken from her drawer. Sampson chuckled. "You're always thinking, aren't you? No wonder we're all so proud." He gave her a big hug. She hugged him back and at the same time, inhaled. She drew in a deep breath of his fresh scent - the scent of the Pacific Kingdom! How she longed to smell just like that again. He pulled away from her then, and took her by the hand. She followed him to the furthest corner of the room, where he sat down and motioned for her to do the same. The two of them sat there like that, hunched together in a conspiratory way. Imogene couldn't stand the suspense. In a hoarse whisper, she broke the silence.

"If only Auntie Agnes could see us now!" And then she giggled. For as long as she could remember, her offbeat sense of humour had a tendency to kick in at all the wrong times. This appeared to be one of those times. Sampson smiled at her kindly, with the patience of a father.

"Now, Imogene, we have to be quick as I explain it all. I'll tell you as best as I can, from the beginning until right now." Imogene nodded, not daring to cut in.

"Yesterday evening, right before Quosmo summoned me, and not long before you had that major telepathic experience, Serenito arrived at the castle. He was not alone. Somewhere along his travels, he was able to recruit other banished members of the underwater kingdoms. They have joined him in his evil plans to take over the throne!"

"But, Sampson! How many could there be? Surely the castle guards outnumber a few bad guys."

"That is quite true, Imogene. But Serenito and his renegades have employed an unspeakable weapon that the castle was not prepared to fight against. It is the one true forbidden weapon."

"Oh, my. What is it?"

"My dear Imogene. It is magic."

"But, Sampson, don't you use magic kind of, when you hypnotize people and things?"

"Yes, but my magic is for the good of the kingdom. The difference is, that Serenito is using it against the kingdom. But that is not all, Imogene, I am afraid that the story only gets worse." Imogene shook her head, for she thought she already knew what he was about to tell her next.

"How can it get worse? I already know about mother and father being held in the dungeon. You're not saying that there's anything worse than that?"

"I am afraid so. Serenito, in a method that is

beyond even my comprehension, must have cast a spell over my own, dear brother. My brother, Duluth is on his side." Desperately then, Imogene pleaded.

"Go to him… talk to your brother. You must make him see that it's all wrong!"

"I'm afraid not, my dear Princess. My brother has always been a stronger doctor than I. And I suppose that's why it's so hard for me to understand how he has fallen in with such an evil man! I don't think he's done this of his own free will, Imogene. I have to unlock him from the evil spell. Only then can we think about freeing your parents and the kingdom." Imogene, as only Imogene could do, crossly folded her arms across her chest.

"So then, what are you waiting for? I mean, don't you need to hurry on this one, Sampson?"

"No, there is more to consider. The number one item is your scent. And this is what's going to happen. At eleven o'clock every second night, when you are absolutely certain that Miss Agnes is asleep, you must return to the kingdom." Imogene's eyes brightened when he said that. But he was quick to correct himself, and her. "No, Miss Imogene. You can only go as far as the bush that sits at the entrance of the main portal. Quosmo will be waiting for you there with the tonic. You begin tonight."

"Isn't there any chance that I could see my

parents, Sampson?" Even as she asked it, she knew that it was not to be.

"No, that's out of the question." He really felt helpless for her and regretted so much, being the bearer of all the bad news. But tell her, he must. "Serenito is looking for you, Imogene. Night and day, his people search the kingdom, high and low. You cannot reveal yourself; it's too dangerous." Imogene frowned, and thought long and hard about it all. There was no use in arguing or putting up a fight. There was just no point in acting immature, she decided. Maybe it was time to act like a true princess, after all.

"Okay," she agreed. "I will go down every second night for the tonic, for as long as I have to. And you, Sampson? Are you going back down, now?"

"No. That's another problem we face. I must stay with you. My first and foremost sworn duty is to protect the princess of the Pacific Kingdom at all cost!" Imogene shook her head, for she knew he would better serve the kingdom where they needed him the most.

"But, Sampson! Surely not if it means the ruin of the kingdom!"

"Yes, Imogene. That's exactly what it could mean. But like I said, at any cost. Don't worry, dear." He placed a hand upon her shoulder. "I will do all that I can from here. I do have people in place down there." Knowing that he was not all on his own, made Imogene feel a little better, but not much. "Now, Miss. I suggest you return to your room, before anyone suspects that you have slipped out of it. We'll talk more, you can count on it." She reached over and hugged him again.

"Oh, Sampson. What would I ever do without you?" He just laughed softly in reply and stood up with her. He walked with Imogene over to the hatch.

"Good luck, Miss. We can do this, you know." And to that, Imogene only nodded. She climbed through the hatch and into the narrow little staircase. She heard Sampson secure the opening behind her, but she didn't look back. Down, down the stairs she went until she reached the sticker she'd put in place to mark her exit. Removing it, she opened the hatch and climbed through. Once she sealed it behind her, she crouched down as she made her way to her chimney. She waited stone still and listened. Nothing. She opened the last hatch and climbed through. Just as she did, there was a quick rapping coming from her bedroom door! Lightning fast, she climbed down and out of the fireplace. She ran to her bed, messed it up, and then stole a quick glance at herself in the mirror, and was satisfied to see no evidence that she'd gone anywhere.

"Yes?" she answered. She went to the door, unlocked and opened it. There before her stood Kristine, holding in her hand, the note from her door that read, *"I'm Sleeping"*.

"I'm sorry to disturb you, Miss. Wow! You must have been sleeping hard! I've been knocking and knocking and was becoming very worried!"

"I am sorry, I didn't hear you until now. I had a good nap."

"Glad to hear it, Miss. I can see you are getting colour back in your cheeks. Miss Agnes wanted me to check on you."

"I'm stilly queasy, Kristine. I think it's best if I rest a while longer."

"Yes, Miss, you take care, now!" And then the maid turned on her heel and darted away, and Imogene closed and locked the door behind her. *Whew*! Imogene paced the room again. Although she had just seen Sampson, it wasn't enough. She needed to know more. Imogene went over and sat down cross-legged on her bed. She relaxed and took a couple of slow, deep breaths. This time, she thought about Marina. She concentrated hard. The tingle began immediately and Imogene realized that this trick was becoming easier each time she did it! At exactly that same moment, another little girl in the Pacific Kingdom began tingling like crazy.

"Marina, it's me, Imogene! Can you hear me?" Marina was very glad to hear her friend's voice, for she didn't know what to make of the strange pins and needle-like feeling that had washed over her. Now she understood.

"Oh, wow! Imogene, how are you doing up there? This is

my first time!"

"*Really? And I thought I was the late bloomer. Your father says that my power is really strong; maybe that's why we are connected already.*"

"*Oh, Imogene. Am I ever so glad you're gone. I mean... I didn't mean...*"

"*That's okay, Marina. I know what you mean. It would have been dreadful for me if I were below when Serenito arrived. What's going on down there, anyway?*"

"*You wouldn't believe it. It's really scary; it's like living in a bad dream. Armies of Serenito's men march like tin soldiers up and down the streets each night. Every child in the kingdom is now accounted for. If one more child should happen to show up, Serenito's orders are to have him or her shackled immediately. He's looking for you.*"

"*Yes, I know. I wonder who is worse, really. Serenito or Auntie Agnes? I suppose Serenito is worse, because I don't think Auntie Agnes would go so far as to hurt me.*"

"*Just promise that you'll stay away until this is resolved, Imogene. It would be no good if he captured you.*"

"*Yeah. Have you seen my parents?*"

"*No, and I wasn't even going to bring that subject up. But since you mentioned it, I guess it'd be okay. No one has seen hide nor hair of your parents, Imogene. We're all afraid to think about what's become of them!*"

"*It's okay, Marina. I spoke with my mother a short time ago. She and my father are locked in the dungeon.*"

"*Thank goodness. Long live the king and queen!*"

"*Where are you now, Marina?*"

"*I'm at home, in my room. Everyone, and I mean*

221

everyone, in the kingdom is to remain in their homes to make sure the body count is right. Mother is busy cleaning the living room for the hundredth time I'm sure, and so I holed up in here. I was just about to start on homework, actually."

"Homework? Oh, no. That reminds me…" Imogene groaned.

"What's wrong, Imogene? Didn't you finish yours?"

"Yes, of course. But if I'll be staying up here a while longer, I'll have to go back to school here and join soccer."

"Oh, how terrible for you. What is soccer?"

"Just a sport. I guess it's not that bad. Something Auntie Agnes wants me to join. But, I was so looking forward to coming back down, today."

"I know, me too."

"Hey, do you know about Quosmo meeting me tonight with the tonic?"

"What? Oh, I hate it when they leave me out of things." And so Imogene went into detail, explaining to Marina about the tonic and the scent and everything else she'd been kept in the dark about.

"Marina, who did your dad talk to when he came down there just awhile ago?"

"Just us, as he had to sneak in and out so he wouldn't get caught. He's not accounted for, and therefore he can't show up unexpectedly. Serenito would jail him for sure, just like he did your parents. Why?"

"Well, Sampson said he'd recruited some men down there. I think he just said that to make me feel better."

"Yes, I think you're right. I don't think he talked to anyone about it, other than Quosmo."

"*Well then, it may just be up to us. How good is Quosmo at the art of hypnosis?*"

"*He's pretty good. He's been studying for two whole years, now. Ever since he was ten. He hypnotizes things around the house, and he has even gotten me a couple of times!*" Imogene laughed out loud.

"*And you, Marina? What have you learned about it?*"

"*Only because it's you asking, I will tell. I have been practicing a little. Father said he'd teach you and I together, but secretly I've been trying my hand at it for quite some time.*"

"*That's great! I think I'll need to take a crash course in it myself. Tonight at eleven, go with Quosmo to bring me the tonic.*"

"*But, Imogene, he'd never let me tag along like that. And for that matter, neither would my father. Especially on such a dangerous mission.*"

"*Yes, he will. You tell Quosmo that it's an order, directly from the princess of the Pacific Kingdom. Wouldn't he have to obey, then?*"

"*Yes, absolutely he would. Good idea, Imogene!*"

"*Great. I will take care of Sampson, so don't worry about him. Oh, and one more thing, Marina…*"

"*Yes, what is it?*"

"*Bring Rafe.*"

And that was that. The connection and tingling sensation left at the same time. Imogene was so excited about the upcoming night. To see Marina and Rafe again, and well, that Quosmo, she would put up with because she had to, but. only as long as

223

he didn't try to kiss her hand, again. The truth was, that she had been avoiding him as much as she possibly could, ever since her celebration. She didn't like the way her cheeks burned red whenever he was near. And he was kind of cute...

Imogene was weary all of a sudden, and decided to have a rest. She lay down on the bed and thought back to the night before; how tiring it had been when her mother had attempted to reach her. And already on this day, she had communicated with her mother, Sampson and Marina. No wonder she was totally wiped out. Imogene set her alarm, and then cuddled into her pillow. Luckily for her, she fell immediately into a deep sleep; one that she knew she was going to need, if she was going to be of any help in saving her beloved Pacific Kingdom.

Hours later, Imogene was still sleeping, although lighter than at first. All of a sudden she sat straight up in bed, for she'd heard a noise. There it was again! She waited, holding her breath. It began again. Imogene rubbed the sleep from her eyes and listened.

"*Imogene!*" Thankfully it was only Sampson. Imogene was much too groggy to use her telepathy at the moment. Rather than answering him, she staggered to her bedroom door, unlocked and opened it. Sampson stepped into her room, and shut the door quietly behind him.

"You must have been really tired, Miss. I don't imagine you slept well last night?" He didn't even know at this point, about all the communicating that she'd done.

"No, I sure didn't. But, that's not all, I've been busy." She yawned and stretched then, before asking. "What time is it?" Sampson told her that it was past noon.

"Oh, no, has Auntie Agnes asked for me?" She reached over and turned off the clock's alarm that hadn't worked, anyway.

"No, Miss. She would prefer it really, if you would be so considerate as to remain in your room so you don't share whatever illness has befallen you." He smiled at her ingenuity.

"Did Auntie Agnes or Kristine ask where *you* were all morning?"

"No, I told them that I was suffering from the stomach flu, much the same as you were. It really was a fine idea, Imogene. It has certainly kept the both of them from bothering either one of us." Imogene was feeling next to new again after her snooze, and decided that it was high time to get down to business. She turned serious.

"I'm glad it worked out well. Good then, Sampson, we need to talk." She took her position at the head of the bed, and he at the foot. Very seriously then, she explained to him how she had spoken with Marina and how she knew that he really couldn't have gotten anyone from the kingdom to help him. Sampson was slightly taken back by the tone of voice this child was using; it was the first time ever that she had demonstrated her place, which was after all, first in line to the throne.

"Miss Imogene, let me explain. I needed the time to figure out what to do…" But it was too late for him to backtrack now, for Imogene already had the makings of a plan formulating in the back of her mind.

"No, it's okay. We don't have time for that. We have to hurry, and I think I've come up with a plan." Sampson leaned in closer, very eager to hear it. Imogene felt insistent upon convincing him and she continued, "It'll work, I know it will! But, I need your help." Sampson only smiled.

"I don't doubt it, my dear Princess. Go on, do tell me what you're thinking." He was patiently waiting for her to explain.

"Okay. I think Serenito will be expecting some kind of uprise from the people, am I right?"

"Yes, Imogene! He's more than likely wondering what is taking us so long to retaliate. The fact is, I would be the one to lead such a counter attack. But from up here, it's difficult. The people are waiting for my word."

"And so you shall give it to them. We will plan a counter attack, but not a real one. The counter attack that you give the go ahead on, will be nothing but a smoke screen for the real thing."

"What do you mean? Why go to all that trouble? I don't think we have the manpower to stage two attacks, Miss." Sampson knew the child's heart was in the right place, but he couldn't see how this could come to a good end. Imogene gave her head a tilt and narrowed her eyes in a mischievous way.

"I don't think my dear uncle will expect an attack from the children of the kingdom." Sampson gasped. She couldn't mean it.

"No, Imogene! Absolutely out of the question! It's too dangerous!" But Imogene stood her ground.

"No, it's not. The children can sneak around much better than the adults can. While Serenito's gang or army is busy with our adults, us kids will be doing what we can." Sampson shook his head in despair.

"And Imogene, I am afraid to ask which children you have in mind. But ask, I must." Imogene smiled at him, before she replied.

"Why, the only ones I know I can trust with my life, Sampson. Marina, Quosmo, Rafe and I will save the kingdom." Imogene spoke with so much conviction; as though she had never been more sure of anything else in her whole, entire life. She repeated, "I'll need your help." Sampson, who was now nearly one hundred percent resigned to agree with her strategy, nodded in compliance.

"I suppose then, that Quosmo is already in place to bring Marina and Rafe with him tonight?"

"Absolutely. They can follow me up to the first basement where we'll hammer out the details." She hesitated for a moment, and then had to ask, "Do we really have a choice, Sampson? And then, "Do you think we have a chance?" She had looked to him for answers so often in the past; she needed his reassurance one more time.

"Honestly, Imogene. I think that you just may be the kingdom's saving grace." And then Sampson reached over and hugged her. He got up quickly then, and walked to the door. "I best be on my way. We can't risk having Kristine or Miss Agnes suspecting us of anything." Imogene nodded in agreement as she watched him go. Very quietly then, the door closed behind him and she was left alone again.

It was long past lunch and even later than the afternoon tea, when Imogene felt confident enough to leave the security of her bedroom. She'd been trying desperately to avoid her aunt all day, but she knew that at some point, she'd have to face the woman. All the way down the grand staircase, Imogene chanted to herself, *just do it. Get it over with. Just do it.* And it was difficult for her to do, as she had matters of greater importance to mull over, than worrying about her pesky aunt. Imogene's Auntie Agnes heard her footsteps and wasted no time.

"IMOGENE!" She screeched from the parlour, just as Imogene entered the room.

"Yes, Auntie Agnes?" Imogene tried to appear sick; she held her tummy with one hand, and bent over slightly. It looked as though the simple job of walking was a strenuous task, indeed. Auntie Agnes pointed her cane toward her.

"You don't look well, now do you? I suppose you've gone and caught the stomach flu, haven't you?" And she asked as though becoming ill was something that Imogene had done deliberately.

"Yes, I think so, Auntie. I threw up and everything. Ten times, even. I'm dizzy and I still don't feel well." Her legs wobbled as she made her way to the chair opposite of where Auntie Agnes sat.

"Very well, then. I shall postpone the soccer thing until you have decided to finish with this sick nonsense. I will also call your school tomorrow and tell them that you shan't be attending until I am satisfied that you are better." Auntie Agnes looked extremely cross as she thought for a moment, before adding, "At any point during your illness, did you bother to read one of the books I told you to choose?" Imogene nodded eagerly.

"Oh, yes, Auntie Agnes, how can I thank you? I read quite a lot last night before bed, and that book is so much more exciting than my favourite mouse book. I guess you're right, I should have outgrown it long ago."

"Well, I should hope so! That book is much too young for you. Now go back to your room before I get sick from just looking at you. You'd better get well soon." The last statement was more like an order than a well-wishing, and Imogene realized just how lucky she'd been, to have never truly been ill. Her Auntie Agnes did not handle it well, at all. On shaking legs and still doubled over, Imogene got up from her chair and began to stagger away.

"Yes, Auntie, I intend to get better. Thank you." And then Imogene left the parlour. She'd done it! Now she'd have at least the rest of the day to herself; out from under the ever-accusing stares of her aunt or Kristine. Neither of them wanted anything to do with the imaginary flu; they were deathly afraid they'd catch it. Imogene smiled happily all the way back to her room.

17

IMOGENE AND THE GRAND SCHEME

Imogene remained in her room for the entire duration of the day. She planned and paced. And then she lay down on her bed and schemed. She picked up a pen and paper and proceeded to plot and doodle.

Imogene began writing down the important questions she needed to ask Sampson. With him on her side, and his son, daughter and Rafe, she just knew her plan wouldn't fail. She was still doodling when at her door, there came a *knock*. Silence. *Knock, knock, knock!* She ran to it, undid the lock and swung it open. There of course, was Sampson, and in his hands he carried a tray full of snacks and pop.

"Oh, thank you, Sampson." She exclaimed appreciatively. She hadn't had a single thing to eat or drink since the stale ginger ale and dry toast.

Sampson set the tray down on her desk as she closed the door behind him. She wasted no time in helping herself; he brought cookies, fresh strawberries and a bowl full of potato chips. Imogene was famished and popped a strawberry into her mouth, right along with the chips. Juice dribbled from the corner of her mouth.

"Slow down, child, or you *will* be sick!" Sampson warned her, as he laughed at the mess she'd made of herself. She calmed down at least enough to chew and swallow, and then washed it all down with a drink of pop. "How are you doing, anyway?"

"Better now, thanks to you. I was beginning to wonder how to sneak down to the kitchen to smuggle myself some food." She was chewing on a cookie now, as she talked. Sampson was looking at her anxiously, with matters much more important than food on his mind. Imogene took another drink and then held up her list in front of her.

"First," she read out, "do you and Duluth practice the same magic?" to which Sampson nodded and replied.

"Yes, Miss. All doctors of hypnosis have the same manual to go by. It is our doctrine and we cannot vary from it. It is impossible."

"Okay, but Duluth has gone astray, so is it possible that he's practicing another form of magic?" Sampson shook his head.

"No, it is not. What's happened, I fear, is that Serenito must have employed another form; I should say, a deviant form of magic to force my brother on his side. It is the only way. Unless..." Sampson's face lit up like fireworks.

"What? What is it?" Imogene demanded to know.

"There *is* another way! Serenito could never get his hands on the deviant magic. That's highly unlikely given his lowered status in the underwater world. But, I think I've got it, now. I can't believe I never thought of this before!" And now it was Sampson who paced the room. Soon he paced furiously. Imogene just sat, watched and waited until he was ready to share. He folded his arms across his chest, and stopped right in front of her. She was surprised to see his face twisted in pain. "All day! All day I have been trying to figure out how that Serenito succeeded in getting his hands on my brother." Imogene wrinkled up her nose at him, but she didn't interrupt. He continued, "I know that Serenito must have gone to the greatest of lengths to get his filthy hands on him." And then Sampson paced some more. Still, Imogene said nothing and waited. She wished there was something she could do to help, but she knew there was not. "I'm afraid, Imogene. I think that Serenito must have sunk as low as anyone ever could, this time around." With his hands, Sampson rubbed his face in frustration; as if that alone would make everything bad go away. Imogene couldn't bear it any longer.

"Please, I can't stand to see you so distraught. What is it? What has my uncle done, now?" When Sampson turned and faced her, Imogene saw something that she had never, ever seen on him before. There were tears running down his face.

"Serenito must have taken Duluth's son and wife as hostages. I swear on my life that is the only way, that my good hearted brother would ever agree to do his evil bidding."

"Are you sure?" And then Imogene felt foolish for asking. Of course he was sure. All she had to do was look at him to know that. Quickly, she added, "I'm sorry, Sampson. I know that it must be true." He sat down on the edge of her bed and so Imogene joined him there, and tried to wrap an arm around his broad shoulders. Her arm wasn't nearly long enough. Sampson bolted to his feet.

"I must go and talk to him now. I have to talk to him before Serenito has the chance to do them more harm." Sampson headed straight for the door. Imogene ran after him and grabbed him by the arm.

"What do you mean, you must go to him? You're not going down there!"

"No, Imogene, I'm not. My place is here with you. What I meant was that I must return to my living quarters. I will induce myself into a deep state of meditation, find my brother and talk to him."

"Do you mean telepathy? The way I did last night and even when I felt my mother's fear?" He nodded.

"Yes, but for most people it takes a lot more work to get to that point. I suspect that I'll be at it for a while." Sampson felt dismayed, as he knew that he really couldn't afford to waste that kind of time. Imogene tugged on his arm again.

"Use me." He looked down at her as though she had completely lost her mind.

"Imogene, I know you mean well, but how can you help?" And then just as he asked, it struck him. Although Imogene's powers were new and unrefined, they were so very strong that she could act as a conductor between him and his brother. And he also knew, that by using Imogene, it would only be a matter of minutes before he was in contact with Duluth. This was an opportunity he couldn't pass up. His mood brightened a little as he backed away from the door and told her, "Princess, you've got yourself a deal."

Sampson and Imogene sat down facing each other, on the floor of her room, next to the bed. They both sat cross-legged and held hands. With their eyes closed and heads bowed, they began to relax. At the exact same moment they concentrated on each other. Instantly, Sampson and Imogene were completely in tune.

"*Imogene, can you hear me?*"

"*Loud and clear, Sampson. I tingled only for a quick minute this time.*"

"*Yes, that's right. After you've been doing this a while, you won't tingle anymore at all. You see, you have already*" *become an old pro!"*

"*Old is right. Are you sure I'm only ten?"*

"*Actually, sometimes even I wonder about that. You are wise beyond your years. Are you ready to get on with it?"*

"*Yes, what do I do?"*

"*Nothing. You and I are already connected, physically and emotionally. Now you must stay relaxed and clear your mind of everything, as best you can."*

"*Okay, Sampson. I'll try."* And so they remained just that way for a moment longer. When Sampson felt Imogene's little hands soften in his, he knew that it was time to begin.

"*Imogene, this is going to feel for you, like you are listening in on a telephone conversation. You mustn't speak at all. You may feel the urge to, but you mustn't. You are just an innocent bystander listening in, okay? Can you do that? The most important job you have is to remain calm."*

"*I can do it. I'm ready."*

"*Good girl."* Sampson took a couple of slow and deep breaths, and then he thought about his brother. He thought about his parents, and the home that he grew up in. He remembered every single detail about the Atlantic Kingdom. He remembered vividly, as he and Duluth listened, learned and watched intently, over and over again, as their father taught them the art of hypnosis. And soon he was not only thinking about it all, but watching it, as one would watch a movie. He watched as he and his brother walked to school together, ate lunch, played and learned. Finally, he saw his brother's wedding. And then with amazement he watched his own wedding, and then the birth of his son. Sampson was lost now; so deep within his self-induced trance that tears ran freely down his cheeks as he relived it all. His entire life was literally passing right before his eyes. And then he began to travel at the speed of light. All around him were splashes of every colour he'd ever seen and some he hadn't. The colours were moving, swirling and joining and then they would separate again with such intensity that in the end all he saw was blackness. He was nearing the end of his journey and tried desperately to remain calm. And then, he found himself looking at a near image of himself. But it was not his own reflection that he saw. There in front of him, appeared the image of his dear brother, Duluth. He was in a cell! It was the dungeon, Sampson realized grimly. Duluth was sitting on the floor in the corner, head bent down, with his legs crossed. All of a sudden, the man's head snapped up. Duluth had immediately felt his brother's presence.

"Sampson! Thank goodness you are here."

"Duluth! Are you well, my brother?"

"As well as can be, I'm afraid. Although when this is over, if Serenito doesn't finish me, I'm sure the king and queen will. They think I have betrayed them."

"Do not worry. I will take care of the king and queen, Duluth. They will understand, I know it. Now you must tell me, where are your wife and son?"

"*You are so intuitive, Sampson. How is it that you never lose faith when everyone else does? For that alone, I am forever in your debt. Serenito has my wife and son with him, as you well know. They are in the king and queen's house.*"

"*Have you spoken with them at all?*"

"*Only briefly. Serenito watches them too closely for them to communicate with me. They are not harmed; that much, I know. Tell me, dear brother. Have you come up with a plan?*"

"*Actually, no. But, the princess has, and I do believe it will work!*"

"*The princess! But is she not merely a child? We are going to risk life and limb on a plan that was devised by a child? No, I don't think so.*"

"*Duluth, Have faith, man! When did you become so pessimistic? Do you really think I would risk it all if I didn't believe her plan stood a chance? Besides that, you don't know this princess. She is no ordinary girl; in fact I feel that she is destined for even greater things. She is the reason I'm able to communicate with you. If it were not for her acting as our conductor right now, I wouldn't be talking to you like this. I would not know, Duluth, that you sit on the floor of your cell like a beaten man with your head bowed down.*"

"*You can see me, too? Oh, my goodness. I've always been the stronger doctor, Sampson. I assumed that it was as it has always been; where I could see the vision of you, but you could not see me. This girl you speak of, she must have quite the power to be able to do this; that is proof enough for me. I apologize, and I will trust in her plan. What must I do?*"

"*Nothing. Act as though nothing has changed, Duluth.*

We can't have Serenito expect anything is amiss. We are going to send in the troops as a cover only. They will be large in numbers but will carry no weapons."

"No weapons! How do you expect to save us all with no weapons?"

"The princess will not tolerate bloodshed. The troops will serve as a screen only, while we go in and rescue your family and the king and queen."

"Sampson, the future of the kingdom rests entirely upon you. Do take care. I hear Serenito coming now; I must stop talking." Poor Sampson watched in horror as his brother stood up and walked over to the bars of the tiny cell that he was confined to. Serenito, with his eyes full of fury, towered toward Duluth with his arms outstretched and his fists clenched. And then everything turned black. The connection was gone. Imogene let go of Sampson's hands and jumped to her feet.

"Sampson, was *that* man my uncle?"

"Yes, Imogene," he replied in a soft, slow voice. "Don't worry about him. You did well. You are truly going to be magnificent someday, do you know that?" He watched as she walked over and sat on the edge of her bed.

"Yes, I think I do know that. And I fear it because I know that my life will never be the same. Sometimes, I just want to be a boring, normal kid again." Sampson looked sympathetically at his little friend who at this moment, felt as though the weight of the world rested upon her small shoulders. He reassured her as best he could.

"My dear Princess. Once we're done up here, and once the kingdom is again under your father's rule, I promise that you will feel very much like a normal kid again, but never a boring one. Even if it takes the rest of my life making sure of just that, it will be so." He got up from the floor and went to comfort her. He lifted Imogene up onto his knee and embraced her with his big, strong arms. And they sat there like that for a good, long while. Imogene felt safe and secure, even if only for the time being. She squeezed her eyes tight; she tried to rid herself of the image that was now permanently branded into her head. She realized she'd be better off if she'd never laid eyes upon her uncle's horrible face.

He too, like the other underwater people, had been wearing a robe. It was not a handsome robe like the ones her father or Sampson wore, nor was it like the robes any of the other men she'd seen. This robe was dark, shiny and too long; it did not belong in the kingdom any more than its wearer did. Over top, his long dark hair cascaded and rolled all the way beyond his shoulders, and he wore a pointed hat. His black moustache curled up wickedly at each end. And there was nothing about him, aside from the colour of his eyes, that even remotely resembled Imogene's father. She was thankful for that, but wondered how two children from the same parents, who grew up together in the same household, could be so completely different? She realized that the same was true where her mother and Auntie Agnes were concerned.

"My dear," Sampson began, interrupting her thoughts. "It is almost time." Imogene looked over at her clock that sat on the bedside table. It read twenty minutes to eleven.

"Is it that time already? Auntie Agnes must have gone to bed by now, right?"

"Yes, I heard her hobble by your door about an hour ago. Don't worry. She thinks you and I are sick in our own beds, having gone to sleep hours ago."

"Thank goodness for that. At least she has not had any reason to bother me to read to her."

"I know, Miss Imogene. That's one punishment you shouldn't have to suffer through, anyway. Now, let us go." Sampson got up and walked over to Imogene's fireplace. He turned and looked back at her; she nodded and quietly followed. Up the chimney they went, and through the first hatch that led to the chute. Sampson had to shimmy on his belly; the passageway was so small. And Imogene thought she'd had it tough. Soon, they arrived at the hatch that led to the narrow little staircase, and then softly down the stairs they crept. Down the stairs, through the wall, into the basement and through another wall, with Sampson lighting candles all along the way. Imogene was sure that the candles were for her benefit, as she guessed that he could have found his way even in the pitch black.

Finally, they reached the pool. Imogene went into the little bedroom that she had been in just the day before, and found her bathing suit right where she'd left it. She changed and met Sampson back at the water's edge.

"Ready?"

She looked him up and down, then up and down again. He hadn't changed his clothes.

"Sampson, aren't you coming with me to get Quosmo, Marina and Rafe?" She had assumed that especially now, that he would want to.

"No, dear. There would be no room for me under the cover of the bush. And if you happen to get caught, I must be left to rescue you." Imogene nodded. That was something that she hadn't considered.

"Okay, that's a good idea. But what if I lose my way?"

"You won't, now. You can't lose your way at this point. All you have to do, is think about where you want to go. You will reach the bush, and then you will lead the others back to me," and then he added, as he tapped the side of his head with his forefinger, "I will be right here if you need me." Imogene hugged him quickly, and then without another moment's hesitation, dove straight down and into the pool of water. In a flash, she was gone. Sampson sat down on the floor and watched the water until even the ripples had disappeared. Sadly, there was little for him to do, but sit and wait. Sit and wait for Imogene, Quosmo, Rafe and Marina to return to him safely.

Imogene, in the meantime, was travelling at lightning speed. Sampson was right; she didn't once have to worry about becoming lost. All she had to do, was picture her destination in her mind. She remembered back to when her mother first saw her come out from the cover of the bush at the lake; her mother had swum to her so fast, that Imogene couldn't believe her eyes. But now, Imogene understood that kind of power. In the tunnel she'd already gone by the first turn and up ahead, she could see the light. In another minute, she knew that she'd be standing at the bush. She reached the end of the tunnel now, and stopped. She looked around at the fish, and saw that there were plenty of them. Perhaps if anyone else were in the water, the fish wouldn't be there? But then, she shook her head, no. In the past, the fish had seemed to know that Imogene posed no threat, and so she had to assume that they wouldn't make themselves scarce for any other person from the kingdom, either. Still, she remained in the tunnel. Imogene was well aware that this was a one shot deal; she couldn't afford to get caught by Serenito or his nasty men. She decided that she'd better talk to someone to make sure the coast was clear before she emerged. Imogene took a couple of deep breaths. She thought about Marina, and concentrated hard.

"*Marina! Can you hear me?*" To Imogene's great

relief, her friend answered right away.

"*Yes! Are you at the bush?*"

"*No, not quite. I wanted to talk to you to be sure that it's safe, first.*"

"*Good. It's not really that safe. Maybe you shouldn't come out at all. I'm just about at the lake; we had to split up so we wouldn't attract attention. Rafe and Quosmo have probably already met up by now, and should be hiding near the shore. Wait!*" Imogene could hear Marina pant fast, and then hold her breath. Imogene also held her breath and waited. What happened to her friend? "*There! I just had to duck into the trees; Serenito's men are everywhere. Don't they ever sleep? Okay, I can see the bush now. There went Quosmo.*"

"*What do you mean, there went Quosmo?*" asked Imogene, suddenly more concerned.

"*Oh, I mean into the water, toward you. You're waiting in the tunnel?*" Imogene looked out in the distance toward the light. She could barely make out a figure coming her way.

"*Yes, I am and I see him. He's coming!*" Imogene watched him make a beeline for the tunnel's entrance. She almost giggled as she wondered if he'd try to bow down or kiss her hand. Not possibly, she hoped. Quosmo stopped beside her, they smiled and nodded at each other and waited expectantly for the others to arrive.

"*Imogene? Rafe is coming now. Do you see him, yet?*" And so Imogene studied the water again, and saw Rafe's small form becoming clearer and clearer the closer he got.

"*Yes, he's here, too. Now it's your turn, Marina. Please do be careful as there is no one looking out for you out there!*"

"*Gee, thanks for reminding me, Imogene. Hang on; the army is making another pass. I'd better stay put for a bit.*" And the girl held her breath again. Imogene imagined that they must be very close by, if Marina was afraid they'd hear her breathe. The longer that the three of them waited, the more anxious they became. Quosmo gave Imogene a nervous look and shrugged. Rafe kicked a shell back and forth from foot to foot. And Imogene kept her neck craned upwards, ready for any sign at all. It was taking too long now, and they were becoming more and more worried for Marina with each passing second. Just then, when Imogene, Quosmo and Rafe were all very near panic, they saw her. Marina swimming for them, full speed ahead! Once united, Imogene motioned for her friends to follow and before long they all filed in behind as she led them onward and upward to the basement.

Sampson was now on his hands and knees, staring steadfast into the pool of water in which Imogene had disappeared. It seemed like so long since she'd left, that he was nearly ready to change his clothes and dive in after her and the other children. At last, just as he was about to do just that, he saw movement in the water. He stared harder and sure enough, he saw them. He breathed a huge sigh of relief, and then stood up to get ready to pull them out. Imogene was the first to emerge.

"Imogene, thank goodness!" Sampson exclaimed the moment he lifted her to safety. He handed a towel to her, and then pulled up his son. Quosmo gave his father a quick handshake as soon as his feet were on solid ground. Imogene threw him a towel. Next came Rafe, followed by Marina. The four kids stood around the pool in their towels, on shaking legs. Sampson studied their worried faces, frowned and asked, "Has it gotten so much worse, in such a short length of time?"

"Yes, Father." Quosmo answered honestly. "Serenito's men are absolutely everywhere. We have to move fast!" Marina was nodding in agreement and hopping from foot to foot. She added.

"Yes, Father, I hope you have a fast acting plan!" Sampson looked at them all. Imogene and Rafe had been silent the whole time. Imogene, he knew, was exhausted from making the record speed round trip. That explained her silence, but it did not explain Rafe's, and he just couldn't shake the feeling of uneasiness that came over him, each time he looked at the boy.

"Imogene, please take Marina to the bedroom and find some dry clothes for the both of you." Sampson nodded toward the door. As soon as the girls were gone, he pulled some dry clothes from a bag, for the boys to wear. "I'm afraid they'll be too big, but at least you guys will be dry while you're up here." Quosmo and Rafe took the clothes from him and immediately changed into them.

"Wow, Father! Can we look around some?" Quosmo begged, as he squinted and peered this way and that over his father's shoulder. He'd never been to the surface before, and he was amazed at the odd construction of the basement. Rafe was equally enthused.

"No, son. I'm afraid there is no time. Not today, but perhaps that's an adventure for another day. And you, Rafe? What are you thinking?" Sampson took the opportunity to approach the boy. How he wanted to get inside his head. But Rafe acted calm, cool, and collected as he replied.

"Nothing, sir. I'm just here to help in anyway that I can." Sampson was disappointed that the boy was not eager to offer more information. And he was positive that there was more to him than met the eye. But, what?

"That's great, Rafe. I'm sure we'll need your help. Now boys," he directed. "As soon as the girls return..." but he didn't get a chance to finish, as the girls had just come back into the room. They were obviously just as eager as anyone, to save the kingdom. Sampson nodded at them all. "Follow me." And they did. From the room, hand in hand down the dark hallway that had no candles lighting the way, until they reached a room at the very end. This room was well lit and in the center of the room sat a large table surrounded by five chairs. In the

247

center of the table, was a detailed map of the entire castle. Imogene and the other kids raced to take their seats. Sampson took his position as well, but he did not sit. All eyes were upon him; he was to be the leader of this very dangerous mission.

"Children. Thank you for banding together with me. Without you, I don't think the kingdom could be saved. Imogene, you especially, are one brave little girl." Imogene blushed red as her friends turned and stared. Sampson tapped the table lightly with his palm. "We will celebrate our victory later, and everyone will get their reward. But for now, we must continue. As you can see, I have only the castle plans here." He waved his hand around the perimeter of the castle drawing. "There is no use in worrying about how to get to the castle. You children will have to make your own way to it." He looked seriously at each one of them. "We lack the luxury of time. If this were a properly executed mission, we would sit and watch and find out just when the guards make their rounds. We would know how many men they have and where they are stationed. But we can't sit and watch. We just have to make do. In short, you children will swim back through the tunnel, make your way back to the castle without being seen, and save it."

He looked at each of the solemn faces sitting before him and beamed with pride. So serious and yet so young. He looked at Quosmo. So brave and mature for a boy of twelve. Most of the other boys his age he knew, were only interested in owning the best looking and the fastest seahorse. And on the other hand, here was his son, preparing to go into battle.

And little Marina? She was trying very hard not to hop around, happy as she was to be included.

Then of course, there was Imogene, who had the most to lose, the most to gain and was hardly buckling under the pressure. She rose gallantly to the challenge that most adults even, would never come face to face with. Sampson knew that when the time came, this girl would rule the kingdom well.

Out of the corner of his eye, Sampson looked Rafe up and down. His mother, Elena was a favoured servant of the king and queen. His Auntie Kristine was as faithful as they come. So maybe, just maybe, with the good and loyal blood that ran through the boy's veins, he would prove to be a true ally to the throne. Sampson could only hope so. Imogene spoke, snapping him out of his reverie.

"All right, then. Sampson, once we're inside the castle, where do we begin?" She was ever so impatient to get a move on and Sampson could hardly blame her. He pointed to the royal chambers.

"This my dears, is where Serenito is keeping my nephew Ian, and his mother, Portia." Sampson's own children looked up at their father with identical bewildered expressions. Marina stood up so quickly that her chair flew backwards.

"Daddy," she whined. "I didn't know that Auntie Portia and Ian were captured!" The poor girl burst into tears. Sampson was about to go to her, when Rafe intervened. He stood, looked at Sampson and held up his hand to stop him. Sampson, mostly out of curiosity, stayed put to watch the boy. He was more intrigued by him now, than ever before.

The room fell silent. Rafe approached the crying girl, knelt down beside her and put his hand on her lap. Marina looked up at him and the moment her eyes met his, she found that she was unable to look away. Nor did she want to. And so they sat there like that, locked in what appeared to be a private, silent exchange. Sampson, Quosmo and Imogene found that they too, although for different reasons, were unable to pry their eyes away from the two of them. What was going on? Marina's tears stopped flowing; she nodded at Rafe, and then turned away. Rafe removed his hand from her lap and returned to his chair. Of all of them, Sampson was the first to react. He stood, turned to Rafe, and demanded.

"Explain what just happened here, boy! What did you do to Marina?" As he asked, he could plainly see that Marina was just fine. But he needed answers. Just then, Sampson realized the very reason Rafe had bothered him from the very start. He couldn't read him. Not one bit, could he see the real boy behind the mask. Was he good hearted or bad? Selfish or selfless? Kind or mean? Sampson had no way of knowing and it frightened him to death. From Rafe, he could sense nothing. Marina wailed.

"Oh, Father, please leave him alone! He only helped me to see that I've got to remain strong, or no one will be rescued. He said that if I lose control now, I would be no good to you, or to Quosmo, or to Imogene." Softly, she added, "And he took away my tears." Stunned silent, Imogene and Quosmo looked from Sampson to Marina and then to Rafe and back again. They watched Rafe as he sighed deeply, shrugged as he looked at the others, and then surrendered his explanation.

"Sampson, I mean, sir? We don't have time for a long story. You need to know only that I come from a long line of Curors. I'm sure you've heard of us?" He looked to the older man hopefully. Sampson was wide-eyed as he nodded to the boy. He realized then, the reason that he couldn't read him. Curors were highly esteemed in all underwater kingdoms, even held in higher regard than doctors of hypnosis.

"That's right, Rafe. We don't have time," he answered thoughtfully. "But can you tell me why no one, and I mean not another soul in the Pacific Kingdom knows about you?" Rafe nodded eagerly.

"Yes, in short. Somehow, two generations, meaning my father and grandfather, were skipped over. Once that much time had passed, we were pretty much forgotten about. As you know, my family comes from the Tasman Empire..." Imogene cut in.

"Tasman Empire? Doesn't this just keep getting better and better. Where is the Tasman Empire?" All eyes were on Rafe. He straightened his glasses as he grinned, and then continued.

"The Tasman Empire is located in the Tasman Sea. We call our land, *empire*, whereas you call yours, *kingdom*. The Tasman Sea is located south of Australia. Anyway, when my grandfather was born with no Curing abilities, the empire just about lost hope. And when my father was born without them, the empire *did* give up all hope. The royal privileges were revoked and we were classified as outcasts, for my family was no longer of any real use to the empire. When my father grew old enough to leave his parents, he moved away. He eventually ended up working in the rice fields of the Pacific Kingdom. The rest is history, as he met my mother, married her, and then they had me."

"Well, Rafe, I am pleased to say that the empire's loss is surely the kingdom's gain. I am glad to have you with us." Sampson meant every word of it as he walked over to the boy and offered his hand. Rafe shook it with enthusiasm.

"Now, back to the pressing matters," Sampson said as he returned to his spot. Again, he pointed to the royal chambers on the map. "First item is to save Portia and Ian. Only then, will Duluth in theory, be free. Serenito will be left with nothing to threaten him with. Quosmo..." he looked straight at his son. "You must get them to the hidden school safely. That is your duty. Once they are in hiding there, return to the castle to help the others." Quosmo nodded, proudly accepting his orders.

"Marina, once Quosmo has communicated to you that your aunt and cousin are safe, you must go to Uncle Duluth. He is being held here." And as he said it, he pointed to a tiny box of a room at the end of the dungeon's corridor.

"But, Father," she protested. "How will I get there without being seen?" The poor girl didn't see how it could be done.

"Don't worry, my dear. By that time, the make-believe army that I am getting together will be making its way to the castle. They'll be making such a racket that Serenito will order his men out to fight them. I don't think you'll run into resistance down at that end of the dungeon. You will then free your uncle." Marina nodded, pleased to be in charge of such an important task.

"Do I bring him to the school, Father?"

"No. He'll know where it is. You need only to tell him that his wife and son are there waiting for him, and he'll find it just fine." Lastly, Sampson turned his attention to Imogene and Rafe, and as a matter of factly, directed them.

"The two of you are in charge of rescuing the king and queen." He pointed to the cell at the opposite end of the dungeon from where Duluth was. "But, I fear that there will be at least one guard there." Imogene and Rafe looked at one another uneasily, and then at Sampson. Imogene stammered.

"But, then what do we do? Surely the guard will not allow us to walk in and demand that he release my parents!"

"No, I don't suppose it'll happen that way at all. That is why I've prepared this." And Sampson pulled from his pants pocket, four little drawstring bags. He handed one to each child and began to explain. "I am anticipating no trouble of course, but we must be as prepared as we can be. Ready for anything and everything. In each of these bags, are exactly six pinches of the sacred Poufo Powder." Each of the children held their bags up and examined them. Rafe was the most anxious and started untying his string.

"No!" Sampson reached over and pulled the bag right out of Rafe's hands. The boy jumped back, alarmed. "I'm sorry, Rafe; I didn't mean to startle you. The mysterious thing about this powder is that whoever holds a bag of it, is immune to its effects. But if even the tiniest amount of the powder is released into the air, whoever is not holding a bag will drop like a fly. Hopefully you will not need it until the end." He tightened the string and handed the bag back to Rafe.

"The end?" The four children gulped and asked at the same time.

"Yes, the end. Once Duluth and his family are safe within the hidden school, and once the king and queen are back on the throne, you must lure Serenito and his men back to the main room of the castle, where the public functions are held. The four of you must be posted on the landing high above, where you can let the powder fall. It will certainly be enough to put them to sleep; long enough for us to secure them in the dungeon." Sampson looked around at all the serious faces that awaited his next command. He'd never been more pleased with anyone in his life, than he was now, with all of them.

"All rise." The children stood. Sampson placed his large fist toward the center of the table. Four smaller fists joined his and they all touched. They were all darkly aware, that this moment could very well be the last that they would ever spend together again. "Let's go." Once more, the children followed Sampson from the room. And as before, they quietly made their way down the hallway, past closed doors, until they reached the room with the pool. Imogene and Marina carried on to the bedroom to change their clothes. It was not long before they rejoined the others. Sampson gave each child a reassuring hug and a pat on the back, and said, "May the kingdom be with you all, children. Do have a safe journey." One by one, they dove into the pool. As he watched them go with a heavy heart, he wished he could have said more. Like perhaps, *be careful*, or *look out for one another*. But alas, those were things they already knew to do. And how do you prepare a child for war? Was there a right or a wrong way?

Sampson shook his head in remorse and sat down on the dirt floor next to the pool. He sat cross-legged with his hands resting on his knees as he tried to relax. He took a couple of deep breaths, and still feeling Imogene's power coursing through his veins, one by one, began making contact. He spoke with everyone; the beekeepers, the merchants, the rice farmers, the teachers and the orchard masters. By the time he was done recruiting them all, Sampson had a willing and able group that was raring and ready to go at his earliest command. And then, all that was left for him to do, was sit and wait.

18

IMOGENE AND THE ROYAL MISSION

Imogene and her friends swam down through the tunnel, around the familiar bend and reached the entrance to the lake. Imogene's heart felt like it was beating hard in her throat; she was so worried about the mission. She had a sinking feeling that the others would automatically look to her for instruction, from here on. Upon realizing that, she became more determined than ever before to succeed. By the time she and the others had made it to the surface, and under the cover of the bush, Imogene was no longer an uncertain little girl. She had taken on the role of a true princess; one who was ready to fight for her beloved kingdom.

"My good friends," she whispered as she stared at them all. "I'm afraid that my dear Uncle Serenito has no idea just who he's up against! We won't fail."

She looked each of them straight in the eye, and saw nothing but fierce resolve staring back at her. They waited for their next set of orders.

"Let's go now, to the castle without being seen. If we should split up for any reason, we'll meet at the garden doors, beyond the patio. There is enough bush there to provide us with cover. And do you have your drawstring bags?" They all nodded and showed them to her. "Good. Follow me." Imogene looked in all directions, and seeing that the way was clear, swam underwater toward the shore until it was too shallow to remain hidden. Marina, Quosmo and Rafe followed. Crouching, they snuck up onto the shore and scrambled into the closest group of trees, just in time. A large patrol came marching by. There were at least a dozen mean looking men, armed for battle. They all dressed in black and carried swords at their left sides. Over the right shoulder of each man hung a large coil of rope. The children trembled, as they hunkered down behind the trees in the long grass and held their breaths. Now, Imogene understood why she'd heard Marina holding her breath earlier; they really did march *that* close. When all was quiet again, Imogene, like a true commander, was the first to pop her head up to survey the area. To her greatest relief, the way was clear. She slunk back down and whispered.

"Let's take to the trees that line the pebble path. That way, all we'll have to do is drop to the ground, should they happen to come back." They all nodded in agreement. Marina and Quosmo held hands, and Rafe straightened out his glasses. Quickly then, Imogene led them from the trees and across the road to the forest. The trees were sparse and only grew in patches, but there was tall grass, bushes and definitely a lot of overgrown weeds that they could easily nestle down into if the need arose.

The four children crouched again as they made their way over the twigs and around the branches and leaves that had fallen upon the forest floor. Imogene was sure they were making such a ruckus that there was no way they'd make it to the castle without being seen or heard. But they in fact would, as there would be no more sentries on the pebble path for some time. Imogene stopped at the crest of the hill. She motioned to her friends and they all lay down together in the tall grass that lined the forest. The castle was in full view.

"How do we get from here to there?" Quosmo asked in a hoarse whisper. The situation looked impossible. They watched the guards below, who incessantly paced back and forth in front of the main doors. The only thing in the children's favour was that the drawbridge was lowered and in place for them to cross the moat.

"Do you think they're using the servants' corridors?" Imogene asked thoughtfully. She didn't wait for an answer and quickly, she continued, "No! They have no need to sneak about; not when they already hold the entire kingdom hostage. Wait. I'll ask Sampson if the corridors lead to the dungeon." Marina, Rafe and Quosmo were silent and still as they watched Imogene begin. This time she didn't take the cross-legged position; she couldn't risk being seen. And she hoped it would work, anyway. Laying flat on her back, she closed her eyes, took a couple of deep breaths, relaxed and focused on Sampson. There was no tingle at all, no tell tale sign that the telepathy would work; nonetheless, in no time at all, Sampson answered.

"Yes, Imogene? Where are you all? Are you together? Is everything okay?" Sampson was clearly upset and spoke so fast that Imogene could barely keep up.

"Yes, we're all fine. We are hiding in the bushes on the hill overlooking the castle. What I need to know is, do the servants' corridors lead to the dungeon?"

"You clever girl. Of course, yes, they do. Be careful!"

"We will, and I'll keep you informed." Imogene opened her eyes, turned onto her belly and looked back at the castle.

"Well?" Marina asked impatiently.

"Yes." Imogene replied. "Quosmo, can you hypnotize from here?" Quosmo thought for a moment, before replying. He looked down at the guards again, then back at Imogene.

"That depends, Imogene." He looked back at the guards, and saw that there were now only two guards that were near the main doors. "Them?" he asked, incredulously.

"Yes, them. Before, when I spoke with your father, there were four guards pacing back and forth. Now there are only two. If you can do something to them so that the four of us can sneak in, we can make it to the servants' corridors. Once we are through the main doors, the servants' corridors begin directly to our left. Can you do it?" Quosmo was still studying the castle scene below, but he could feel Imogene's intense stare. She was right; it would be easier to do now, while there were only two guards. But he had never before even attempted to hypnotize from such a distance; for until now there'd been no need. And thankfully, the chances of either of the guards possessing any telepathic powers were extremely slim. Quosmo suddenly felt Imogene's strength radiating toward him, and only then did he know he could do it. With her help. Quosmo reached over and took hold of her hand. Imogene gasped! He was quick to explain, for she'd quickly turned red and pulled her hand back.

"Imogene, yes, I can do it. But you have to help me." He held out his hand again and this time she willingly placed hers in his. Now she understood what he was doing.

"Don't worry, Princess. I only need the use of your great conductivity, much the same as my father did when he spoke with Uncle Duluth." Rafe and Marina looked on in awe, but neither of them said a word. Quosmo continued explaining, for their benefit as well.

"Lend me your power. Relax and let me flow through you. It is only through you that I'll be able to work on them." He tilted his head in the direction of the guards. Wordlessly, Imogene nodded and then closed her eyes and relaxed, still holding Quosmo's hand. She knew exactly what she must do. Quosmo closed his eyes and began. The two of them concentrated on one another until nothing else mattered. Within seconds, Imogene and Quosmo were united as one.

"*You guards! Guards at the castle doors!*" The astonished guards each suddenly stopped marching, stood completely still and cocked their heads to the side. To Marina and Rafe, it looked as though they were listening intently... but to what?

"*Yes, you! Listen to me!*" Quosmo held their attention like nothing had ever before. "*Look up to the sky! That's right, the sky! You can't see me, but do you see my pendant?*"

Marina and Rafe watched the guards look upward. How each of them wished they could hear what Quosmo was telling them. Suddenly Marina had a thought. An excellent idea, she had to admit. Quietly, she nudged Rafe with her elbow. He watched her as she reached over and took hold of Imogene's free hand. She was so gentle that Imogene didn't even stir. Rafe figured out exactly what Marina was up to, and he reached over and held onto Marina's free hand. In unison they closed their eyes, took a couple of deep breaths and relaxed. All four of them were linked now; Marina tingled slightly, and Rafe not at all, for his own powers were far too great. Within moments, they were inside Quosmo's mind and could hear all that was going on.

The guards were still searching the sky in vain for the mysterious pendant. And in the meantime, Quosmo was struggling with all his might to conjure up the image. It was a similar pendant to his father's and hung on a gold chain around his neck. He was about to give up, having become entirely frustrated when all of a sudden, it appeared, as clear as day. His pendant hung high in the sky, as big as life itself. The guards were tormented, and they were unable to look away. That floating pendant was the most beautiful thing they'd ever seen, and they were indeed, fully spellbound. Quosmo smiled. He had them right where he wanted them.

"*Yes, you fools. That pendant.*" Expertly, Quosmo began to chant in a very low and mechanical kind of voice. "*Watch the pendant, guards. Watch the pendant. Watch the pendant. Back and forth, back and forth, back and forth. Watch the pendant, guards. Wave your left arm if you are watching the pendant.*" Quosmo watched as the guards each waved their left arm high up into the air.

"*Watch the pendant, guards. Jump up and down if it is going back and forth.*" The guards, still waving their left arms in the air, jumped up and down. *"You guards are so tired after such a long day at your post. I'd like you to have a nap, now. Lay down and go to sleep!"* The guards wasted no time in obeying him. They dropped to the ground like rag dolls and fell fast asleep. Quosmo let go of Imogene's hand, and watched as she and Marina and Rafe opened their eyes. They were all amazed, but Marina was the first to congratulate him. She could barely keep her voice down to a whisper; she was so excited.

"Quosmo, you did it! I can't believe it; that was the most incredible thing I've ever seen!" And just as she finished, she realized that she'd let the cat out of the bag. For how would she know what had gone on, unless she had been connected? Quosmo noticed the look of guilt on her face and was quick to console her.

"Don't worry, Marina. And Rafe, for that matter. If it were truly a bad thing, the two of you sitting in like you did, I would have told you not to do it before I began. There was no harm in it, because the two of you remained quiet. Really, it's okay." Rafe and Marina were each greatly relieved. Imogene interrupted.

"What Quosmo has just done is a great thing." She turned and looked directly at him, "Never doubt again, what you can or cannot do." She looked at them all, "Isn't this a fine example of what we can do together? We can't waste any more time. Let's go now, and save the Pacific Kingdom!" And she was the first to scramble to her feet and run down the hill full force, straight toward the main doors. Quosmo, Marina and Rafe were close at her heels. They ran like the wind to the bridge, but had to slow down to cross it as quietly as they could. They tiptoed around the sleeping guards and through the castle doors. Imogene summoned them to follow her again, and then she all but disappeared within a wall directly to her left. The servants' corridors were just where she said they'd be, and within seconds they were all safe and secure within the castle walls. Imogene led the others all the way to a spot near the spiral staircase that Quosmo would need to take to reach his relatives. She pointed to the staircase and explained softly.

"Quosmo, that leads to the royal chambers. Please do be careful, as it is the only way that I know of to get in or out, aside from going through the house. Can you communicate with your aunt or cousin to find out whereabouts they are?" Quosmo nodded anxiously and whispered.

"Yes, that's a good idea. We don't exactly have time to look all over for them, now do we?" She shook her head, no. He held out his hand and she immediately gave him hers.

"Ian! Ian! Can you hear me? It's Quosmo." As Quosmo waited for Ian's reply, Marina held hands with Imogene and Rafe. Quosmo felt the added energy almost immediately. But he still hadn't had contact with Ian! And then very faintly, he heard

him.

"*Quosmo, tell me you've come to get us out! Where are you?*"

"*Later. First, where are you? And how many guards have you got?*"

"*Mother and I are together in the princess's room. There are no guards in here with us, but they are at the door. I fear there is no way out. I could possibly make it out the window and climb down the castle wall, but my mother couldn't in her... well, you know... condition. You know I can't leave her behind.*"

"*I understand that, Ian. We have to get you through the royal chambers, to the spiral staircase that leads to the servants' corridors. Don't you worry about how. Just make sure that you and Auntie Portia are ready to go at merely a moment's notice.*"

"*Ready? My dear cousin. We have been ready to go for some time, now. May the kingdom be with you.*" The connection was gone; as Imogene let go of Quosmo and Marina, she wondered out loud.

"So. We have no way of knowing how many guards are in the royal chambers, now do we? But we can bet there are quite a few and I imagine that my uncle is in there as well. We can't afford to cause a commotion of any sort. Think, think, think." Imogene's nose wrinkled habitually as she tried to figure out a way of getting Portia and Ian out safely. Quosmo only watched her. Rafe straightened his glasses and Marina hopped softly from one foot to the other. At last, Imogene knew exactly what to do.

"Quosmo, if they are locked in the room with no guards inside, how long do you think it would be before the guards realize that they're missing? I can't see a way of getting them out through my bedroom door without attracting attention, it's just not possible." She looked at him intently. Quosmo nodded in agreement for he knew that all she'd said was entirely true.

"Are you suggesting that they *do* take the window, Imogene? You heard my cousin. Auntie Portia wouldn't be able to make it down in her condition." Imogene shook her head at him.

"Oh, yes she can. And what condition, anyway? Is she crippled?" Marina and Quosmo exchanged looks, and then both shook their heads, and so Imogene continued. "Ian can take my clothes from the wardrobe and my sheets, if he has to. If he ties them all together into one big rope, surely they can each can climb down. And besides, they wouldn't have to climb down the entire distance. The floor below the royal chambers holds the servants' apartments, which is hardly ever used. The only way to get there is through those quarters and I'm sure Serenito is not using those. Directly under my window is a balcony that leads to one of the servant's rooms. Portia and Ian need only to climb down to that balcony and into that room. And that's where we'll be waiting for them!" She offered him her hand and closed her eyes. Quosmo held it and without hesitation, they began. Marina and Rafe simultaneously held on again; they weren't about to miss a thing.

"*Ian!*"

"*Yes, Quosmo. Are you coming, now?*"

"*No. It's too risky to come through the door. If Serenito catches us, there will be no hope of saving the kingdom. And that's not all, Ian. I have the princess with me and I won't risk her life.*"

"*What are you saying, then? That you're not coming for us?*"

"*No, I'm not saying that. You and your mother must take the window.*"

"*Out of the question.*"

"*Ian, I regret to say this, but it's the only way. You and Auntie Portia must tie all the clothes and sheets together to form a rope. You need to climb down only to the balcony below the princess' window, and then I'll have you and your mother safely on your way to freedom!*"

"*Yes,*" Ian sighed. "*I see the window. We'll do as you ask.*"

"*Good. Make as little noise as possible, for the longer we have before they know you're gone, the better off we'll be. Once you make it to the balcony, enter the room. Unless we make it there before you do, the room should be empty. The door leads to the servants' corridors. We will meet up with you, and I'll take you and your mother to a safe place.*"

"*Thank you, Quosmo. We'll see you soon, I hope.*"

"*Of course.*" Quosmo let go of Imogene's hand. Imogene led them up the stairs to the floor below the royal chambers. They turned as though they were going toward her bedroom, and ended up at the door to the room below hers. They had past so many doors along the way that Marina had to wonder if Imogene had stopped at the right one.

"This has got to be the one, I think." Imogene claimed, as if she'd read Marina's mind. Perhaps she had. She tried the door handle and smiled as it turned easily in her hand. She pushed it open, peeked her head inside, and saw that the room was indeed empty, just as she'd expected. Quosmo, Marina and Rafe followed her in. Rafe closed the door securely behind them. Imogene headed directly for the window and looked straight up. Suddenly, from the corner of her eye, she caught the passing of the guards. Imogene shrank back against the wall and slid down to the floor. The other children immediately ducked out of sight.

"What is it?" Quosmo asked, as he lay on his belly on the floor.

"The guards are awake and making their rounds. I hope they didn't see me! We have to time them; we need to know how often they come around so that your aunt and cousin can climb down." Imogene, as pale as a ghost, frightened as she was from her close call, hugged the wall as she looked out the window again for the guards. Quosmo shimmied over to another window to monitor the situation on the ground below. Imogene nodded.

"Just as I thought, my room is the one right

above this one. Quosmo, the guards haven't come back yet; do you think Portia and Ian are ready?" Quosmo shrugged.

"There's only one way to find out, Princess. Let's talk to Ian again." He and Imogene took their cross-legged positions on the floor. "You two," he directed to Marina and Rafe, who were still taking cover, "Watch the windows and keep timing the guards." They headed straight toward the windows and did as they were told.

"Ian! Are you done? Is the rope made?"

"Yes, cousin. The rope is long enough to reach the balcony. How will we find you?"

"Don't worry; we're already in the room below yours. Just wait for my signal and then you and your mom can climb down. And when the time comes, you must hurry!"

"Yes, we understand that. Mother, in fact, is waiting near the window now. She's more adventurous than I ever imagined!"

"That's great news, Ian. I'll talk to you again shortly... just be ready." Quosmo, still holding Imogene's hand, asked his sister and Rafe, "Well?"

"They've just come back this way." Marina piped in.

Rafe added, "We have a three minute window of opportunity... starting... now!" Quosmo squeezed his eyes shut and instantly summoned his cousin.

"Ian! Go for it!"

"Here she comes, Quos!" Quosmo dropped Imogene's hand and raced to the balcony just as

Imogene's knotted clothes and sheets came tumbling down. In a matter of seconds, an extremely large woman, undoubtedly Auntie Portia, came sliding down and landed with such a bang on the balcony floor, that Imogene was sure the sound could be heard from miles around. And now, judging by the size of the woman, Imogene had a pretty good idea what exactly her *condition* was. In a heartbeat, Quosmo was at her side, pulled her to her feet, and back into the room. He left the red-faced, breathless woman with Marina and ran back for his cousin. But, by this time, the rather athletic young man was already on his feet, having landed safely on the balcony floor. The other occupants of the room watched as he deftly spun around and with one giant tug, brought the entire makeshift rope down. He backed into the room, pulling with him the only evidence of his and his mother's escape. Ian let the rope drop to the floor and wiped his hands against his robe. Quosmo met Ian in the middle of the room and extended his hand in greeting. Ian ignored it and embraced him instead.

"Ian, so good to have you with us!" Quosmo then turned to his aunt, and bowed slightly. "Auntie, so nice to see you." Auntie Portia let go of Marina, whom she'd been hugging the entire time, and hurried to her nephew.

"Oh, Quosmo. When will you stop being so formal? Handshakes and bowing all the time? Give me a hug!" Her voice was as thunderous as her appearance and it was too late for him to reply, as he was already stuck tight within her massive arms. She swung him around the room, as if he were as light as a feather. Imogene hated to break up their brief reunion, but they had to move. She was about to interrupt, when Ian fell to his knees before her.

"Princess, please forgive me for forgetting my place." He hung his head in sorrow. Marina smirked as she tried to pull her cousin to his feet.

"Ian, don't worry about it. It's just our friend, Imogene!" The young man stood up, obviously embarrassed. Portia introduced herself and her son properly.

"Princess Imogene, it is nice to meet you!" She held out her plump hand and Imogene took it. They shook vigorously, and then let go. Imogene laughed out loud at the woman's boundless energy. "My name is Portia, as you know, and this is my son, Ian." Ian smiled sheepishly at Imogene, and she smiled back and extended her hand to him.

"Pleased to meet you, Portia and Ian. Really, don't bow down to me. We don't have time for that kind of thing today." Quickly, she turned to Quosmo and suggested, "It's time to bring them away, don't you think?"

"Yes, you're right. We haven't a moment to lose. It won't be long before the guards realize what had happened to them, and then the rest of those hoodlums will be looking for us. Let's go!" And with that, Quosmo led his aunt and cousin out of the room. As soon as they were gone, Imogene decided to contact Sampson to give him a speedy update on the events so far. She held out her hands for Marina and Rafe to take, which they gladly did.

"*Sampson!*"

"*Imogene, thank goodness. I've been worried sick.*"

"*I know, but we're all good. We made our way into the castle after Quosmo put the two guards to sleep! You should have seen him; he was terrific!*"

"*Sounds exciting, Miss. Then what happened?*"

"*Then we snuck into the servants' corridors and Quosmo communicated with Ian. We had him and Portia climb down into the balcony below my room.*"

"*Good, then. Did Quosmo get them to the school safely?*" Marina cut in suddenly, for she was dying to talk to her father, too. Imogene didn't mind.

"*Hi, Father! We're just now waiting to hear from him.*"

"*Marina! I knew I felt something... exciting! Are you well?*"

"*Bouncing like usual! We are well.*"

"*And Rafe, are you there, too?*"

"*Yes, sir.*"

"*Are you well?*"

"*Yes, sir. Learning, always learning.*"

"*Oh, I imagine that you are, Rafe. Now before long, children, you will hear the sound of my men making their way to the castle. I will give them the signal, soon. And you know that you'll have no time to waste. The next time I hear from you children, it will be to celebrate our victory, I'm sure. Am I right?*" And then with voices strong beyond their tender ages of ten, Sampson heard, "*Absolutely!*" Then the connection was gone. The children let go of one another and looked questioningly to Imogene. She did her best to explain.

"Sampson hasn't a minute to spare. He had to summon his men." And then she was silent for a moment, and leaned her ear toward the window. She smiled. "Do you hear that, Marina and Rafe? They're coming!" Imogene was right. All three of them crawled to the window and poked their heads up just enough to see a wide army of men marching up the valley toward the castle. And just then, unexpectedly, Imogene began to tingle. "Quick! Take my hands!" The three of them formed a circle and waited.

"*Imogene!*" They recognized Quosmo's voice immediately. "*Send Marina to Uncle Duluth! Make sure she has the powder with her in case she needs it. And Imogene, at the same time, you and Rafe had better go to your parents. Too much time has gone by. We have to take full advantage of our father's diversion!*"

"Consider it done, Quosmo. Are your aunt and cousin safe?"

"*Yes, but it took me longer than I thought it would. I'm afraid that the three of you will have to continue on without me. I'll be back only in time to join my father's men. Take good care!*"

"Oh, no, Quosmo, what about the Poufo Powder? We'll need yours, too!"

"*That's okay, Princess. My father made sure that there was enough in each bag, in the event that I couldn't make it back in time. You don't really need me to complete the mission.*" And in the next breath, he was gone.

"Okay, Marina. Once we step outside this door," Imogene ordered as she pointed to it, "You'll go left all the way to the end of the corridor. Go down the stairs at the end, and by the way, there will be many stairs. Don't leave the staircase. You'll pass four doors at four different landings on the way down, but none of them lead to the dungeon. You will have arrived at the dungeon floor only when there are no more stairs. Rafe and I will be going the opposite direction and don't worry, we'll be facing more danger than you will." And then she stopped and listened again. "Hear the men! They're closer and we have to hurry. Once your uncle is free and gone, make your way back to the stairs, but this time to the very top. Back to the spiral staircase in the middle of the servants' corridors that leads to the royal chambers. We have to all meet at the very top, where we can let the powder fall on Serenito and his men!" Imogene watched as both Marina and Rafe let out their breaths. Marina, with newfound courage, stood tall and for once did not hop from foot to foot. She held her head high, and announced to them both.

"Don't worry, Imogene and Rafe. It will be done." They all clambered to their feet and padded softly to the door. Seconds later, Imogene and Rafe were sprinting down the corridor in one direction, Marina in the other.

Marina ran as she had never run before. It was not long before she reached the end of the corridor. She found the stairs at the end, exactly as Imogene had described. She took them two by two. She did not once consider that she could fall, as she was in way too much of a hurry to worry about such things. She rushed past the doors on the four separate landings and kept going until she reached the very bottom. Quietly, she slid down against the wall, and squatted there. She took a quick glance around the corner and to her total surprise, saw no guards! Could she be this lucky? Uncertain, Marina waited and when she looked again, there was still no one about. Marina stood straight up.

BANG! CRASH!

As Marina touched the top of her now tender head, she looked down to the floor to see what had fallen. Could she be so lucky a second time in a row? Ordinarily, Marina would think not, but nonetheless, she smiled from ear to ear as she reached down and picked up the key chain she'd knocked right off the hook and onto the floor. Just then she heard her name being called.

"Marina, is that you, child?" She recognized his voice instantly.

"Yes, Uncle. I'm coming!" She ran to the cell where he was being held. He reached out for her through the cold, steel bars. He shook his head at her while she turned the key in the lock.

"No, Marina! You mustn't release me! You see, Serenito has your aunt and cousin as prisoners!" Wide-eyed he watched as his usually obedient niece blatantly ignored all that he'd just said; she proceeded to unlock his door, opened it wide, and smiled at him.

"No, Uncle Duluth. We've freed Auntie Portia and Ian. They're waiting for you in the hidden school!" Duluth slumped back against the cell wall in relief. *Could it be?* And then judging by the look on her face, he knew that it was. In the next instant, he regained his composure, stood straight and then embraced his niece.

"You are more brave than you should ever have to be, Marina. This is a great thing that you have done. I'll go to my family now, and thank you! Will you come with me, child?" Marina pulled away from her uncle's grip and answered firmly.

"No. I can't. My job is not done here, Uncle. Don't worry! Everything will be just as it should be, and soon. Go now, quickly!" Duluth nodded at the young girl, and then scurried off down the dank and dimly lit hallway. He could feel the direction in which he needed to go, and he instinctively knew how to get there. It was not long before he was gone - completely out of sight. Marina sighed contentedly and closed the cell door. She went back down the hallway and back to the staircase from where she'd come. She had done it! Her chest swelled with pride as she climbed the stairs, slowly but surely, making her way back up to the servants' corridors. From there, she would find the spiral staircase that she hoped would eventually lead to a reunion with her friends.

In the meantime, Imogene and Rafe had made their way down to the opposite end of the dungeon. Just as they'd suspected, there *were* guards in front of the king and queen's cell; three of them! Imogene saw her parents huddled together on the single-wide cot that sat against the wall of their dreary prison. Imogene knew that her parents could not possibly see her squatted down in the dark, but her mother's head jerked up all the same.

"Imogene! I knew you'd come. I hoped you wouldn't, though. I'm afraid there is no chance of escape for your father and I. You'd better return to Auntie Agnes, sweet muffin."

"No, Mother. There's always a chance. I'm not leaving you, ever. You and father just be ready to go when it is time. We're breaking you out!"

"NO! Imogene, please go."

But it was too late. Imogene ignored her mother's orders; she watched her parents for another few minutes. It pained her to see them with their heads bowed low in defeat. She had never been more sure of anything than she was now; she would not let them down.

"Rafe," she whispered to her friend. "It's got to be now. I'm going to run that way," and she pointed down the hall, beyond the cell where her parents were being held. "While I'm distracting the guards, you open the cell. See the keys?" She pointed to where they hung on the wall. Rafe nodded, and straightened out his glasses that Imogene noticed weren't crooked in the first place. "Quietly let them out and tell them to hurry to the royal chambers. Then you follow the guards who have followed me. I'll stop running; you come up behind, and at the same time, we will give them a pinch of the Poufo Powder!"

Rafe chuckled and then said with a slight shake of his head, "Imogene, what do they teach you surface kids?" Imogene replied, without skipping a beat. "How to respect your parents! Ready? NOW!"

In the next instant, Imogene ran out from behind the stairwell, bolted mere inches away from the guards who hadn't been very alert, and was well out of their reach by the time they were on their toes. She stopped and waved at them mockingly. She rolled her eyes into the back of her head and folded her arms across her chest, in true Imogene fashion. She stuck her tongue out and shook her hips from side to side.

The guards were so angered and took chase so fast, that the two in behind tripped and fell over the guard in front! Imogene smiled wide, which enraged the tangled up trio even more.

By the time they really took off after her, Rafe had the keys in one hand and the lock in the other, and he stood beside the open cell door. Rafe had just freed the king and queen.

19

IMOGENE SAVES THE KINGDOM

The bewildered king and queen scrambled to their feet and rushed out the open cell door. Elsie gently took the young boy by the shoulders and asked, "Rafe, what is...?" But, Rafe just shook his head.

"No. There's no time to explain." He pointed to the stairs and shook free of her hands, and then ordered, "Go that way and return to the royal chambers while there's still time!" He turned and darted away; not even staying long enough to make sure they did just that. Rafe was in such a hurry to help Imogene, whom he imagined by now, had to be cornered by the three guards. He went as fast as his short, scrawny little legs would allow. Would he reach her in time?

Back at the cell, Roland tugged on his wife's arm, and pulled her along to the staircase. "Come, my dear. I think its best if we listen to the boy. He must know what he's doing, or he wouldn't have been able to free us the way he did." Elsie was reluctant to go.

"Roland, no. We can't leave Imogene!" Roland instantly released his wife's arm.

"Imogene? What are you talking about?" He didn't know that his daughter was involved.

"Yes, Imogene. I spoke with her briefly. I fear it was she who distracted the guards; led them away so Rafe could set us free! You and I were both looking down and we missed it, my dear." Roland understood now, but once more, took hold of her arm.

"Then, Elsie. We must trust that the children know what they are doing. We must do as Rafe has instructed, and return to the security of the royal chambers. It will do the kingdom no good, should a guard or worse yet, should Serenito return only to lock us up again." Elsie put up no resistance this time; and with heavy legs, followed her husband up the stairs. Deep down, she knew that he was right, and each of them could only hope that Imogene would survive this misadventure completely unscathed.

At that same moment, Rafe squinted through his glasses, and spotted the guards near the other end of the dungeon, just as they were closing in on his friend. He ran full speed ahead, then skidded to a stop and at the same time, shouted.

"NO!" The bumbling, clumsy guards were

caught completely by surprise. Just as they turned to see who had come up behind them, Imogene and Rafe each opened their drawstring bags and brought up a small pinch of the Poufo Powder. Instantaneously, the children brought their fingers up in front of their lips and blew it straight into the guards' faces! The guards didn't even know what hit them as they fell to the floor in a heap. Imogene, to say the least, was grateful that Rafe had shown up right when he did.

"Oh, my! That was close. Thanks, Rafe!" Rafe reached up, straightened his glasses and replied with a sheepish grin.

"That's okay, Imogene. That's what friends do." And then he took one of the guards by the legs and attempted to drag him to the nearest cell. "Help me lock these three up, will you?" Imogene was happy to oblige and within a few minutes, the guards were safe and sound under lock and key. As Imogene pocketed the keychain, she asked her friend hopefully.

"And my parents, Rafe? Please tell me they got away?" Rafe nodded enthusiastically.

"Yes!" And then he realized that he hadn't actually seen them go. "At least, I think they did. I told them to, anyway, and then I took off after you." Rafe could feel beads of sweat forming on his forehead as he began to panic. "Do... do you think they're okay, Imogene? What if they didn't get away, after all?" Imogene was quick to soothe him.

"I think so, Rafe." And then she laid her hand across her chest, right above where her heart would be, and then added, "I think I'd feel it in here, if they weren't." She then swung her other hand behind her back and crossed her fingers. At least she hoped they had gotten away. Together, she and Rafe hurried back to the staircase and began to climb their way up and up and up. Up to the royal chambers, up to Marina, and they hoped, up to the freedom of the Pacific Kingdom.

It was about the same time that Rafe and Imogene were ascending the stairs, that Sampson arrived back at the kingdom. His timing was perfect, as he turned up at the crest of the hill just as his defense force did. And then, Quosmo appeared; very much out breath after having dodged Serenito's men all the way back from the hidden school. He took his rightful place at his father's side, and together they assumed lead positions at the head of the group. Quosmo and Sampson proudly led the scores of men; the beekeepers, the merchants, the rice farmers, the orchard masters and the like, to storm the castle they loved so much. Serenito, intent on keeping the throne for his own, retreated back into it. All of his loyal, but cowardly followers returned to the safety of the castle walls. As soon as they were sheltered inside, the bridge was drawn and the great castle doors were bolted shut. They would not know until much later that these actions would actually assist in sealing their own fates.

Serenito took his place on King Roland's throne and addressed his people.

Marina, all this while, had been sitting on the floor, underneath the hall table at the top of the stairs that reached the royal chambers. A heavy blue velveteen tablecloth provided her cover and there was no way that she could be seen. It had been so long now, that she'd been cramped up under there, that she was becoming stiff and sore. And where were the others, anyway? Surely they should have arrived by now. She could hear Serenito making his speech down below, but with the great many stairs between them and the heavy material draped around her the way it was, she couldn't make out a single word. Her curious nature got the best of her, and she couldn't stand being shut out from the rest of the world any longer. Just as she laid her head down on the floor to peek out from under the cloth, she felt them. Vibrations on the floor. Marina knew right away that someone was coming. Did she dare look? She decided she'd better, and so with her head still laying flat upon the floor, she lifted the cloth just a smidge; barely enough to see out from under it.

Unfortunately for Marina, she was not to be very lucky a third time in a row. She had half expected to see the feet of her friends standing right in front of her nose... but that was not the case. Instead, right at eye level and much to her surprise, stood a large pair of hairy, dirty, stinky feet. The rest of the body that belonged to the feet noticed the movement of the tablecloth right away. In a heartbeat, two strong arms reached under the table and grabbed Marina by the waist, sending the table flying in the process. It all happened quicker than quick. Marina was too scared to utter a sound, as the giant of a man threw her against the side of his hip and carried her just that way, down the stairs. Her head bobbed up and down against the man's filthy robe, and her feet swayed this way and that. She was held in such a fashion that she could not see where they were going, though Marina had a pretty good idea, where they would end up. She squeezed her eyes tight as she hung on his hip, and tried to imagine herself being anywhere else but there.

Serenito saw the big man lumbering down the stairs. His eyes narrowed at the girl child that was hanging at the man's side, and he smiled the most wicked kind of smile. He stopped addressing his people, stood up and held out his arms in greeting. The man stopped at the stage and stood the child up before the supposed new king of the Pacific Kingdom. Marina trembled with fear as her eyes locked with his. Worst of all, Serenito cackled. It was a hideous, twisted outburst that sent shivers up and down Marina's spine. And then, as soon as his racket ceased, the room fell deathly quiet. He reached over to Marina and pulled her towards him.

She had no choice but to let him. With rough hands, he spun her around to face the waiting audience of renegades.

"My people! New inhabitants of this kingdom! Do you see what we have found here?" And then Serenito placed one hand upon her head, and spun her around and around with the other. Marina, had become dizzy, squeezed her eyes even tighter, and hoped with all her might that her friends might come and rescue her soon. Serenito cackled again and then introduced the girl to his army. "May I introduce you all... this is the moment we've been waiting too long for..." Dramatically, the evil man paused, and the men below began to stomp their feet in rhythm. "This little girl, this child that stands before us, can be none other than my long lost niece, IMOGENE!" Marina's eyes shot open and nearly bugged out of her head, but still, she said nothing. Hoots and hollers echoed throughout the castle as Serenito and his men rejoiced in their newfound treasure. They knew now, that nothing stood between Serenito and the throne. The kingdom was as good as his.

Imogene and Rafe had arrived on the high landing, just as Serenito wrongly introduced Marina, and they knew they hadn't one second to spare. If she'd had time, Imogene would have certainly crossed her fingers in the hopes that the Poufo Powder in her and Rafe's bags would be enough. The two of them stood across from each other, on opposite sides of the balcony, and on the count of three, opened the bags. They ran like the wind and crossed paths in the middle of the landing, allowing the contents of each bag to pour downwards the entire distance, in parallel sheets of the magical substance.

Imogene and Rafe stood at each end of the landing, puffing and panting as they watched the scene below. One by one, the men began to fall. Imogene looked toward her uncle standing beside her father's throne. His hands had dropped to his sides in defeat. He was in a state of shock as he watched the complete failure of his revolt; one he'd thought he was sure to win. Marina bolted down from the stage, and hopped over and around Serenito's fallen forces. She bounded up the stairs toward her friends. And luckily for her, almost lucky for the third time in a row, she held tight within her fist, her drawstring bag. Her father had been right! Because she'd held the bag, she had felt no ill effects from the powder at all. Imogene and Rafe met her at the top of the stairs, and then the three of them leaned over the railing and continued to observe their victory. In the end, and rightly so, Serenito was the last man standing. Imogene was glad that he'd had no choice but to watch all of his hopes and dreams crumble to the castle floor. She was still staring at him, rather curiously, when all of a sudden he turned directly toward her and stared straight into her eyes. It was so unexpected that

Imogene almost jumped back a step. But as soon as she regained her composure, so began the staring contest; a true battle of the wills, between good and evil. A war of two worlds. Imogene wrinkled up her nose and concentrated with all her might. *"Fall, Uncle Serenito. Fall. Lay down with the others."* She didn't know if he'd heard her or not, as he did not answer, nor did he flinch. Imogene shuddered under his unwavering stare and from him, she felt more hatred than she ever would have thought possible. She was tempted to look away, when all of a sudden, he lifted his hand high in the air, and pointed a bony finger straight at her face. He trembled, his whole body shook as his mouth twisted around and he tried to call out. But his voice would not cooperate now. He produced no sound at all, and he fell with a bang, face first from the stage, then onto the floor. And then, all within the castle was still.

"Whoopee!" Marina yelped, breaking the silence as she hopped up and down between her two friends. Imogene joined in and the two girls jumped up and down together with joy.

"Ahem?" Rafe, who was standing to the side, cleared his throat to get his friends' attention. He thought they were being rather silly, since they still had work to do. The girls stopped fooling around and looked at him expectantly. "Ladies, don't you think we should lower the drawbridge and get the king and queen from the royal chambers?"

"Yes, Rafe!" Imogene sputtered as she grinned. "Why don't you and Marina go lower the drawbridge and I'll fetch my parents!" Like a shot, the trio split up again. Rafe and Marina hurried down and skipped over the sleeping, snoring villains and made their way to the great castle doors. Imogene ran down the hallway to the royal chambers, where she knew her parents were waiting anxiously. She skidded to a stop right outside the doors and tried the handle. It wouldn't budge. Imogene was near panic; she knocked on the door and waited. Nothing. And now she was really beginning to worry. She couldn't holler out, for fear of waking Serenito and his men.

"Imogene! It's you, isn't it?" Imogene heard the unmistakable voice of her mother, Elsie. Imogene nearly cried out with relief when she heard it.

"Yes, Mother! Are you and father okay? You can open the doors now, the kingdom is free!" All at once, the doors flew open and Imogene was staring straight at her parents. Roland beamed at his daughter, knelt down and held his arms open wide for her. She ran into them, and he held her tight.

"It seems our little princess has saved the day, doesn't it, dear?" He turned and asked his wife. Imogene turned to Elsie and embraced her.

"Well, my husband, I think we have always known we could count on Imogene, now haven't we? Imogene, where is your Uncle Serenito and his men?" Imogene looked up into her mother's beautiful eyes, smiled, then answered.

"They must have worn themselves out, trying to take over father's throne. The last I saw of them, they were sleeping downstairs!" Imogene and her parents laughed, and then headed to the balcony to see it all for themselves.

There was much commotion on the lower level now, and the royal family watched as Sampson and his son barked orders to the kingdom's men. Each of Serenito's men were shackled together by their wrists and ankles, before they regained consciousness, in groups of ten. They were soon brought to their feet, and led away to the dungeon, right where they belonged. The men were to be held under lock and key until the true king decided their fates. Imogene watched them go, then quickly scanned the room for Marina and Rafe, but to her dismay, they were nowhere to be seen.

"There they are, dear." Elsie quipped, and pointed to a spot on the floor, nearest the throne. Imogene and her parents chuckled at the sight of her friends chaining Serenito's feet together. Imogene giggled as she looked to her father.

"Daddy, what will happen to Uncle Serenito, now?" His expression had become very serious. He looked down at his daughter and replied gravely.

"I am troubled over that, child. I honestly don't know what to do with him. And the others," he waved his arm toward them, "well, some of them could be reformed; many of them are young enough to relearn; some may desire the opportunity for change that I will offer them. But not him. Not my brother. I am afraid that he has chosen his path, and he will not stray far from it." Elsie laid a comforting hand upon Roland's shoulder; she knew there was nothing she could say to soothe him. Imogene only nodded and snuggled up to him just a little bit closer. The royal family stood there like that, watching the activity below, until the very last villain was hauled away.

The next few days in the castle were busy ones for the royal family and servants alike, as everyone did their best to put everything back in order. The queen had the castle scrubbed from top to bottom, in a vain attempt to rid every nook and cranny of the evil doings that almost took it over. She and Imogene even spent days on their hands and knees, washing and cleaning and erasing.

The king had important dealings as well. He was forced to create an actual, official army, rather than a put-together sort at the last minute, that they'd had the good fortune of succeeding with. He set up highly efficient lookout posts that would be manned twenty-four hours a day. Although they had survived Serenito's most recent escapade, Roland knew they might not fare as well, should there be a next time. In fact, had it not been for Sampson and the children, the outcome may have been entirely different, indeed. Speaking of Serenito and his men; the king would allow them to sit and stew in the dungeon for a good, long time, until he decided what to do with them.

By the end of the first week, the castle was spotless. Imogene was very glad that school would be starting up again soon, for then it would really feel like life had returned to normal. Besides, she had grown tired of scrubbing things. It was noon on Monday, when finally, she and her parents had time to sit down together for a meal. Imogene was glad for it.

"Well, Mother and Father. Now what?" She looked anxiously from one parent to the other. They both laughed easily at their daughter's non-stop antics.

"What do you mean, now what?" Her father shot back. "Have we not had enough excitement in our kingdom to last us a good, long while?" Elsie grinned and nodded her head in agreement.

"Your father is right, Imogene. Usually things down here are pretty calm! And don't look so disappointed, sweet muffin." Imogene shook her head at them both.

"It's not that I'm disappointed. I'd like to go to school three days a week again, and play with Marina and Rafe like before, in the evenings and on weekends. It's not that at all! I don't want any more excitement, either." The king and queen looked curiously at their daughter as she fell silent and looked down at her lap. Suddenly, she brightened and added, "Do you know what? It's nothing, really.

I was just thinking, that's all." Before her parents had a chance to ask, Imogene wrinkled up her nose and made a face at both of them. She jumped up from her chair and quickly backed away from the table.

"Where are you going?" Roland asked with a smirk. Elsie only watched, slightly concerned over her daughter's sudden and rather erratic behaviour.

"Um," Imogene began, as she crossed her fingers behind her back. "May I go outside and play, now?" She hoped desperately that they couldn't tell that there was something kind of important on her mind. As a last resort, she forced herself to think happy thoughts. She thought about school, her seahorse...

"Of course!" Roland and Elsie answered at the same time, and they watched her as she turned and skipped happily out of the room. Once outside, Imogene strolled around the castle. She drank in all of the beauty of the kingdom that she was now very much a part of. She worried a little about what would become of her uncle and his men, but she trusted that her father would be fair in sentencing them. Then, as she breezed through the bountiful flower gardens in the backyard, she thought ahead. Next week, she and her friends would be the guests of honour at a grand victory celebration! Now, that was sure to be fun! And soon, Imogene would finally meet her seahorse and begin taking lessons. Later, she would be able to go on those ocean expeditions with her family and friends. She had so very much to look forward to.

But... she wondered, *why does there always have to be a but...* There was one problem that nagged Imogene. It was always there, right at the tip of her tongue, but she had been so busy getting her kingdom life back to normal that she didn't want anything or anyone to interfere. No, she sure didn't. And so, as she skipped back through the main doors of the castle, snuck to the left and hurried through the servants' corridors, she made her mind up for good. She would not ask her parents, *but... what about Auntie Agnes?* No. Not tonight. And then, with an honest and pure smile plastered upon her face and perfectly content with her latest resolution, she rejoined her parents at the dining room table.

20

PEACE IN THE KINGDOM

The following day at school was an exciting one for each and every child in attendance. The principal could do very little to tone down the level of excitement and so after the morning assembly, he ordered everyone outside, teachers included, to play games in an attempt to work off their extra, euphoric energy. Imogene, Marina and Rafe engaged in an exaggerated version of hide and seek, and included in the play area were the west orchard, the mammoth garden and the patch of forest that separated the two. Imogene, unfortunately for her, was *it* and her first task was to lay face down in the grass while she counted to one hundred. And as she began, her friends ran away in desperate search of the perfect hiding spots.

"... thirty-four, thirty-five, thirty-six..." Just as she was about to count the next number in line, she felt a tap on her shoulder. Fully expecting it to be either Marina or Rafe, she quickly snapped her head around to see what it was they needed. She was surprised to see that it was neither of them; it was none other than Quosmo, who'd plunked himself down on the grass beside her.

"Hey, Imogene!" He smiled a little and looked down at his feet almost sheepishly, as she sat up to face him. She hadn't really seen much of Quosmo since they'd saved the kingdom together, and that was quite some time ago. Mind you, she hadn't *expected* to see him around often either, for they traveled in different circles, given their age difference.

"Oh, hello, Quosmo!" Then she waited for him to get on with whatever he had approached her about. She was beyond blushing now in his presence, thank goodness for that. She was nearly at the point of regarding this hand-kissing pre-teen as a little girl might treat her best friend's older brother; with nothing more than polite nonchalance.

"Imogene, I just wanted to say... well, it's just that you see..." The poor boy was lost for words. Imogene smiled courteously and waited patiently for him to continue. He looked up at the sky, took a deep breath, and then tried again. "It's like this, Imogene." And then silence, again. Then he had it; he knew exactly how to tell her.

"My *dad* is really proud of you. He thinks you are

way braver than any other person in the kingdom. He finds it hard to believe that a girl of your intellect and maturity is only ten years old. And you know, he usually keeps to himself about such things." All of this though, Imogene already knew. Sampson had either told her directly, or she was able to deduce such facts from the round about ways that he sometimes spoke. Still, she nodded politely at the stammering, stuttering young man who sat beside her. And then suddenly, she smacked her hand to her forehead.

"Oh, no! Quosmo, I must be at one hundred by now!" She jumped to her feet. "Want to come and help me find the others?" She held out her hand for him to take, but he declined her offer with a shake of his head.

"No, you go on. I'll see you around." And he watched her take off down the hill toward the trees. His own face reddened a bit, as he silently admonished himself for trying to talk to her at all. As he got up and walked away to rejoin his own group of friends, he hoped she would forget all about it. And more than that, he really hoped that she wouldn't ever, ever realize that the things he'd told her, actually weren't from his father at all.

By now, Imogene was in the middle of the little forest, creeping along over twigs and leaves and branches. It was impossible for her to not make a sound, but she so hoped to catch her friends talking or making some kind of noise that might lead her to them. And then, she heard it. A *scritch* and a *scratch*, and then the smallest, tiniest *thump* possible. She fell to her hands and knees and crawled cautiously in the direction of the noise, but saw nothing. She sat down on her behind, crossed her arms over her knees, and waited. It was right then that she noticed it sitting helplessly across from her on an old tree stump.

As she watched it, she heard the *scritch* and the *scratch* again. The difference this time, was that now she could see exactly what the source was, of these curious little noises. On hands and knees again, but slower than she'd ever moved before so as not to frighten it, she inched closer.

"Well, hello there, you noisy little creature," she whispered as she reached over and picked up the dragonfly carefully by its wing. It obviously wasn't able to fly, for surely if it could have, it would not have let Imogene pick it up. Speaking of little, it was only little in comparison to the child who held it. This particular dragonfly had come from the mammoth garden to the west, and like everything else that grew there, was quite large. So large, that it was almost the size of Imogene's hand! The dragonfly tried to stand tall on her palm; it was steady on its feet only for a moment, before toppling over on its side again. Imogene became more concerned as she peered closer at it. The dragonfly lifted its left leg and *scritch-scratched* it against the other.

"Oh, you poor thing. You've gone and hurt your leg, haven't you?" The dragonfly fluttered its wings only slightly, but it looked as though it had just agreed with what Imogene had asked. Gingerly, she set the insect back upon the stump, and examined the leg. She compared it against the good leg and found exactly what the problem seemed to be. The bad leg was bent in the opposite direction, right at the joint. Ever so quickly, Imogene reached her hand behind her back and crossed her fingers. How she hoped that she was about to do the right thing, and so, she set about straightening the poor creature's leg, talking to it in a soothing tone, the entire time.

"Now, now. This leg won't do, now will it? How can you fly away if your leg is weighing you down? Here now, I will take care of it for you." And so she did. Imogene very carefully took hold of the dragonfly's leg on either side of the knee joint and snapped it back into position. The poor insect just lay there, stone still and panting as though it was about to take its last breath. Just as Imogene was about to burst into tears, convinced that she'd gone and killed it, it fluttered its wings, *scritch-scratched* its legs together and flew high into the air!

And then Imogene *did* cry a little, but her tears were those of relief. She watched as it circled around and around overhead, and then dropped back down gracefully and landed on the stump again in front of her. The dragonfly stared her straight in the eye as it gave its wings another gentle wave. And then, to her complete surprise, it walked to the left, then to the right, and then stopped at the center of the stump again; the dragonfly was showing her that it was better now! Could this be a magical dragonfly? Just as Imogene was about to argue that fact in her head, her friends came crashing through the trees, and sadly for her, the dragonfly panicked and flew straight away. Marina hopped up and onto the old tree stump.

"There you are, Imogene! What happened to you? We've been waiting and hiding forever!" As Marina interrogated her, she naturally hopped from one foot to the other. Before Imogene had the chance to answer, Rafe straightened out his glasses and sat down cross-legged beside her.

"Yeah, what are you doing, just sitting here?" Both friends looked earnestly at Imogene and waited for her to answer. She took one look at both of them and assumed that never in this life time, would they ever believe her if she told them about the magic dragonfly. And so what was the use?

"Sorry, Marina and Rafe. I just found an insect and lost track of the time." She tried to downplay it as best she could, but nonetheless, Marina and Rafe began searching the ground for it. Imogene laughed as she shook her head. "Oh, no. It flew away when you guys came. Come on, let's go back to school!" The little dragonfly was immediately forgotten, by all but one, and they made their way through the trees, up the hill and back to school. As she hiked along, Imogene looked to the skies now and then, hoping to catch a glimpse of the mysterious creature she'd helped. It was of course, nowhere to be seen and Imogene smiled contentedly as she imagined that it had found its way home.

Later that afternoon, after Imogene had put her school things away and washed up for supper, she joined her parents in the dining room shortly before the evening meal. She knew that this would be the day she'd have to ask her parents about Auntie Agnes. It bothered her too much, to not bring the subject up; but at the same time she dreaded the idea of ever having to go back to the surface. Roland and Elsie were pleased as usual, to see their daughter entering the room.

"Sweet muffin," her mother began fondly. "How was your day at school?" She was genuinely concerned as she watched Imogene take her usual seat at the table.

"It was great, Mother!" And then she thought for a moment, before continuing. "If all the days ahead, go like today did, maybe things really will return to normal!" Roland cleared his throat and all eyes automatically turned to him.

"My dear Imogene. There is no reason why life shouldn't go on as it normally would, now that the kingdom is back in order! Pray tell, did you learn anything in class today, or was the overall mood of the student body a little on the hyperactive side?"

King Roland and his wife knew full well that the students had been given a two-hour break in the middle of the day; he just wanted to know what his daughter had to say about it. Imogene smirked.

"Oh, Daddy, something tells me that you already know what mood we were all in! But it was great fun outside, and once we were all called back in, we really did do our school work." The incident with the dragonfly was at the tip of her tongue; she was dying to tell them about it, but in all fairness, she'd better ask about Auntie Agnes first. Now it was she who cleared her throat. Elsie grinned, for she knew precisely the thing that had been so disturbing to her daughter. All this time, she had remained as silent and patient as only a mother could, until Imogene felt the time was right to ask. Obviously, that time had come.

"Mother and Father." Imogene reached back behind her chair with both arms, and crossed the fingers of both hands this time, for this was going to take a lot of hope. "I really don't want to ask, but I have to because I need to know. What about Auntie Agnes?" She made a face as she asked, and she looked so comical with her arms stretched behind her back, that her parents burst out laughing. Imogene swung her arms to the front and crossed them defiantly across her chest. "What?" She demanded. This had been so disturbing to her that she could not fathom why she had suddenly become the laughing stock of the dining room.

Softly, and in an effort to make him stop, Elsie kicked her husband under the table. They both sobered immediately. Roland cleared his throat, but said nothing and tried to concentrate on his hands, clasped tightly on the table in front of him. Elsie knew that this task had fallen completely on her, but she didn't mind. She smiled delicately at her young child.

"Imogene, it's okay. It is so sweet and so like you to always be concerned for others. Your father and I couldn't ask for a better child; not even if we lived for two hundred years! The fact of the matter is, that we adults have come to the conclusion that you have been through enough. You have endured far more than anyone should ever expect of a child of ten." She hesitated as she watched Imogene's expression soften, and her arms dropped to her lap. "Sampson has taken care of the business concerning Auntie Agnes." Imogene couldn't believe her ears. Just like that? Done? That sounded way too easy.

"But, what do you mean he's taken care of it? How can that be? Does he *really* not need me to go back up?" Imogene wanted so much to believe all that she was hearing. But, could it really be? She crossed her fingers again. Elsie was still smiling.

"It is done, sweet muffin. You know how Sampson imprinted an entirely different past onto Auntie Agnes' memory?" Imogene nodded, and her mother kept going. "Well, he's done it again, dear.

Auntie Agnes believes that your father and I came back and took you with us. We will have to go and visit her though, from time to time. But, do not worry, my dear. We'll go as a family and we'll come back as a family. Don't worry about Auntie Agnes; she will be just fine." Imogene was so relieved that she let out a gigantic sigh. How she had hoped and hoped that she wouldn't have to go back up and... and... lie. And now, all of a sudden, and just like that, she felt like she really hadn't a care in the world.

Later that night, after Imogene bade her parents goodnight at her bedroom door, she pulled the heavy drapes closed as usual, to keep the light out. She washed for the night, then changed into her pajamas and climbed into her nice, soft and comfortable bed. As she lay there, she realized that life just couldn't get any better than it was at this particular moment. Her parents were in the next room, the kingdom was safe, and she'd see her friends again the very next day. Before she knew it, Imogene had fallen into a deep and blissful sleep. Her last thoughts of the evening were of the brief, and strange conversation she'd had with Quosmo. Fortunately for him, even that was short-lived, for in the next instant she was out like a light. She slept so soundly that she didn't hear, on her bedside table right next to her head, the softest *scritch* and *scratch*, and then the smallest, tiniest *thump* possible. She was not at all aware of the mysterious little creature that stood watching over her, for the entire night. Nonetheless, it just so happened to be the best sleep that Imogene had experienced, since she'd first arrived in the Pacific Kingdom.

A sneak preview into book two.....

AN EXCERPT - DAGER OF THE TASMAN EMPIRE

The miserable old woman glared at her young charge with those all too familiar steel grey eyes. Instantly he cowered and shrunk back against the wall, causing the hag's mood to soften. But only a little. And even that was short lived. She straightened and leaned toward him.

"You little pond scum! How many times have I told you? I want this floor spotless!" Her intimidating voice was deep, rough and loud. She threw the pitch fork that only moments before, had been raised high above him like a battle weapon ready to strike, to the ground at his feet. She lifted her heavy skirts, and stormed out of the chicken coop. He heard the lock click shut behind her, and only then did he breathe a sigh of relief. At least she was gone. He knew that no matter how hard he tried, or how clean he got that floor, it would never, ever be good enough to satisfy his master.

The little guy picked up his fork, turned it to its side and began scraping the stubborn chicken droppings from the old, worn out floor. His movements were quick, experienced and rhythmic; and so they should be. He'd been doing this now for more than two years. With calloused hands that had no business belonging to a five-year old boy, he scraped and scratched and pulled the dung to the far corner of the little room, then opened the trap on the floor. In the next moment, the little room was bare, except for him and the fork. Now all that was left for him to do, was wait for her return.

He slumped down onto his bottom, against the wall across from the door and rested. Chances are that he would have nodded off right away, sitting there like that in the dark and quiet, if not for the hunger pains that gnawed ever so constantly at his empty insides.

It so happened though, that he did eventually fall asleep. After all, a child his age could hardly be expected to work from dawn to dusk with no grub nor a break in-between. He dreamt. Did he ever dream, and his dreams rarely changed from one to the next. He dreamt of magical, faraway lands, which during the waking hours, he knew did not truly exist. He dreamt that he was a free boy who had a family that loved him. In his dreams there was no old hag and no stinky, dirty chicken coop. There were only fun and games and most importantly, laughter. Not the wicked laughter that he was sadly used to hearing, either; this was good laughter that came straight from the bellies of kind people. And then as most dreams do, this particular dream came to an end. An abrupt, cruel end. The boy did not wake up of his own accord either, oh no. It was the chickens that roused him. The old hag had left him locked up in the coop, and then proceeded to let the chickens in. He jumped up from the floor and let out a yelp. And then, high above the clucking and pecking noises from the hens, he heard it. Her laugh; her horrible, spine tingling laugh that surely was not of this earth. She opened the door.

The morning sun was already high in the sky, and was far too brilliant for his little eyes to take in all at once, and he was momentarily blinded by it. She laughed again as she reached in and grabbed him by the shoulder.

"Come now, boy! Did mama go and leave you in the coop all night?" And then she cackled again, as she roughly pulled the boy toward her. He still couldn't see and would have stumbled if not for her holding him up. As it was, she threw him to the ground anyway, the minute he was out of the coop. It would have been a little kinder if he had fallen on his own. The boy's hand landed directly upon a sharp object, which had been hidden underneath the dirt. He looked down at his injured hand surprised, and watched as droplets of his very own blood turned a small piece of the earth an angry shade of red, and then mysteriously disappeared. He glanced back at his hand again, and was even more startled to see that the wound was now gone. As sly as could be, the boy wrapped his small fist around the object and hid it safely within his grasp. And although it was still early morn, and the sky was as blue as blue could be, thunder roared and lightening shot across the sky.

At that same moment, unbeknownst to him or to the hag, in a world that very few knew existed, an old man's hand began to bleed.

Dager of the Tasman Empire is available on amazon.ca and directly through the author at

www.teresaschapansky.com

ABOUT THE AUTHOR

The author works, plays and writes in the beautiful Cowichan Valley on Vancouver Island, British Columbia, Canada.

While writing for children has been and likely will always be her primary focus, she's found a little niche in writing memoirs aimed toward the adult audience, beginning with *Memoirs of a Pakhtun Immigrant.*

More books by Teresa Schapansky:
Some Christmas
Coinkeeper series, books 1-4
One Little Coin
Along the Way series, books 1-12

For more information
about the author, please visit:
www.teresaschapansky.com

www.ingramcontent.com/pod-product-compliance
Lightning Source LLC
Chambersburg PA
CBHW020335180626
46812CB00001B/208